Valedictorian

A Story of the Hidden Glory
of a Troubled Life

CONSTANCE W. HALL

authorHOUSE®

AuthorHouse™
1663 Liberty Drive
Bloomington, IN 47403
www.authorhouse.com
Phone: 1 (800) 839-8640

Published by AuthorHouse 02/09/2016

ISBN: 978-1-5049-7851-4 (sc)
ISBN: 978-1-5049-7852-1 (hc)
ISBN: 978-1-5049-7850-7 (e)

Library of Congress Control Number: 2016902125

Print information available on the last page.

Dedicated to
Wilbur Lee Williams
October 23, 1941–August 18, 2005
RIP

Chapter 1

A cold wind blew through the large crack of the shanty door as the black night faded to a steel-gray morning, swiftly arousing the cock perched outside, complacent about his morning crow.

Inside the chicken house, young Wilbur shifted on his makeshift bed—a heavy cotton tarp stretched across four wooden stakes tethered with twine. His patchwork quilt offered little protection against the unexpected cold. Usually, his brother, Jesse, slept with him, lying in the opposite direction with his feet in Wilbur's face, their bodies sharing warmth. However, this morning, Wilbur awoke shivering and alone. But he didn't mind. Every morning was a new adventure, and as he opened his eyes, a smile spread across his face. He was happy to have awakened before the others.

Across the crowded room, only four feet away, his parents slept together on a thin mattress made of ticking stuffed with hay, suspended off the dirt ground by four horizontal logs. He noticed his little brother's small feet sticking over the end of their bed as he clung to its edge next to his mother, seeking refuge in the night from a bad dream.

After quietly turning back the covers, Wilbur dirtied his bare feet as he tiptoed over to his three-year-old brother.

"Wake up, Jesse. Daylight's burning," he whispered. Jesse's angry hand shoved him aside, and Jesse rolled over, showing Wilbur his backside. *No matter. Little brothers just end up crying anyway*, he thought, and he safely made his way outside.

The colors of the morning sun bled into the sky, streaking the tops of the hills with red, threatening to tattle on Wilbur's escape before he had the chance to spot any game. He crept past two-by-fours stacked in the entry to their unfinished house and past the tarps covering bags of cement that flanked the front door. He couldn't wait until the house was finished and they could move in. Sleeping in the chicken house had lost its novelty long ago.

When he could see the woods beyond their yard, he sighed with contentment. There, above all else, he felt as if he belonged. He scurried past the chicken coop and then slowed his pace, stalking past the first few trees of his woods. Always quick on the take, he spotted a squirrel before he was a hundred yards past the barn. Without considering how close he was, he took a hasty shot, missing by a few feet. The report woke the still-somnolent rooster on the far side of the stoop and set it squawking, crowing for all his hens to awaken, erupting the chicken yard into a full chorus of chaos.

"Goddammit, Punk! I told you a thousand times not to disturb me in the mornings!" Wilbur was still close enough to the house to hear his father, Webb, hollering from inside, using the nickname Wilbur's parents had coined for him shortly after his second birthday, when they'd realized they had a hardheaded know-it-all son who wasn't afraid to state his opinion on any topic, whether or not he'd ever heard about it before. Only his parents called him that name, for no one else understood its meaning. "I'll tan your hide for sure!"

Wilbur shrugged off the threat. His parents needed to get up anyway. His father, Webb, should be working on the house already, if for no other reason than the chicken house was freezing in the mornings. His father spent most of his days in the coal mines, which was why the house was taking so long. But today was Sunday, and Webb had a whole day to work on the house. Wilbur's mother, Sarah, would start fixing breakfast soon before going to work as household help somewhere in town.

Since Wilbur was still close to their chicken house, he lingered a while, wondering if his parents would get moving. He heard his father grumble with a voice still thick from sleep, "I coulda slept a whole 'nother hour. What's with that boy? Waking us up before dawn? He'd best stay outta my way, Sarah. I'm in no mood for his foolishness, especially today."

His mother kept a nice, even tone when she said, "I'll take him and Jesse up the crick to your ma's. She can watch 'em. I'm suppose to cook and clean for the Beaumonts today."

Wilbur heard his father respond but couldn't make out much more than "too old to keep up." A second later, his mother came outside. She didn't see him in the trees, but she called to him. She smiled when he emerged.

"You come inside, boy," she said, "and help me get you and your brother washed and dressed. Make sure your daddy sees you doing something worthwhile before he gets his mind set on a whoopin'."

"Yes, ma'am," replied Wilbur meekly. Back inside, Webb had finished putting on the rest of his clothes, and he sat by the door, tying his bootlaces. It didn't take long. They slept in slimmed-down versions of the only clothes they owned, which meant long johns at night. Then they donned overshirts, coveralls, and jackets for day.

"I want the eggs gathered and a pullet cleaned 'fore you get off today, Punk," said Webb as he mussed his hand over his son's towhead. "And behave yourself at Granny's."

"Yessurr." Wilbur smiled, eager to wring a chicken's neck. Though only five, he appreciated his designation as the man in charge when Pop needed help, being too busy to take care of matters himself.

Efficient at the task, Sarah and her boys had supper plucked and hung to bleed by eight o'clock. Afterward, they headed to the home of Mary Weaver, their granny, which was a twenty-minute walk down the hollow. "I hope Uncle Ned's there," said Wilbur, throwing rocks at the grazing cows.

"There's better things for you to do with your time than hang around that good-for-nothing," replied Sarah.

They reached Granny Weaver's, and Sarah said her hellos, not seeing Ned in his usual spot—asleep on the cabin floor. She kissed her boys good-bye and then walked back up the hollow to meet Mrs. Beaumont by nine.

Their visit didn't last long. By noon, the boys had grown bored, so Granny Weaver sent them home with some bread to eat. The morning chill had given way to a crisp late-September breeze by the time they arrived back home. They saw Webb put down his hammer and get out his own lunch of leftover biscuits and lard. "The house is looking good," said Wilbur.

"It's coming along," said Webb. "Now that I've got the framing finished, I'm waiting for Carl to come and deliver the plywood and plaster." Carl Jamison owned Jamison's Building Supply in nearby Clarksburg. It was a one-man operation handed down from father to son. During busier times, a delivery might or might not come when scheduled, but local construction was in a slump, and Carl couldn't afford hired help. In 1941, vivid memories of the Depression still weighed on people's minds. Back then, only backyard gardens had staved off starvation, and the unfortunates who hadn't planted had begged and stolen food to survive. Nowadays, people hid surplus money behind walls, buried it in jars, and stuffed it under mattresses in preparation for the next inevitable economic crash; the future looked bleak in the eyes of the elders.

The boys occupied themselves in the yard. Webb wet his fingers, dabbed the bread crumbs from his lap, popped every visible morsel into his mouth, and then reached for a cigarette. He'd just lit the unfiltered Camel, when he heard Carl's familiar engine round the bend. He stood to greet him as Carl's truck lurched into the driveway.

"Hey, Carl, right on time."

"Well, seeing as you're my only drop today, I ought to be."

"Sorry to hear. Business still slow?"

"Yep. I'm gonna have to go into the mines myself if'n it doesn't pick up soon. You're my only paying customer. That said, here's the slip for today's load." Carl handed him a bill for $700.

"God almighty. Is this everything to finish the inside?"

"Yep. I reckon one or two more orders will do. All's you got left is the siding and the whatnots your missus will want put in—you know, 'frigerator, stove, lights."

"She wants an inside commode too. Better figure that in."

"Will do. Come by the store when you're ready," said Carl as he collected seven crisp hundred-dollar bills from Webb and bid farewell.

Wilbur marveled at that amount of money. It didn't occur to him that it was odd for his father to pay in cash or that it was unusual to conduct business as they did, on a handshake. All he cared about was moving into the house, which Webb insisted would be possible before winter if his help showed up.

Webb went to work nailing plywood, and the rooms began to take shape. Wilbur watched him hammer, thinking that this house was going to be a mansion. It certainly dwarfed the three-room cabin where Granny Weaver lived without running water or a bathroom. Like exclamation marks, privies dotted every property among the hollows; the more-fortunate inhabitants lived upstream.

Wilbur could already see the house taking shape. A set of concrete steps ran up the side of a steep hill just off the main road, leading to the front door. In the hill, Webb had dug out a basement, and a lower doorway exited the back. The basement steps went up to a main foyer, which fed a small sitting room, master bedroom, bathroom, and kitchen. Another staircase ran opposite the front door, in the sitting room, and led to the second bedroom. Webb had pointed out a large stairwell landing, telling Wilbur that it would be his and Jesse's spot because the family would save the bedroom for guests.

Ned showed up to help at three o'clock. "Hey, Webb. Sorry I'm late." He nodded to the boys.

"Where you been—sleeping one off?"

"You know how it is. I planned on turning in early, but Charlie showed up at Ma's right as I headed to bed. He wanted me to go riding, and well, I couldn't be rude. Before you know it, the sun's coming up, and we were in the hole ten dollars," explained Ned.

"Gettin' hustled in pool again?"

"We were ahead twenty at midnight. Don't know what happened."

"Who? How'd you pay 'em?" Webb had heard this before, the only variation being Ned's creativity of payment.

"A couple of slickers from Jane Lew. Never seen 'em before. Said they were scouting troubled companies to buy. They let me slide with an IOU after my girl told them where to find me. Bitch. I'm suppose to meet 'em again tonight. So ya see, I gotta work here today and get something to give those boys or stay away from Ma's."

"You ain't gonna be here long enough to earn shit."

"I can work till dark, and you can pay me what you will. Okay?"

Webb handed his brother a trowel and pointed to a large bucket of plaster. "Get busy, you sorry son of a—"

Wilbur and Jesse made for the woods.

The sun hadn't yet set when Sarah returned. Wilbur and Jesse ran screaming to their mother, faces smeared in dirt, Jesse's nose caked with snot. Wilbur held a dead groundhog by the tail. "Lookie, Mom. I got supper."

"He's chasing me, Mama! I don't wanna hold it!" cried Jesse.

At sunset, they began the nightly chores: feeding chickens, collecting eggs, and stewing chicken. The boys had plucked and gathered dandelions while walking home. Sarah boiled them and added them to the table's bounty. She sent Wilbur and Jesse to summon their father for the meal. "Hello there! I'll be right along!" hollered Webb from the construction site.

"Are we done for today?" asked Ned.

"I reckon. Here's two dollars' pay—and more than you've rightly earned," said Webb. Ned took the money and loitered about as he listlessly tried to help Webb clean up. "I'll get it, Ned. You can go now." Ned left swiftly on foot, wearing a bulging army-surplus jacket. Webb started picking up his materials for the night but halted and swore.

"What is it, Dad?" asked Wilbur.

"Goddamn good-for-nothing son of a—he took two new hammers, a saw, and my level."

Chapter 2

Before settling his family in West Virginia, Webb held a steady Monday–Friday job working for the Public Works Administration on the Blue Ridge Parkway in Waynesboro, Virginia, blasting through rock and granite to create the roads connecting Shenandoah National Park to the Great Smoky Mountains National Park. Sarah found work cooking and cleaning for a wealthy family in Williamsburg in exchange for room and board for herself and her two sons; Webb would visit only on the weekends. This arrangement continued until the federal money ran out and Webb's employment was terminated.

While in Williamsburg, Wilbur had learned to fish with regular success at three, catching brook trout and bass from a stream. Wilbur's father had previously shown him how to whittle a pole and rig the line. After weeks of catching only enough to eat, Wilbur hated to stop fishing once he caught his legal limit, because he knew he could easily catch more. Earning money by fishing entrepreneurially, he arbitrarily raised his limit to ten and began knocking door-to-door with his string of goods, selling fish for a nickel each. The general store in Williamsburg sold rods and reels for $1.25, and by the end of the summer, he'd earned enough money to buy himself a brand-new rod.

When Wilbur was four, Webb had taught him the art of trapping by learning how animals lived. They watched rabbits, groundhogs, and possums in their natural habitats. Wilbur sat for hours, blending into the forest, until he could predict each critter's movement, and then he'd set traps along their expected pathways. His lust for hunting was so great that it became the only time when he sat quietly. Sarah gladly let him go off on his own, getting him out of her hair while she tended her chores in Williamsburg.

Once the Blue Ridge Parkway was complete, Sarah quit her job, Webb packed up his family, and everyone moved home to West Virginia. On one cold Saturday night—the second weekend in November—Wilbur and his family sat on their cots in the chicken house, eating a supper of stewed squirrel, potatoes, and onions obtained by their own efforts. Their small garden yielded a variety of root vegetables, cabbage, and lettuce due to Sarah's planting after the summer harvest. Being a natural hunter, Wilbur had bagged three squirrels with his father's 20-gauge shotgun (a prized possession given to Wilbur after he mastered his trapping skills) earlier in the morning.

Wilbur first saw the 20-gauge when his father hung two shotguns on the chicken house wall, just out of his reach. The other was a 12-gauge over-and-under. Both had belonged to Webb since his childhood, and he used them to provide food for his family. Sarah had bragged about their son's remarkable hunting skills, but Webb didn't imagine the depth of Wilbur's talent until he saw the bounty Wilbur regularly brought home. It made him proud to see how well his son provided for them, and he also felt somewhat relieved, because Wilbur's contribution allowed him to concentrate on building their home.

"Would you like to learn how to shoot?" he'd asked Wilbur one night after noticing him stare at the guns again. Wilbur would be six years old soon, and since he'd proven himself responsible, Webb felt he was ready to handle a gun.

"Sure would, sir. Can I shoot the big one?"

"You're a worthy trapper, Son. Maybe it is time you went after the big game. Let's see how you do with the littler one first."

Webb had spent the first two weeks back home settling onto the land, making supply preparations to build, and teaching Wilbur to shoot. He'd then returned to the coal mines full-time.

Six months later, he ate supper with his family after putting the last coat of varnish on the living room floors of their new house. "Well, Sarah, this is the last supper we'll eat here," he said.

"Do you mean it? Can we move in tomorrow?"

"Late tomorrow. Give the floors time enough to dry. But yes, I think we can." His proclamation lent a special significance to supper, and they enjoyed their meal in honor of a life they'd soon leave behind.

Granny Weaver; Ned; and Webb's sisters, Eula May and Cora, and their husbands, who'd all traveled from the adjoining county, made a rare appearance and joined the family Sunday afternoon to celebrate the move, meeting Sarah for the first time. They sat in the sparsely furnished house after touring the rooms, giddy over someone in the family having indoor plumbing, when a knock at the door interrupted their revelry.

Webb went to the door. From his seat, Wilbur couldn't see who was there, but the stench of cigar smoke wafted inside.

"You Webb Weaver?" Wilbur heard. It was a man's voice, rough and gravelly.

"Yeah, that's me."

"Nice house you got here."

"Thank you. Can I help you?"

The stranger chuckled deep in his throat and said, "You get your materials from Jamison's?"

"Yeah. What I can I do for you, Mr.—what's the name?"

"Name's Smith. I got this here lien against the house, saying it's mine unless you pay me for the supplies." The sound of paper crinkling reached Wilbur's ears. Everyone at the table was silent.

"This house is paid for, buddy. I suggest you take leave before I take offense," replied Webb. He stepped outside, out of Wilbur's view completely.

"Nah, sir. I sent Jamison twelve thousand dollars' worth of materials for this place and ain't never been paid a dime. Being a couple of months overdue now, I'm here to collect what's owed. Or take possession of the property."

"You can take your paper and shove it. I paid Carl, and this place is mine. Bought and paid for. I reckon you need to talk to him."

"Jamison's Building Supply ain't in business no more. I bought it yesterday. You got till tomorrow to come up with my money. I'll be back then. Good day," he said. The paper crinkled again, harder this time, and the sounds of footsteps signaled that the man was leaving.

It took Webb a moment to come back inside. He closed the door and examined the paper in his pocket. "You know anything about this, Ned?"

"What's that man talking about?" asked Sarah, looking at Webb, who waited accusingly for Ned's answer.

"Now that you ask, that might be the man who hustled me at pool. He'd have to take off his hat for me to be sure, but he did say he bought out Carl, and that's what the other guy was after—troubled businesses."

"I just saw Carl—Tuesday, when I paid him cash for the last delivery," said Webb. Webb crumpled the lien in his hand and began swearing, using words Wilbur had never heard before. Wilbur wanted to know what a lien was but figured this wasn't the right time to ask.

Shaking with anger and stomping as he paced the floor, Webb told Ned, "You're coming with me. We're gonna settle this tonight. Eula May, Fred, I need your truck. Y'all can go home in it when we get back." He took Ned by the arm and dragged him out the door. They stopped by the chicken house. Wilbur and Jesse watched from the window. Webb came out of the chicken house with his double-barrel 12-gauge. Ned met him in the yard. Wilbur, afraid to join the others, who had gone onto the porch, saw Ned practically jumping up and down with excitement. They went to the truck, where Ned pulled a bottle from his jacket. Webb looked at it for a moment and then took a long drink. Nodding, he got behind the wheel, and they drove off. Sarah came back into the kitchen. The color had drained from her face.

Webb and Ned were gone for two days. His family, immediate and extended, spent the first night in the house, anxiously awaiting their return. They woke to find Eula May's truck parked out front—empty. Late Monday, the sisters and their husbands went home after spending the day searching fruitlessly. Granny left Tuesday morning, having to feed her animals.

Sarah thought her in-laws acted too calmly, as if they'd seen this kind of behavior before. She felt she was at her wits' end, wondering if her husband was alive or not and, if so, whether he was capable of murder—not to mention whether or not she'd have a house to live in.

With all these unanswered questions, apprehension enveloped the house. Jesse clung to Sarah for protection against the unknown evil. Wilbur felt it too: a crack in his childhood. Something bad had come to fester. With his father gone, he now felt responsible for their happiness. He found himself staying awake later every night and getting up earlier every morning, hoping to see his father coming home. Every day he told them repeatedly, "Everything will be just fine."

Wilbur was up in the predawn hours of Wednesday morning. He didn't see a truck pull into their property, but he saw Webb come shambling to their door. Wilbur wanted desperately to run to him and ask what had happened and if Ned was all right, but he knew that would be a bad idea. He couldn't even afford to let Webb know he was awake. So he just watched as Webb lurched into the bedroom. After a few seconds, his mother groggily but intelligibly said, "That you, Webb?"

It was a long time before an answer came, and in that time, Wilbur thought he heard someone crying. Then his father said, "We're safe, Sarah. Ain't nobody gonna bother us now."

Chapter 3

On Jesse's first school day in September 1943, Wilbur held his brother's hand as they walked to school, showing him the quickest route: through McQuarter's cow pasture, across the fallen tree bridging Lost Creek, and then up Pridgeon's Hill. Wilbur had scouted the route two years ago when starting school himself, and now, being an experienced third grader, he happily took charge of Jesse's welfare. "Don't sit in the front row unless you know the answers. Teachers call on the kids up there. Of course, that's where I sit, but I'm real smart," said Wilbur. Jesse nodded with understanding. "And watch out for Mrs. Bullock. I remember when I had her in first grade. She'd get nasty if you talked in class—make you stand up front with your nose in the corner. Never happened to me, but it did to Earl Thompson almost every day."

Wilbur loved school. He made straight 100s—not just As—in every subject and expected nothing less than perfection of himself. He set an incredible standard, but his insatiable desire for approval led him to crave praise wherever he could find it.

Home didn't offer such rewards—at least not since his family had moved into their house. Before then, he fondly recalled, while living in the chicken house, he'd felt special, even loved, because his parents had appreciated him. They'd needed him. Nowadays he just felt underfoot. It seemed his parents fought all the time since moving, and when he thought of his father, he envisioned him drunk. Wilbur couldn't remember the last time his mother had smiled, and whenever he tried to cheer her up, she'd yell at him and tell him, "Leave me be!" He and Jesse worked hard to stay clear of both of their parents.

Now Wilbur's life had improved with school, and he hoped Jesse could find solace there too.

Wilbur couldn't remember exactly when he'd first noticed the strange scent on his mother's breath, but it made him uneasy. He knew what it was well enough, but he didn't know what it meant.

Webb came home shortly after five in the afternoon. The boys had been outside since lunch. After cooking for them—but not eating any herself—Sarah had lain on the couch, claiming she just needed a moment to rest her eyes. She'd been asleep for hours. Webb didn't even glance at them as he went inside. The window was open, so when Webb yelled, "Where's supper?" the boys heard him clearly.

Their mother must have said something, because the next thing they heard was Webb saying, "It's time you got busy. What time do you think it is?" He followed that with "I'll be goddamned. You're drunk."

Another silence followed. Wilbur figured Sarah was denying the accusation.

"Don't lie to me. I smell it on you. How many other times have you been drinking while I'm working my ass off providing for you? You ain't making a fool outta me, woman." The more he talked, the madder he got, as usual.

Wilbur and Jesse stopped playing. Wilbur had strung a stick with twine, making a bow, and was convincing Jesse to stand still while Wilbur shot an apple off the top of his brother's head. The yelling escalated to screams. The boys ran inside just in time to see Webb raise his hand and slap Sarah in the face.

"Let's go, Wilbur! Take me back outside!" cried Jesse, hugging his brother tightly, afraid he'd be next.

Webb turned to his sons and said, "Did you know you boys got a drunkard for a ma?" Torn between fear for his own safety and the desire to protect his mother, Wilbur stood frozen. "What're you staring at, boy? Go on—get outta here."

He looked to his mother. She nodded to him, as if saying, "Go on. I'll be all right." With this slight approval, he rushed Jesse back outside. As they stood in the yard in misery, listening to the shouting, Wilbur had an idea. "Come on, Jesse. Let's go somewhere quiet." He led Jesse to the basement, where they got a rod and reel. Wilbur shoved three apples in his coat pocket and made sure he had his pocketknife and matchsticks, and the boys headed into the woods.

They set up camp on the creek bank about a half mile from home. Wilbur picked a spot with an old stump so they'd have a place to sit, and he told Jesse to gather sticks for a fire. "I'll catch us some supper, Jesse. We'll just stay right here until they stop fighting. Heck, maybe we ought not ever go back," he said, feeling safer and happier outdoors.

Jesse remained silent while gathering wood, occasionally snuffling back a runny nose from crying. He would have felt totally lost if not for his brother. Wilbur sat down on the stump and began fishing as he too lamented their life. A large brim was soon on the line. "Fetch me that long, skinny stick over there," he said to Jesse as he unhooked the fish. "This'll be enough for us." After whittling a sharp point, he threaded the stick through the fish's gills and out its mouth and then anchored one end deep into the muddy creek bank; the rushing water would keep his catch fresh while he built a fire. "Make a teepee with the wood, Jesse, like this." Wilbur demonstrated and then snatched handfuls of dried grass to place in the center. He lit a match, and the fire caught easily. "Now we gotta wait. Let the sticks burn down good before we can cook."

"I'm hungry," said Jesse. These were the first words he'd spoken.

"Yeah, me too." They hadn't eaten since having lunch at school. Wilbur cut an apple in half and handed Jesse his share. "Eat this." They ate quietly, listening to the crackling of burning twigs and the crunching of apples, thinking about the sun as it set low behind the hills, still offering a few more minutes of daylight. *If we were home, we'd be finishing homework and getting ready for bed about now,* Wilbur thought, dreading the idea of going back. *Why should we?* Caring for her children—or even acknowledging their presence—only burdened his mother at a time when she needed to fend for herself. Finding no reason to return to the house, he decided he and Jesse would sleep under the stars. *We'll go home after Pop leaves for work.*

When the fire burned down, Wilbur found two forked sticks and sharpened their ends before sticking them upright in the ground on either side of the fire. He retrieved his fish from the water, shook it dry as best he could, and then placed it on the forked stick ends, making a spit and roasting it above the coals. "Let's gather more wood while this cooks. We're gonna sleep here tonight, okay, Jesse?"

Jesse answered with a silent nod.

They sat, watching the fish cook, hypnotized by the crackling fire. When the skin blackened and the juices started to drip, the young boys tore apart the fish like seasoned pioneers, pulling the meat off until nothing but bones remained attached to the head. Wilbur then piled all the wood he'd gathered onto the fire, creating a cozy warmth for him and Jesse as they cuddled together on a bed of leaves and fell fast asleep.

They awoke the next morning cold and dirty, smelling of wood and smoke. Wilbur guessed they had another two hours before school; the sun hadn't yet risen above Pridgeon's Hill. His father would be leaving for work about now, so he felt it was safe to return home.

"Do we have to? Let's just stay here today. I don't like school anyway," said Jesse as they prepared to leave, offering one last plea to delay the inevitable.

"We gotta go to school, Jesse, whether you like it or not. Besides, aren't you hungry?"

"I'd rather be hungry out here than go back, but okay. I do miss Mama," he said, not yet brave enough to live up to his words. Wilbur gave him an apple for breakfast and ate one himself, and the boys set out for the hike home. "Are we gonna be in trouble? I don't want a whoopin'."

"Naw. If'n it looks bad, I'll tell 'em I made you come."

Reaching the house, Wilbur made sure he didn't see his father's truck before they went inside. They entered the basement first to wash up for school and then crept up the stairs into the living room, keeping quiet. Sarah came out of her bedroom and saw them standing in the hall. "What are you all doing here? Overslept? Get a move on, both of you, before you're late for school."

Wilbur waited for her to say something about their being out all night, but she hadn't even noticed. "Sorry, Mom. We'll get going."

They grabbed their satchels and left, no one the wiser.

Years passed in the same way. Webb continued to drink every day, but now Sarah regularly joined him. Unable to continue her fight for the life she'd envisioned, she'd surrendered, numbing her disappointment with alcohol. When they were together, concepts like love, support, commitment, and affection were alien. Webb and Sarah didn't act like man and wife but like strangers who'd only befriended one another as drinking partners. Their marriage became about escaping their haunting secrets and disappointed expectations.

Now Ned, whose apparent purpose in life was to stay inebriated, practically lived in the house too. Most days, Wilbur and Jesse came home from school to find their mother asleep, catching up from a late night and early morning drunk. She'd usually wake sometime after supper (prepared and eaten alone by the boys themselves). When Webb and Ned finished their postwork beers at the pool hall, Sarah would get ready for her day. To Wilbur and Jesse, those few hours were the only time she seemed happy: she put on lipstick, dressed, and was briefly sober before another night of drinking. When Webb and Ned arrived home, the three would entertain all comers, people coming and going, until long after the boys put themselves to bed.

Wilbur grew to hate this life. Jesse, on the other hand, loved it. To him, his parents seemed happy; they smiled and laughed. In his opinion, their nightly parties made life fun. While Wilbur stayed outside hunting or in his room studying, Jesse sat unseen at the top of the stairs and watched the carousing. He would be either asleep or would refuse to acknowledge when the gaiety turned sour—when the drunkenness turned mean and angry—and when the partiers looked to blame someone else for life's injustices. Not every time but often enough, Wilbur listened as his father swore, calling his mother a whore and wishing her dead, though, thankfully, Webb hadn't raised a hand against Sarah in a long time.

In the autumn of 1947, Wilbur turned twelve and started the seventh grade. He and Jesse, who was now in fifth grade, sat in the same class in school. Wilbur and Jesse saw things differently. Jesse hated school—not so much the people but the homework and the studying. Wilbur sat in the front row and always raised his hand first to answer, while Jesse would sit in the back and fall asleep. Jesse tried to emulate Wilbur in the beginning, but once living up to this standard proved impossible, Jesse quit trying altogether. "Just do the best you can, Jesse. Bs are still better than Fs," Wilbur would say. But feeling that no amount of work would ever come close to his brother's performance, Jesse consciously chose to stand apart from his overachieving brother by becoming the exact opposite: since the best he'd ever do still meant being second to his brother, he'd be number one in failure. Jesse didn't do so out of spite—he loved Wilbur dearly—but Jesse wanted to be a person in his own right.

Jesse's so-called individualism constantly got him into trouble and, in his brother's eyes, made Wilbur's own perfectionism an absolute necessity, another burden in compensating for alcoholic parents.

In October, Sarah and Webb had been up late fighting for four days straight, and Wilbur's lack of sleep affected his grade on an important science test—he made a 92. Jesse had been suspended for two days after being caught with an emptied shampoo bottle full of whiskey and had been sent home, aggravating their mother.

Weary from thought, Wilbur walked home on Friday afternoon, trying to find a way to reach out to his brother. He feared Jesse's destiny might lie in their father's footsteps. Already lured to drinking as a ten-year-old—what could Wilbur do or say to stop him? Wilbur also had wondered what had provoked his parents' recent fights. He'd learned the night before that they had been about Ned. Wilbur had overheard his father shout, "I can't believe Ned'd do me like that!"

Bored after two days at home, Jesse met Wilbur at the creek. "Hey, Wilbur. How's school today?"

"Not good. Almost made a B on my science test. What've you been doin'? How's Mom?"

"Not much. Mama's fine, I reckon. She got up and fixed me lunch but seemed to have a lot on her mind."

"You heard them fight too?"

"Yeah. I think Ned's been stealing money. At least that's what Mama told Pop. He doesn't believe her—thinks she's been stashing it away for herself."

"I wouldn't put anything past Uncle Ned."

"Me neither." They walked in silence until reaching home.

"Pop's home?" Wilbur asked, seeing their father's truck.

"Not when I left. He's never out of the mines before five o'clock. Wonder what's wrong."

"Can't be anything good."

They stood at the back door and listened for shouts but didn't hear anything. As they walked up through the basement, the house was ominously silent. Suddenly, a shotgun blast exploded. Wilbur and Jesse burst into the living room and saw their father pointing his gun at Sarah, having fired into the wall beside her. Sarah sat on the couch, glaring back defiantly. "Go ahead—shoot me, you son of a bitch. Being dead would keep me from living with you—hell, I wish it. Go ahead."

Webb held his gun ready, shaking, pondering his next move. He turned on his sons, knowing they stood behind him. "What about them?" he asked as he turned, staring down the gun barrel, which he now pointed at Wilbur's chest.

Wilbur's heart stopped. Was his father really pointing a gun at him? He stood in shock and disbelief. Sarah leaped off the sofa and attacked from behind. "Leave them alone, or I'll kill you!"

Webb dropped the gun and turned back to Sarah, resuming their name calling as if nothing had just taken place.

Overcome with grief, Wilbur ran outside and fell to the ground crying, hating what he knew deep inside: his father, at that moment, had wanted to kill him. Wilbur had seen it in his eyes.

Jesse tried to comfort his brother, but words weren't enough. "Come on, Wilbur. I know what to do," he said, helping him to stand. He went to the basement for supplies as Wilbur sat down on the steps, speechless and numb. Thirty minutes later, they were in the woods, setting up camp with blankets, food, pots, pillows, the old 20-gauge shotgun, and a healthy supply of shells.

Jesse had planned for a lengthy stay.

The weather held for their first four days but turned colder on the fifth night. At the campsite, they'd made a tent from a blanket strung between two trees. They had designated areas for cooking, sitting, and sleeping around the fire and had created a safe home. Neither was uncomfortable until the wind changed direction and blew in from the north.

"Hey, I got an idea. Let's go over to Joe Ryder's house and get some of his pop's old tires to burn. I bet he'd like to come out here too and sit a spell," Jesse suggested. Joe, another seventh grader, lived close by and sat behind Wilbur in school.

"Sounds good to me," Wilbur said, his spirits almost back to normal. They hadn't mentioned their parents since arriving; they just busied themselves with the tasks of hunting and gathering, enjoying each other's company with the unspoken but powerful bonds of brotherhood.

Joe Ryder eagerly accepted the invitation to camp, even on a school night. He told his mother he'd be staying the night with Wilbur, and she agreed, thinking, of course, that the overnight would be at Wilbur's house. Joe's father owned a salvage yard offering a plethora of supplies, and several donkeys roamed it freely. The boys rigged a makeshift sled to one of the donkeys and piled on as many tires as it could hold, a gallon of gasoline, and two sheets of rusty tin to reinforce the sleeping quarters. The procession arrived back at camp before dark.

Wilbur went to work skinning a rabbit caught in a trap he'd set earlier, while Joe and Jesse unloaded supplies and rebuilt the tent into a three-sided shelter: two sides made of tin and one made from the hanging blanket so that cold air wouldn't blow in. Enough hot coals remained burning in their fire, so Wilbur threaded the rabbit on a stick and set it to roast as they sat and told tales.

"Dang, it's cold," said Joe.

"Coldest it's been all week. We'll burn those tires after supper and get a good fire going to keep us warm all night long," said Wilbur.

"You been out here all week? I wondered where you were in school yesterday and today. Mrs. Nutter asked after you," said Joe.

"Did anyone say anything?" asked Wilbur.

"No. No one knew what to say. It's not like you to miss school."

"I know. I'll get back soon and catch up. We're just taking a vacation," said Wilbur without further explanation.

After a supper of roasted rabbit, canned beans, and bread swiped from Joe's house, they soaked two tires with the gallon of gasoline. "We got to throw these tires on from a distance. Gas explodes, you know," warned Wilbur.

"Yeah. I learned that the hard way after looking for the bottom of a can with a lighted match and burning my eyelids shut," said Joe. They guffawed at the mental picture.

They threw the tires onto the fire and watched them burst into flames with a booming *swoosh*, and then they put two more dry tires on top when the gas burned off. A glowing, slow-burning fire kept them warm while they laughed and talked well into the night, creeping closer and closer to the heat as the temperature dropped and snow clouds rolled in. Sometime after midnight, they considered going into the tent, but since the fire was still going strong and they weren't cold, they decided to stay put.

Wilbur awoke hours later, freezing. It seemed brighter than it should have been. The white-blanketed landscape illuminated the dead of night; he could see as if it were day. What he first mistook for rain turned out to be small flakes of snow falling. *Oh my God, it's snow. It's snow!* "Joe, Jesse, wake up. It's snowing."

Everyone rose, excited about the snow, and proceeded to throw snowballs at each other until dawn.

With the sun up, Joe, Wilbur, and Jesse stopped to stare at one another and then examined their own hands. "Joe, am I as black as you are?" asked Wilbur.

"Me? All's I see of you and Jesse are eyes and teeth."

"We've turned black," said Jesse.

Three sets of eyes and smiling teeth stared through black faces covered in smoke and soot from the burning rubber tires. Once they put together the facts, they laughed so hard they cried, their tears streaking white paths down their black faces.

Joe left them the next morning, but Wilbur didn't feel it was time to go back yet. The only thing he missed was school. He figured Jesse felt the same, but when he mentioned this, Jesse surprised him.

"I don't see why you care," said Jesse. "We don't learn nothing important. Just a bunch of time being wasted."

"You're just saying that because you don't know anything." That wasn't true, and Wilbur knew it. Jesse knew plenty. He could have been a good student if he'd put any effort into it. "But at least at school we don't have to …" He found he couldn't say what he was thinking.

"Just a waste of time," said Jesse.

After being gone for nine days, Wilbur and Jesse returned home on a Sunday afternoon. Somehow, it didn't matter whether they stayed in the woods or went home. They thought someone would eventually come looking for them, and when no one did, they figured nobody cared enough to punish them either. Mostly, Wilbur ached to return to school. He needed a home to sleep and eat in and a place to study. He'd endure anything to succeed in school; it was his only way out.

When they arrived, Sarah got up from the table and hugged her sons, briefly conveying her worry through her embrace, and then said, "Get a bath, and go to bed, both of you. School's tomorrow." Webb continued to eat his supper uninterrupted. Nothing more was said.

Chapter 4

Living independent from their parents' emotional turmoil, the brothers forged ahead in their daily lives, going to school, mowing the yard, putting up hay, feeding the chickens, and building fences. The boys also spent every spare moment hunting in the woods; Wilbur's passion for hunting was second only to his schooling. A natural-born hunter too, Jesse went along—but just for company and entertainment, not because he loved the outdoors.

Sharing the same genes, Jesse had abilities that equaled his brother's in every way: he was just as smart and just as coordinated; they'd both inherited Webb's unerring mechanical intuition and were able to fix anything; and both boys were great marksmen. They also shared deep doubts about themselves, but the difference in how they reacted to life's turmoil defined their chosen paths.

Wilbur embraced his natural abilities, building upon what he could do and striving for higher achievements; Jesse took his abilities for granted. The knowledge that things came easily to him made him lazy and bored. If something proved challenging, he'd rationalize not trying, because in the end, so what? He'd eventually achieve, but so what? It didn't really matter in his alcoholic, bitterly pessimistic view of life. Besides, if he accomplished more, then others would expect more of him, and he'd rather save himself the trouble and save everyone else from his or her inevitable disappointment.

Maybe they differed so only because Jesse had had the misfortune of inheriting the alcoholic gene, and Wilbur hadn't. In any case, the boys loved each other. Their bond provided them with the emotional strength they needed to survive. Whenever their home life became unbearable, they'd escape to the woods, hoping that a few days away, a week at most, would offer some peace. The time away did help, but they found themselves living outside their own home more than inside it. Especially during the summer, when having her kids underfoot created more tension than usual, Sarah reached for the bottle earlier and more often. In the past summer, after one of their parents' dish-throwing, screaming arguments, the boys had stayed away for a solid month, living in the woods and only returning home because they missed their parents, drunk or not. For all the sense of adventure and independence they were developing, they were still boys who needed a mother.

Wilbur and Jesse didn't have access to any money of their own. If they wanted something beyond necessities, they had to find ways to earn cash. The neighbors had come to know Wilbur as a reliable hired hand. In his sophmore year, the school's Future Farmers of America, or FFA, chapter sponsored the annual Sadie Hawkins dance, the social highlight of the year for students. This year was extraordinary because the school had received, for the first time, a donation from a sporting goods store of a brand-new Winchester .30-06 deer rifle to raffle off as a fund-raiser. All the boys in the school coveted the gun. Most were hunters, and bringing their guns to class was commonplace; they brought new acquisitions for show-and-tell, and every young man knew what everybody else owned. Wilbur had already presented his 20-gauge in first grade and his double-barrel in second.

He fantasized about winning the raffle, and for once in his life, he felt lucky. He took the unprecedented event as proof of the gun's destiny to be his. Why else would this opportunity have come? A ticket cost one dollar. It was a hefty sum to Wilbur, but he had three weeks before the raffle to earn some money and buy tickets.

On Monday, the afternoon on which the impending raffle was announced, he walked over to Jake McQuarter's to offer to shovel out his barn. As Mr. McQuarter had been blessed with only daughters, Wilbur frequently helped him around his farm for no charge. "Hello, ma'am. Is your husband here?" asked Wilbur when Mrs. McQuarter, an elderly woman who was hard of hearing, answered the door.

"He's feeling poorly today, Wilbur. What can I do for you?"

"I was hoping to earn some money." He explained about the FFA raffle. "And I thought he might need his barn shoveled."

"Eh? You want to muck out the stalls?"

"Yes, ma'am. For, say, twenty-five cents an hour?"

"You say twenty-five cents?"

"Yes, ma'am. An hour."

"I reckon so. Just holler at me when you finish."

Wilbur grabbed a hayfork and shovel from the toolshed and headed to the barn, calculating the hours he could work and envisioning himself buying at least three tickets from this job alone. The McQuarters owned more land than anyone else and made good money raising cattle. They had three barns. The main one had twenty stalls where the heifers came to whelp. Another barn held horses, and the third housed chickens and pigs. *Maybe they'd want those mucked too*, he thought. He worked until dark, cleaning eight stalls before heading home to have supper and do his homework.

By the end of the week, since Jake McQuarter still felt poorly, Wilbur had mucked all three barns. Mrs. McQuarter had nodded with approval each time Wilbur asked to do the next. On his way home from school on Friday, he knocked on their door, wanting payment. "I'm done, ma'am," he said when Mrs. McQuarter answered.

"My, Wilbur. You've surely worked hard this week. I checked them myself, and I swear the barns ain't never been so clean."

"Thank you, ma'am. I was hoping to collect my money today."

"Oh, sure." Mrs. McQuarter ambled away from the door and disappeared from view. She emerged moments later, smiling with gratitude as she placed one quarter into Wilbur's outstretched palm.

Wilbur stood on the stoop, holding his hand out, waiting for more.

"Well, there you are, boy. What else can we do for you?"

"Nothing, ma'am. I just thought I'd get this much an hour."

"Eh? You said a quarter—there's your quarter. I'll be sure to tell Jake what a fine job you did too. Bye now," she said, shutting the door.

Wilbur stood dumbstruck. The McQuarters were kindly neighbors; he knew she'd paid him honestly what she thought they'd agreed on. He couldn't argue with her, but his aching back, sore arms, and stiff neck mocked him. He'd just spent a whole week bent over shoveling manure for twenty-five cents.

The next week, he managed to earn fifty cents cutting hay for Mr. Sanderling, a neighbor who'd lived up and across the road with his wife and two daughters for the last twenty years. Afraid he wouldn't get enough for even one ticket, desperation set in when his other contacts didn't need any hired help. Finally, on the day before the raffle, after scrounging every ditch and junkyard and knocking on doors and asking friends, he'd gathered enough refundable soda bottles to collect the remaining quarter. On Friday morning, he optimistically purchased his one ticket. He watched with envy as a few other boys bought up to five tickets, and he felt cheated, thinking about Mrs. McQuarter. He reassured himself, *They can buy a dozen and still not beat destiny. That rifle's mine.*

He and Jesse walked home from school in high spirits, Jesse always liking a reason to party and Wilbur knowing the rifle would soon be his.

Traditionally, the girls asked the boys to the Sadie Hawkins dance. Wilbur and Jesse had both been asked, but Wilbur had declined his invitation from Betty Ann, a sweet girl who'd let it be known that she liked him since first grade. He didn't have money to buy her a corsage. Jesse guiltlessly accepted both of his invitations, regardless of income. The girls he gave attention to never seemed to mind sharing or to mind that he never paid for anything.

Good looking and charming, Jesse had thick black hair slicked back in a large ducktail, and he wore jeans and T-shirts like James Dean. His bad-boy image made girls swoon, whereas Wilbur's intellect made him appear aloof. Also handsome, Wilbur had kept his blond hair from childhood, wearing it deeply parted on the left and greased back in a smaller ducktail. Average in height, trim, and fit, Wilbur preferred work pants and collared shirts. His hard work and innocent face won the love of his teachers, but he also possessed an internal hardness due to years of struggling for his parents' affection. Sage adults easily recognized his look as one that begged approval, recognition, and love.

After supper, Wilbur and Jesse showered and dressed, and they were ready with an hour to spare. The anticipation of waiting proved too much for Wilbur, so he headed out and arrived at the dance thirty minutes early. Ten student club members wearing dark blue corduroy FFA jackets stood milling about the stage, bored, as they too waited for the dance to begin. Benny Anderson, secretary of the club, dumped the tickets into the chicken-wire barrel and cranked its handle, turning the chits as Wilbur looked on, mentally channeling every bit of energy into his one ticket.

"Hey, I've got an idea," said Benny. The twenty-five minutes to kill seemed like an eternity. All eyes looked to him. "Let's have a practice drawing."

"A what?" asked Wilbur. An incredulous feeling of injustice came over him. "You can't do that," he objected, but they couldn't hear him above their excitement.

"That's a great idea," said the others. Despite his protests, Wilbur watched as Benny reached in and pulled out a ticket. The practice drawing took place in slow motion like a bad dream. Benny took center stage with the ticket in hand.

"And the winner is ..." Benny's lips puckered slowly, as if he wanted to kiss. He smiled and looked to Wilbur.

"Don't even say it." Wilbur shook his head.

"Wilbur Weaver," announced Benny. Everyone on stage clapped and roared, congratulating him for winning.

Then Benny happily returned his ticket to the barrel. Wilbur's disgust went unnoticed.

The experience only confirmed his deepening pessimism about life.

Yeah, I'm a big winner all right. A big winner of nothing.

His anger became justified a short while later, when Benny drew a second ticket from the barrel and read someone else's name.

Chapter 5

Sarah's hands shook as she held the bottles, causing her to spill the sticky pink syrup of the one she emptied along the outside of the other. *Dammit.* She had to hurry, and she had to be careful. If Webb caught her, he would kill her for sure.

Someone had told her (though she couldn't recall who it was) about how spiking liquor with ipecac would cause an aversion for drink, and having done so the last week, she understood why: Webb had vomited profusely, his eyes swollen nearly shut, their lids bursting with small hemorrhages from his constant retching. As of yet, he hadn't a clue and blamed his sickness on food poisoning, on Sarah's bad cooking. She'd taken his abuse, knowing it was her doing but hoping the end result would be a sober husband. She couldn't keep up with his drinking anymore, and something had to change: either he'd stop, or she'd leave him. Ever since she'd quit a month ago, his anger toward her had grown. Alone in his addiction, he'd become downright mean, and she feared for her safety.

She didn't know exactly why she'd decided to quit. Probably it was nothing more than being tired of being tired—tired of looking at herself in the mirror and seeing a woman of thirty-four staring into the face of an aged and haggard woman of fifty.

She recapped the ipecac and wiped down Webb's bottle of rotgut; he no longer cared if his alcohol was bonded. She shook the mixture, distributing the two ounces of syrup throughout, and then replaced it on the kitchen counter. She made sure to dispose of the evidence. Sometimes she'd carry the small bottle in her purse until she went to the market and then ditch it there. But she was stuck at home this week. She dug in the trash for something to hide it in but found only paper trash, which Webb burned; glass didn't burn. *Damn, he'll be home any moment.* After scrubbing away the label, she rinsed the bottle and threw it in the garbage anyway. *If he asks, I'll just tell him it's hair dye.*

The boys were already home from school. Excited about his date, Wilbur ran upstairs to preen and dress, getting ready to take Betty Ann to his senior prom. They'd become an item over the last two years. Sarah liked the girl and privately hoped they'd marry. A pretty hometown girl like her would keep him close after graduation and maybe dispel his nonsense about going to college, and he'd get a good job in the mines, settle down, and raise a family.

She didn't know where Jesse had taken off to; she'd last seen him head out the door, mumbling something about going out with friends.

"How do I look, Mom?" Wilbur asked, coming downstairs dressed in a white sport coat, black pants, and a tie she'd rented with money held back from the grocery budget. He looked splendid.

"Betty Ann will be pleased."

"You think? I need to pick her up soon. Is Pop home yet?"

"I hear his truck pulling up now. I can't wait for him to see you."

Webb came in through the basement. The sight of his son caught him unawares. He couldn't help smiling. "What're you doing all gussied up, Son?"

"I'm taking Betty Ann to the prom tonight."

"Prom, eh? I thought they were for rich kids. We ain't rich, boy. Where'd you get money for that suit?"

Wilbur tried not to let him ruin his mood and hurriedly lied, "I borrowed it from William. You know William—his father owns the bank."

"That's what I'm saying. There's no need to set yourself up for disappointment by acting rich. I ain't no banker, and neither are you."

"I know, Pop. But a man's got to woo his girl somehow."

Webb managed another smile. He gave him his car keys for the night, and Wilbur left with thanks after kissing his mother good-bye.

"Whaddya have to say that for?" Sarah asked Webb when they were alone.

"What?"

"Try to bring him down on his special night? He very well could become a banker—or anything else he wants. You know he's graduating at the top of his class. Number one, to be exact."

"Big dreams he has. Just like me when I first met you. But he'll learn. And it's best he learn now: dreams are for fools. Now get off my ass, and get me a drink."

Betty Ann looked radiant in the pink gown her mother had made; it had wide shoulder straps and an empire waist. Wilbur pinned a corsage of pink and white carnations on one of the straps. She wrapped herself in a chiffon stole and wore her hair curled and piled on top of her head in a loose bun. After twelve years of school, he'd never seen her look so beautiful. The Betty Ann he knew wore plaid skirts and oversized shirts with her hair pulled back in a ponytail. Tonight he carried a woman on his arm.

The prom's theme was "Moonlight and Stars." Tinfoil stars hung down from the auditorium ceiling with cardboard paintings of a full moon and dusky midnight clouds strung among them. Wilbur held Betty Ann close for a slow dance as his favorite song, "Tragedy" by Roy Orbison, played in the background.

"How does it feel, Mr. Valedictorian?" asked Betty Ann.

"How does what feel?"

"You know, graduating first in your class, having all those choices regarding your future. What will you do next?"

"I'm hoping to go to college. I've already been accepted to WVU, Ohio State, and Princeton—I got in there because of my National Merit scholarship—but I haven't decided on anything yet." With graduation two weeks away, Wilbur had already been awarded nine academic scholarships, though none would pay full room and board.

The smile faded from her face. Wilbur noticed but thought nothing of it. "What would you study?" she said.

"Something in science. Last year at camp"—he'd been chosen as one of thirty nationally selected students to attend summer camp at the Institute of Math and Science in Oakridge, Tennessee—"I got a taste for research. Maybe I'll become a research scientist and discover new ways to split the atom."

"Will you promise not to forget about me?"

"Aw, Betty Ann, it'll always be you." He leaned in and kissed her on the mouth. She responded in a manner requesting more, causing Wilbur to entertain thoughts beyond their kiss.

At eleven o'clock, they stood around chatting in pleasant conversation with friends and sipping punch, when Coach Lewis, who was chaperoning the event, tapped Wilbur on the shoulder and pulled him aside. "Wilbur, your brother, Jesse, needs you in the bathroom."

"Jesse? What's he doing here?"

"Evidently, getting drunk."

Wilbur went to the boys' room and found Jesse lying on the floor, facedown in vomit. Wilbur tried to rouse him but couldn't. "He's out cold, Wilbur. I tried getting him up before calling for you, but as you can see, he's done. And not a friend in sight. You need to take him home now," said the coach.

Wilbur left his brother to tell Betty Ann. She wanted to stay and arranged a ride home with friends. After apologizing, Wilbur returned to the bathroom. He rolled Jesse over, cleaned the vomit from his face with a wet paper towel, hefted him over his shoulder, and then walked to his truck and threw him in the front seat. Damning his brother all the way home, he thought about putting Jesse to bed and returning to the prom—to Betty Ann and the promise held in her kiss—but the scene at home immediately destroyed any other plans.

A police car and ambulance stood parked in his drive. Men in uniforms assembled, half in the doorway and half in the living room. He faintly heard his mother crying amid his father screaming, "I'll never set foot in this house again!"

The cars blocked him from parking in back. He stopped on the road and walked to the front door, where everyone stood, just in time to see his father escorted out by two men, one on either side, holding him by the elbows. A white jacket encased his upper body and held his arms tightly around him, tied together in back. As he kicked wildly and screamed obscenities, they forced him into the back of the ambulance.

A straitjacket? "What's going on, Mom?"

"Oh, Punk. Thank God you're home. I was so scared—I had to call someone. He tried to kill me."

"Oh my gosh, Mom! What happened?"

"He—he had a drink after you left for the prom. He had a drink of that rotgut he's been swilling, but I—I had put some ipecac in it. Oh Lord, I didn't think he'd notice. He's always so sick anyway, and it made him puke right away, within just a couple minutes. And somehow, I don't know how he knew, but he knew! He went into the basement. He must have a bottle stashed down there. I didn't know what was going on, but he and Uncle Ned went out drinking. When he came home, he ..." She sobbed, and it took awhile for her to tell him the rest.

"I was asleep when he came home. He picked up a pillow. Oh, Wilbur, I'm so sorry! He tried to smother me. That was the end of me, I thought. Except I managed to grab the lamp and coldcock him with it. Then I called the police. It took four of them to wrangle him—four of them. They had to get out a straitjacket to keep him from flailing around."

Wilbur held his mother as she retold the story, unsure what to feel. He wasn't scared or angry but relieved. They'd lived under Webb's wrath for so long that Wilbur welcomed the idea of knowing that, good or bad, their lives would soon change. "Don't worry, Ma. You did the right thing. I'll go with you to the hospital tomorrow." After reassuring her, he got Jesse, who was still out cold himself, and put him to bed.

The phone rang at six the next morning, waking Sarah and Wilbur. "It's the hospital," said Wilbur, handing his mother the phone.

She didn't say anything after hello. The doctor spoke at length as Sarah's face went blank. She thanked him for calling and hung up.

"Your father's had a stroke."

Sarah sat at Webb's bedside for three days, staring at his comatose body, before he died.

Jesse and Wilbur visited as often as they could, more for their mother's sake than for his.

"I'm taking him home," Sarah told her sons when making his funeral arrangements. "I want the wake held at home." *That's my mother*, thought Wilbur. *She'd be damned to let Webb have the last word.*

31

He wondered if she'd decided to have the wake at home specifically because Webb had said he'd never set foot in that house again.

By late afternoon the next day, Webb's embalmed body lay in a simple casket open for viewing in the middle of the living room. Sarah greeted nearly fifty friends and relatives (mostly relatives) as they paraded past, paying their last respects. Ned, his sisters, and their mother attended his body the whole time with Sarah and her sons but were emotionally distant. They cried openly for Wilbur and Jesse yet made a point to avoid Sarah—and they made sure she knew it.

One week after burying his father, on May 16, 1952, sixteen-year-old Wilbur stood at a podium, delivering his valedictory speech.

He spoke of the Communist threat and the need to protect individual freedom and noted that only in America did people have opportunities to overcome their stations in life, profiting through hard work and merit. For the young adults of his generation, the world was a wonderful place waiting for them to make their mark.

He'd written his address weeks before, and the recent events at home overshadowed his zeal in delivering it but, at the same time, made him more determined not to end up like his father. Wilbur saw himself as capable of great things, and this was the proudest moment in the history of the Weaver family: he was the first person in the family to graduate from high school, let alone as valedictorian.

Only his mother and brother attended the ceremony. He doubted his father's family even knew of his accomplishment, for Webb's death had caused a serious rift. The family blamed Sarah; they claimed he'd drunk because of her, he'd worked too hard for her, and she'd expected too much from him, trying to live above the rest of them. Their most-damning evidence was that Ned knew about her spiking his liquor with ipecac.

"I'm so proud of you, Punk," said Sarah, planting a kiss on his cheek after the ceremony.

"You're the king," said Jesse, and he shook his hand.

His favorite teacher, Mrs. Nutter, who'd taught him for the last six years and taken a motherly liking to him, approached Wilbur with hugs and a gift. "I bought you something to remember me by."

Wilbur unwrapped an expensive Bulova watch. Flabbergasted by her generosity, he tried to give it back. "You shouldn't have done this,

Mrs. Nutter. It's too nice." He choked back tears of gratitude; it was his only graduation gift.

"You deserve it, Wilbur. You're the best student I've had in all my thirty years of teaching."

He thanked her with a kiss and put the watch on his wrist, feeling rich beyond measure.

Betty Ann found her way to Wilbur's side, assuming her place as first lady. The graduates planned to celebrate for the rest of the night, and as Wilbur was the man of the hour, they expected him to attend. He looked for Jesse to take his mother home, but noting that Jesse had disappeared sometime after shaking his hand, Wilbur drove her himself with plans to return to his friends and to Betty Ann for a night of revelry.

"What are your plans, Son?" Sarah asked on the way home.

"You know I want to go to college. I've already sent in my acceptance to WVU. Classes start in the fall."

"I know. But I want you to think of how it is now that your father's dead. Your scholarships pay for tuition, but what about everything else? What will I live on?"

"Can we talk about this later?"

"Yes, you're right. No need to put a blight on your big night. Go have fun with Betty Ann. I'm sure she's waiting for you."

Wilbur left, feeling unsure of his future.

The next day, Sunday, Wilbur woke around nine, having gotten home late the night before. He'd had a few beers but not enough to get drunk. The memory of Betty Ann lay fresh on his mind.

At her request, they'd left the party early and gone for a drive, her mood turning somber as she thought about her life without him. "You'll meet some rich, pretty girl in college and never look back," she'd said.

"I've told you before—that's not true."

"How can I be sure?" Silent tears had rolled down her cheeks. Wilbur had found a quiet turnoff, parked, and turned to her for a promising kiss. It had seemed his duties that night required him to reassure everyone.

"Will you take me home?" she'd asked.

33

"Now?" Wilbur had thought the night young. "Don't you want to be with me?"

"Yes, I do—all of you—but not here in a car. I want you to take me home and then sneak into my bedroom." She'd kissed him deeply and whispered into his ear, "We'll be quiet. You know my parents; they're old and sleep like logs. I want our first time to be in my bed so I can lay down every night and dream about it."

"Well, since you put it that way."

The experience had been everything he'd fantasized it would be. He remembered saying, before falling fast asleep in her arms, "I love you, Betty Ann. You're going to be my wife."

Having slept only an hour, he'd awakened with a start around midnight, suddenly realizing where he lay. *I'd better get out of here*, he'd thought, not wanting to leave her but glad her parents hadn't caught them. He'd caressed her lips with a good-bye kiss and made it safely home thirty minutes later. As he'd walked inside the basement door, he'd noticed Jesse lying passed out on the concrete floor, stinking drunk.

Sarah finished cooking a meatloaf for lunch and called them to eat. Jesse made his first appearance since the night before and sat at the table with his mother and Wilbur, who'd been busy making a list of potential summer jobs.

"Both you boys need to get good-paying jobs. I just don't know how I'm going to make ends meet. Wilbur, I know everyone will hire you, but, Jesse, what about you?" she said.

"I know people who'll hire me."

"Yeah, who? You're building up quite the reputation for drinking. I can't abide that now. In fact, I don't want one more drop of alcohol in this house ever again. You understand?"

"I ain't Webb Weaver," Jesse replied. He shoveled his lunch down and turned to leave.

"You ain't going nowhere but searching for a job with your brother. Punk, you look after him and go around to those places on your list. I want you both back here before supper."

They were successful in their task; Wilbur got a job bagging groceries at the local IGA and also persuaded Mr. Parker, the owner, to hire

Jesse—but under one condition: Wilbur would be held accountable for his brother's dependability. Both were to start Monday.

After supper, Wilbur showered and went upstairs to change clothes. He had a date planned with Betty Ann. Jesse cried for one last night of freedom before working and left on foot, meeting his friends to hang out in front of the pool hall.

Wilbur felt the familiar shake of the house as the basement door shut, and he casually wondered who it could be. He buttoned his shirt and tucked it neatly into his trousers before heading to the mirror to comb his hair.

Voices drifted up the staircase to his hall bedroom—familiar voices. *Uncle Ned and Granny*, he thought, hearing them call for Sarah as he preened, cutting his part straight and forming his ever-so-slight ducktail.

The instantly recognizable sound of an engaging shotgun got Wilbur's attention. A threatening tone of voice made him rush downstairs. The visitors obviously thought Sarah was alone. "I know what it took to get this house," said Ned to Sarah.

Wilbur hid on the top stair, poking his head from behind the banisters. He saw his grandmother and uncle—who held a shotgun pointed at his mother—as they stood inches away, their backs to him. He saw the look of fright on Sarah's face.

"With my help, Webb committed a mortal sin to save this house from repossession. It was our doings that paid for it, not yours. The way we see it—Webb's real family: Ma and me—this house is ours. And we've come to take what Webb would've wanted us to have."

The reality of what he saw seemed impossible. Wilbur looked at his grandmother, at the side of her face and her posture, for some sign of humor. Could this be some sort of cruel joke? But they were dead serious. He could not miss the contempt in his grandmother's face.

"As his wife, this house is mine," said Sarah through a voice steeled in anger. "Now get out."

"He never did marry you," said Granny Weaver. "Told me he never intended to either."

Could that be true? Wilbur couldn't recall their anniversary date.

Sarah fumbled for a defense. "Common law is just as legal. You worthless beggars aren't getting anything."

Wilbur had heard enough. Stunned at the truth about his parents' nonexistent marriage, Ned's suggestion of murder, the reality that his own grandmother was a hateful thief, and, most disturbing, their attempt to take his own house, he acted quickly and instinctively. *By God, I'm the man of this house.*

His own shotgun lay under his bed. Careful not to tip them off, he quietly got his gun and waited until he walked downstairs to break the barrel, shocking them with the sound of his presence, and loaded two shells in Ned's sight. "This is my house now, and you two ain't welcome anymore." Wilbur spoke with contempt, pointing the readied gun at Ned and staring him down, creating a standoff where a moment's indecision on Ned's part would be enough to push Wilbur into action. He fired into the staircase, grazing Ned's head. Feeling for his wound, Ned dropped his gun, and Sarah quickly grabbed it. "Next time, I'll aim between your eyes," Wilbur said.

"Good God, boy. It ain't you we got a grudge against. You'd live here with—"

"I said leave. And don't ever darken this door again. Neither one of you."

"Come on, Ned. These folks ain't kin to us," said Granny Weaver. She and Ned left through the front door with Wilbur's gun trained on their every move. Sarah ran to lock the door behind them.

"You can't leave, Punk. I won't be safe without you."

He had no words to say in reply. Nothing could describe the crazy, hateful world that he longed to escape.

Despite her fears, their showdown brought an end to the Weavers' intrusion, and Webb's family never bothered them again.

Through the summer, Wilbur and Jesse worked at the IGA in town. Both of them grew tired of what seemed to be ceaseless hours of toil for never enough money to satisfy their mother. Wilbur spent money on gas and occasionally treated Betty Ann to a movie; otherwise, he gave his mother the rest. On paydays, Wilbur drove to the bank where he and Jesse cashed their checks, and Jesse would beg him to let him keep a few dollars for himself, but Wilbur always said no, knowing he'd drink it away. However, no matter what they earned, they couldn't escape hearing about the bills. "I just don't know what we're gonna do. This isn't enough to live on," Sarah repeated each payday.

Her constant complaining about Wilbur's going to college began to wear on him too. He'd have to work to meet his own needs for food and shelter in order to attend and had yet to figure out how to support both himself and his mother. With each passing day, he felt the odds stacking higher against him. But college or no, he was determined to make something of himself. The hills of West Virginia offered no such opportunity.

Jesse quit work in the fall and began his tenth year of school, leaving his brother to what appeared to be his career in the grocery store. Wilbur decided to forego college for one year to appease his mother, who promised to find a way for him to go if he'd just give her time. The decision ate at the core of his soul. He knew the longer he waited, the more his chances faded as he tethered himself to Sarah's needs.

Over the year, he tried keeping his dream alive by telling his mother every few weeks, "I'll need this dress shirt when I start college next fall," or "These new shoes will last for years when I go to school." His mother would simply reply with a mumble of agreement, never really responding.

Only Betty Ann supported him. She listened to him talk about every detail of his coming life, but even she grew tired of his incessant rambling as their romance took a backseat, overshadowed by his obsession with school.

The next summer, Mr. Parker offered Wilbur the job of assistant manager. "I can't, Mr. Parker. I'm going to college in a few months," he said.

"Just think about it. Go home, talk it over with your mom, and then let me know. You could have a secure future here."

"Thank you, sir. But I've had my mind set for years. No offense, but I don't want to stay here all my life."

As soon as he got home, Sarah approached her son. "Well, what did you tell Mr. Parker?"

"About what?"

"About his job offer? Taking his job would solve everything."

"You knew about that?" It all dawned on him: his mother and his boss had set him up. Nobody wanted him to leave.

"Of course. He told me the last time I was there about what a good job you were doing. He said that he hated to let you go, and I agreed."

"I told him no because I'm going to college." They argued again, each pleading his or her case, until Wilbur walked away, leaving the issue unresolved.

On the way home from cashing his paycheck two weeks later, the unrelenting pressure from everyone led Wilbur to a desperate decision. He knew when he handed his mother the money, he'd again have to endure her litany of worries.

The fall semester started in less than a month. He should have been packing his bags and feeling excited, but he wasn't. Instead, he felt depressed, trapped by guilt and obligation. Every day on the way to work, he passed a marine corps recruiting office, but he'd never given it a second glance. He noticed it now, and the life it offered enticed him into stopping in and talking to the recruiter.

After filling out some forms, Wilbur sat down with a young sergeant and answered questions about his education and desires. The more he told, the more gregarious the sergeant became. "Quite impressive, Mr. Weaver. With your achievements, you could pick and choose whatever and wherever you want to be in the corps. You're our kind of man."

"What about the pay?"

"A new recruit's base salary is one hundred and thirty-five dollars a month, and you don't have to pay for room and board." This payday, Wilbur's wallet held twenty-two dollars from the check he'd just cashed—two weeks' pay. The sergeant's offer sounded like a fortune. He'd have enough to send home and money to spare. That was all he felt his mother really wanted—money. She wouldn't care if he left as long as she got it. "I promise you, Mr. Weaver, a man of your talents will go far as a marine. We appreciate and reward intelligence and hard work. Sign here, and your new life starts tomorrow."

"So soon?"

"The sooner the better. We've found implementing our way of life immediately upon signing promotes independence—a must for all good marines."

What about Betty Ann? If I write often and call, will she understand?
"Can I think about it?" asked Wilbur.

"Specialist opportunities come and go. The highest enlisted level of entry we have open—one you qualify for—is air traffic control. They only accept the top recruits, and I see one space available. You're welcome to wait, but I can't promise you the top spot tomorrow."

"No one around here's going to fill it before then."

"Maybe not here, but a recruit in another state might. What's a day or even a week matter?" The sergeant pressed him. "You'll get leave in a few weeks—plenty of time to see your sweetheart."

Anything is better than here, he concluded, and he signed his name.

"What took you so long? I've been waiting to go to the post office," said Sarah upon Wilbur's arrival.

"Hi, Mom. Sit down, and let's talk. Would ending your money troubles make you happy?" Wilbur broke the news and explained his reasons for enlisting.

"How could you do this without asking me?" She was angry at first, but his compelling arguments eventually made her understand his motives: he only wanted to forge his own life and be a good son. She couldn't fault him for that. Her eyes welled with tears of pride once she realized how hard he was trying to please her and take care of her, and no matter what she said, she couldn't undo the decision. "Oh, Punk. You'll never know how much I'm going to miss your sweet face."

"Betty Ann will keep you company, and I'll come home as often as I can and write in between." Wilbur started crying too, feeling the full weight of what he'd done.

After a night of sorrow, tears, and passionate good-byes from Betty Ann, Wilbur boarded the bus the morning of August 10, 1953, bound for Parris Island, South Carolina, for six weeks of boot camp.

Chapter 6

The drill sergeant told the recruits not to move a muscle while they lay belly down in a sandy pine forest for twenty minutes, wearing only T-shirts and running shorts. Wilbur found the exercise excruciating: the ground full of gnawing chiggers had tested his own limits of self-control. At one time, he'd have given a month's pay just to scratch. Private Raynor evidently couldn't resist, and the drill sergeant unleashed his fury on the lineup afterward. His remark—"Next time I see you scratch yourself, I'm going to make you a eunuch"—caused Wilbur to smirk, but he thought he only did so in his mind.

With a week of boot camp left, his adventure thus far had been disappointing. *Any idiot can take orders. When does the cream get to rise?* The twenty-nine men he bunked with seemed, to him, no more than land grunts with IQs well below average. If air traffic control school didn't challenge him, he'd have to find someone in charge and straighten this whole mess out.

Boot camp ended. Wilbur and his new friend Sammy, who lived a few hours north in Ohio, were set to take their two weeks' leave and hitchhike home together. "We gotta wear our uniforms hitching," said Sammy.

"Why? I'd rather not risk ruining it." Since the army had issued him only one dress uniform, he'd have to purchase another on his own if anything happened to it.

"Women love men in uniforms. With fifteen hundred miles to cover, we'll get rides much easier."

"How long you reckon it'll take us?" Wilbur had never hitched a ride farther than through his hometown, and he liked sharing Sammy's experience. Sammy had come up with the idea of hitchhiking after hearing Wilbur groan about bus fare. The prospect of their adventure excited Wilbur.

"Three days and nights ought to do it. If we plan it right, we'll catch a ride before dark on an eighteen-wheeler and sleep through most of it. That's the trick, because if we don't, our lonely asses will be walking the roads at three in the morning."

Two and a half days later, Wilbur said good-bye to Sammy, thanked the gentleman who'd driven them the last sixty-five miles, and got out in the center of his hometown. Sammy and the driver would continue north. "Hey, Wilbur, I'll meet you right here in eight days at eight a.m. for the trip back. Okay?"

"Okay. Call me if anything changes."

A half hour later, Wilbur walked into his home. He first peeked in at his mother, finding her sound asleep in her bedroom, and then, with trepidation, went to check on Jesse, hoping he'd be in bed, where he should be, especially on a Monday morning. He was. Wilbur paused at his bedside, taking note of his brother's look of innocence when asleep; at fifteen, he was a beautiful boy. *Why does he have to be like Pop?* It pained him to think of Jesse's wasted potential. Wilbur went back downstairs and lay on the sofa, deciding to sleep until his family awakened.

A happy reunion took place for Wilbur, the first true happiness he'd felt since he was a young boy. After hugging, crying, and talking nonstop with his family, he spent most of his time with Betty Ann. They again hugged and cried as he prepared to leave one week later.

Their tears abated as Wilbur enthusiastically spoke about his next stage in the United States Marine Corps: after returning to Parris Island, he'd leave in two days for Olathe, Kansas, and begin his three-month schooling as an air traffic controller. It was not the research science he'd once thought of doing, but this field accepted only the brightest enlisted marines with the mathematical skill and technological perception required to read radar. He'd eventually be responsible for the lives of USMC's finest: the pilots. The broad advancement opportunities in and out of service also satisfied

Wilbur, for civilian controllers made large salaries all over the world: Singapore, Saudi Arabia—anywhere he dared to dream of.

The happiness he felt offered convincing proof that his enlistment had been the right decision for everyone.

"I must say, you look very handsome in your uniform. You've got more muscles than ever," said his mother. Jesse agreed, awed by Wilbur's appearance. Betty Ann liked the man he'd become too, as evidenced by her constant fawning; she couldn't keep her hands off him.

He said his good-byes, and Betty Ann drove him into town to meet Sammy. On the way, Betty Ann kept her hands firmly on the wheel. She was tense, and Wilbur rubbed her shoulders in a futile effort to help her relax. "Look," he said, "it's just a few weeks. After that, we'll be able to make some concrete plans, once I have my assignment." Betty Ann kept quiet. "It's all going to work out. This is the right thing. For us, I mean." He tried a few more times to get her to talk, but whenever she looked at him, she teared up. Soon enough, they saw Sammy waiting outside the post office.

"I love you, Wilbur. Be careful going back," she said.

"I will. I love you too." Wilbur wiped the tears from her eyes, and they kissed good-bye.

He found air traffic control, ATC, school challenging but easily rose to the top among the forty students in his class. The military base in Olathe intrigued him; it was full of young, fresh faces from all over the country and from all branches of service: the marine corps, navy, air force, and army. After classes, the men and women met in town nightly to socialize, dance, and drink. In his second week, one evening, he and his roommate, Tom, went to a place called the Shame. They couldn't help but notice a tall, leggy dark-haired woman standing at the bar. He recognized her from class and decided to introduce himself.

"Hi. My name's Wilbur. Don't we go to school together?"

"I'm Marilyn, and I know who you are," she said with a smile.

"Why would you know my name?"

"Because you sit up front and answer all the questions. One can't help remembering a name when the instructor repeats, 'Yes, Wilbur,' or 'That's correct, Wilbur,' every day."

"Oh, I didn't realize," he said, hoping she'd been impressed. "How are you finding school?"

"Frankly, a lot harder than I thought. Since you're so smart, maybe you can tutor me."

"Sure, anytime."

A tall Italian-looking man came up beside her and whispered something in her ear. They were obviously familiar with each other. She laughed at his remark and then excused herself from Wilbur, saying, "I might just take you up on the tutoring if things don't improve." She left with the man.

Struck by Marilyn's beauty, Wilbur returned to his beer and to Tom, feeling disappointed by her abrupt departure. He tried to rejoin the festivities at the bar but couldn't stop thinking about her, so he left shortly after.

Eighteen-year-old naval cadet Marilyn Matthews hailed from St. Louis, Missouri. She wore her thick, curly dark hair short and swept away from her face, exposing her fair skin, hazel eyes, and perfectly arched brows. Tall and lean, her figure grabbed Wilbur's attention. Her long legs ran clear up to his hips; he couldn't help but envision her naked. *I bet she's even prettier without clothes.* In his opinion, she looked cultured and fancy, not plain like the girls back home. She looked worldly and sophisticated. Trying not to feel guilty about this negative comparison to Betty Ann, he rationalized to himself that his interest in Marilyn was purely educational. *Besides, she apparently has a boyfriend.*

Wilbur began helping Marilyn when she cornered him after class and asked him to explain the day's lecture. Over the next two weeks, they'd sit alone together in the classroom after dismissal, each day staying longer, as he helped her understand the equations and terminology involved for calculating coordinates. He loved spending time with her, but the tutoring tested his patience: she marginally passed the assignments with his help, and though he hated to admit it, he suspected she'd fail without him. The material was simply beyond her abilities. Eventually, she'd have to choose a different career.

After their third week, he realized his frustrations over her grades were more about wanting her near him than about her educational welfare. He wanted her despite his feelings for Betty Ann, and he felt her interest in him, though seemingly purely academic, simmered just under the surface of pretense. Seeing her out regularly with her boyfriend, Lenny, Wilbur believed Lenny's presence deterred her from showing her true feelings. *If only he were gone,* thought Wilbur, hoping the military would step in and resolve his dilemma by posting Lenny somewhere far away. Anxiously, he waited for the opportunity—and nerve—to ask her out.

On one occasion, he saw them sitting in a booth together at the Shame, arguing. Lenny had said something in anger, pointing his finger in her face, and then stormed out, leaving her alone and crying.

"What did he do to you, Marilyn?" asked Wilbur, walking over to her, seizing the opportunity to be the hero. His appearance startled her. She looked up at him, at a loss for words, and cried harder, her emotional state far worse than he'd thought. "Come, now. It can't be all bad, can it? That guy's not worth crying over anyway," he said as he slid into the booth beside her and offered a napkin to wipe her tears.

"Yes, it's that bad. I don't know what I'm gonna do. Everything's so hopeless."

"Let's get out of here and go talk somewhere quiet."

"I don't want to talk about it. But yes, let's get out of here."

He held her hand and led her out of the bar, walking toward the commons area, a park near the water. A gazebo stood in the center, currently unoccupied. "This looks private enough. Tell me what I can do to help," he offered. Marilyn looked into his eyes and started crying all over again. He wrapped his arms around her in comfort and let her weep. Noticing that she was fraying her tear-soaked napkin as she wiped her eyes, he said, "Let me get you another tissue." He started to get up.

"No, don't leave me." She looked up into his face. He felt the overwhelming urge to kiss her and leaned closer but stopped short, unsure of her desires. She answered him by closing the distance and kissing him tentatively and then passionately.

He'd wanted her since the first moment he saw her, and knowing that she finally reciprocated his secret longings, he could barely control himself as he kissed and groped her. Suddenly afraid, he stopped. "Maybe this isn't a good idea."

"You don't want me?"

"God, yes. But it's just that—"

She encircled his face with her hands and kissed him again. "I want you, Wilbur," she whispered, placing his hands high around her waist. The images of Betty Ann that had been flashing in his mind suddenly went dark.

This early, the park was empty, and they were left alone to surrender to their desires. Once Marilyn caressed his groin, Wilbur couldn't stop himself, and she didn't move to stop him. He rolled from the concrete bench, laid Marilyn on the grass-covered floor, and made love to the second woman he'd ever known—an unexpected gift on his eighteenth birthday.

He'd never been so consumed with desire, and afterward, he felt shamefully regretful as his thoughts returned to Betty Ann. "I'm sorry, Marilyn. I didn't mean for this to happen."

"Don't be. I wanted you too."

"Good," he said. Overcome with passion in the heat of the moment, he'd been so focused on suppressing his thoughts of Betty Ann that he hadn't been as attentive to Marilyn as he should have been.

She laughed and kissed him again. "No. I always had a choice."

Wilbur laughed, relieved, but only for the moment. "Then happy birthday to me."

Though they saw him around town, Lenny, surprisingly, never came to stake his claim for Marilyn after that night. She didn't offer an explanation for their breakup, and Wilbur didn't press her. *His loss, my gain,* he thought. That explained it well enough for him.

Always analytical and responsible, Wilbur forgot himself with Marilyn. He became carefree and less inhibited, he laughed more, and her smallest actions charmed him. While passing the next three weeks as her constant companion every day at school and every evening, he was only slightly aware of his commitment to Betty Ann. On the occasions when he did remember (when writing her his weekly promised letter), he'd bury his guilt, believing his relationship with Marilyn was temporary: she'd move on when school finished and when she got her station orders from the navy. Betty Ann had nothing to fear.

He didn't allow himself to visualize a life with Marilyn, mostly because she didn't seem to want it. Thankfully, she never asked him, "What next?" If she had, he wouldn't have known. With two weeks of school left, he wanted to focus solely on his time with her, passing each day together more lovingly than the last. Though neither had said, "I love you," Wilbur knew he felt love for her, but he wanted to hear her say it first, if either said it at all. In his estimation, he was in a win-win situation. One the one hand, Marilyn could say nothing, and they would continue to enjoy a passionate fling and then move apart; Betty Ann would be none the wiser. On the other hand, if Marilyn did come forth with a proclamation of love, then he'd have two wonderful and loving women to choose from. How could he complain? *I could break up with Betty Ann without breaking her heart,* he thought, unaware that he'd already chosen.

"I'm so proud of you, Marilyn. You're doing much better in school," said Wilbur over dinner in the mess hall two weeks later.

"Thanks to you, but it's still hard. To be honest, I had no idea what I was getting into when I signed up. My first day after boot camp, they gave us our dress uniforms and said to put them on and go speak to the counselor. So we did, and then we stood in a line fifteen people deep while the other girls before us went in. We watched as they came out of the office looking nervous and upset. When my turn came, some mean, nasty woman yelled at me to sit down and demanded to know what I wanted to do. I didn't know anything. I asked her to explain the choices, and she yelled, 'I don't have to babysit you! Just pick something!' Well, when you're eighteen and fresh out of high school, people like her are intimidating. I saw a pretty lady in a different kind of uniform across the hall, and since this woman was pressuring me to make a decision, I just pointed to her and said, 'I want to do what she does,' and the counselor stamped my papers for ATC school. Stupid way to choose, huh?"

"That's incredible," said Wilbur. He'd thought the ATC students were handpicked as the brightest. "I'm glad you got here, no matter how. At least I got to meet you."

"I hope you'll always feel good about us," she said in a serious tone. "Will you meet me at the gazebo tonight?"

"Sure. Whatcha got planned?" He grinned flirtatiously.

"I need to talk—that's all."

"Sure. How about six thirty?"

She agreed and left after eating. Wilbur stayed behind, mulling over the words she might say. *Does she want to break up? Maybe she's in love too. What if...* The possibilities weighed on his mind until he met her again.

"Hi, sweetheart," he said, arriving at the gazebo. They kissed.

"Hello there," she replied, already sitting and waiting for him.

"What's on your mind?"

"A lot. I'm afraid."

"Afraid?"

"Yes. I'm afraid for you and me and us." She had come prepared with her own tissue supply and was wringing one in her hands.

"I know there's only two weeks left before we'll ship out, but we'll keep in touch," he said.

"I'm pregnant."

Wilbur was speechless as her words registered. He stammered. "What? But we were careful, weren't we?"

"Not the first time. Remember? Here in this gazebo?"

"Yes, of course I remember." He paced, feeling stifled in the confined gazebo, and walked out into the open park, remaining in her view.

"I'm sorry. I started not to tell you but thought you'd want to know since you're, you know, so kind, responsible—hell, I don't know what to think." She started crying. Wilbur returned to her side.

"I need to know how you feel, Marilyn, about me. Do you see me as your husband? Do you love me?"

"Yes, I do love you. That's why I'm telling you. If I didn't care, I'd have taken care of it myself. But being Catholic, I've not got many choices in the matter. One thing is certain: they'll discharge me from the navy."

"I hadn't realized. So without me, you'll soon become an unemployed, unwed, unholy single mother."

"Do you have to be so blunt?" She cried harder.

"I'm sorry. This is my fault too. I won't let you be alone." He struggled with his words. Not once did he think about abandoning her, but this news had come as such a surprise. He tried to formulate a plan—about his future, hers, a baby—in a matter of minutes. "Come home with me after school. Will you? We'll spend our leave together and figure out what to do then. Heck, maybe you'll come back with me as my wife."

"Can I? Will your family have me?"

"No need to tell anyone about being pregnant. What are you—five, six weeks now?"

"I think so."

"Nobody can tell by looking at you. We'll keep it our little secret, okay? Are you sure about this—you're really pregnant? It's so early to know for sure."

"I'm sure. Believe me."

"Okay. I'll call home and say I'm bringing my girlfriend home to meet them. We'll take a bus the day we get out."

"Thank you, Wilbur," she said pitifully, as if he'd saved her life. Shamed, she berated herself for being so stupid and sobbed, breaking Wilbur's heart with her dejectedness. He held her tightly, pressing her head to his shoulder.

"Don't worry another minute. We'll be fine."

The following week, they got their duty station orders. Wilbur would report to Cherry Point Marine Corps Air Station in North Carolina for the next three years, and Marilyn, having failed her ATC final, had to repeat six weeks of school in Olathe or choose another career field.

Wilbur called his mother the day before leaving to tell—to warn—her about Marilyn. He couldn't think of anything to say to Betty Ann except the truth. He had to make her understand. Simply bringing home a girlfriend seemed more devastating than telling her; she'd think he'd easily cast her aside by choice. Maybe he had, but how else could he explain his actions? When he got his mother on the phone, he couldn't bring himself to lie, and he confided his dilemma, hoping to lighten his burden and gain her support. "Will you tell Betty Ann, Mom? Tell her I'm sorry. I didn't mean for this to happen."

"Oh, Punk. That's for you to do. I won't let you hide behind me."

"You're right, Mom. I'll call her next." They discussed some of the details of the trip and then said their good-byes. He dialed Betty Ann's number. Once she was on the phone, Wilbur found that he almost couldn't go through with it. She sounded excited to hear from him. He stammered his way through a bit of small talk, but apparently, Betty Ann saw through it.

"Wilbur, what's going on?"

"I'm so sorry, Betty Ann, but I have to stop. We have to stop this."

"Stop what? What are you talking about?"

"Our relationship. I've met someone else."

Betty Ann kept silent. The silence lasted an eternity as far as Wilbur was concerned. When he couldn't stand it any longer, he said, "I'm sorry."

"Don't bother," said Betty Ann. She hung up.

It wasn't the way he'd wanted it to go, but he couldn't help thinking he'd gotten off easily.

Wilbur and Marilyn arrived on a Saturday afternoon after a twelve-hour bus trip. His mother greeted them at the station. Nauseated from her pregnancy, Marilyn had vomited four times while traveling through the mountains, and she looked pale and weak when she met Sarah. "Why, you're as skinny as a rail and a might peaked too," said Sarah.

"I hadn't expected the roads to be so curvy," she replied.

"Oh, you'll get used to them. Come along, and let me fatten you up." Sarah took her by the arm and walked her to their truck.

"Where's Jesse?" asked Wilbur.

"He's at work. I don't reckon we'll see him till tomorrow. It's Saturday night, you know. He won't come directly home. God love him—I don't know what I'm gonna do with that boy."

With a gregarious personality and more loving nature than Wilbur, Jesse had carved a soft spot in his mother's heart. He'd called her Mama (opposed to Wilbur saying Mom) until the age of twelve. Jesse got away with things Wilbur never dreamed of. Sarah had set their individual standards while they were young and had come to expect Wilbur to achieve and take care of her, whereas Jesse was allowed—and expected—to earn his keep simply by entertaining her with his warm personality. Wilbur thought Jesse could get away with murder.

Sarah prepared lunch and then showed Marilyn to the spare bedroom upstairs to rest. "This'll be your room, dear. Wilbur'll sleep with his brother in the stairwell right outside your door. Just holler if you need anything. Maybe you should rest a bit now."

"You go ahead. I'll stay up and talk with Mom for a while. I'll be right here when you wake up," he said encouragingly in response to Marilyn's look, and he kissed her on the cheek before returning to the kitchen with his mother.

"I talked to Betty Ann last night. I hope you know how much you devastated her. She was crying and talking about how you were supposed to marry her. I thought you were the smart one, Punk. Not six months away from home, and you go off and get some stranger pregnant."

"I'm sorry, Mom."

"I ain't the one you need to apologize to. What you done to poor Betty Ann ain't right." She raised her voice, getting angrier as she talked.

"Shhh. You'll wake her." He pointed upstairs. "She doesn't know anything about Betty Ann."

"Dammit, Punk. How many lies are you gonna weave? I don't like this whole situation. And I don't much like that city tramp you brung home either."

"Don't say that. You haven't spent more than an hour with her. Give her a chance—for me. Please?"

"Mmph," Sarah grunted. "How far along is she?"

"Not very. I'm guessing about six weeks."

"And she's sick already?"

"I think traveling's made it worse."

"Maybe."

"Now, don't get your mind set on the negatives. Just relax, and give us a few days. We'll talk some more later. I think I'll go for a walk and get a little exercise after being cooped up on the bus." He kissed his mother and went outside.

When Marilyn awoke three hours later, she found Sarah baking a cake in the kitchen, and she asked for Wilbur. "He's in the garage, changing the oil in the truck," replied Sarah, taking note of the girl's ill manners in not inquiring about her. "Have a nice nap?"

"Yes, thank you. I think I'll go downstairs and find him."

"Suit yourself."

In the basement garage, Wilbur lay elbow deep in grease under the truck. Marilyn lightly kicked his shoe for attention and said, "Gotcha working already?"

"Huh?"

"Your mother. She's got you working already?"

"No. This was my idea. Fixing things relaxes me." He crawled out and sat up. "Hand me a towel, will you?" Wiping his hands clean, he meditated on the hostility he perceived in her tone of voice, which he'd felt from his mother too. "Is anything wrong?"

"No. Just surprised to find you here. So this is where you grew up? Beautiful countryside, even if it does make me queasy."

"Come on—I'll take you for a walk." They headed down the hollow, climbing the hilly dirt road. The meandering stream ran swiftly beside them. Wilbur pointed out his favorite places to hunt, fish, and camp. Marilyn laughed at the dilapidated shacks perched on stilts in the hillsides with smoke billowing from their chimneys.

"People actually live in those?"

"Sure. My grandmother does."

Marilyn's request to meet his grandmother prompted him to confide the details of his past—of his father's death and the rift it had caused. When he finished, Marilyn nodded. "Wow. I had no idea. I don't know if I could have handled that sort of thing happening in my family."

"I'm sure you could have. When we don't have control over these things, we figure out how to make it through."

He liked the way she smiled at him when he said that.

The road crested into a forest of old beech trees overlooking a valley where the stream forked. Split-rail fences sectioned off areas of grazing cattle below. "What a lovely spot. Let's stop here," she said. She walked easily between the trees, heading to a cleared landing, when a prominent carving caught her eye. She stopped to examine it more closely. "What's this?" A large heart with an arrow through it was chiseled deeply into a huge birch tree, engraved with "WLW loves BAD." "Yours?"

"Well, yes."

"Talented artwork. When did you carve it? And who's BAD?"

"That's Betty Ann Dupree, my high school sweetheart. We'd better start back. Mom will have supper ready soon."

"And where's she now?"

He ignored the question, changing the subject by asking about the baby—if she wanted a boy or girl and what they'd name it—temporarily escaping her inquiry.

Two days passed uneventfully as Jesse got acquainted with Marilyn (and remarked to his brother that he'd captured a hottie) and as she sat about, chatting with Sarah. Wilbur stayed busy with home repairs: painting the chicken house, tuning engines, and sealing concrete.

On the morning of their third day, Marilyn again awakened nauseated. Previously, she'd managed to wretch and vomit without attracting notice, but not this time. Awakened by the noise, Sarah knocked before she opened the bathroom door, offering crackers and a glass of ginger ale. "Here, dear, try this. It always settled my stomach when I was expecting."

Marilyn sat, bent over the toilet, shocked by Sarah's words and kindness. "So you know?"

"Yes, but not because anyone told me. Women can just tell. How far along are you?"

"Somewhere in the first six to eight weeks. I guess I need to see a doctor soon."

"Well, you've certainly got a bad case of morning sickness. It mostly comes around week twelve, give or take a few." *If she's further along, that baby ain't his. He's only known her a few weeks.* Sarah kept her figuring to herself, awaiting further proof.

The crackers and ale eased Marilyn's nausea enough for her to walk. Not wanting to draw any more attention to herself, she mustered the energy to offer Sarah help. "What can I do to help prepare for Thanksgiving? Can I do some grocery shopping for you?"

"That'd be great. I'll make a list and send it with you and Punk later today."

"Who's Punk?"

Sarah laughed. "Why, that's Wilbur's nickname—something only his Pop and I call him, because he always thinks he's so smart. Been that way since birth."

"It fits him," agreed Marilyn. The women shared a laugh, and Marilyn listened to her mother-in-law's tales of Wilbur's childhood antics as they finished preparing the day's meal.

At four o'clock, the women put out a bountiful Thanksgiving feast complete with two meats and four desserts to choose from. The family of four, including Marilyn, ate and talked easily through the meal, until the conversation turned to the landscape. "Wilbur took me for a walk down the hollow. The vista from the top was one of the prettiest sights I've ever seen, including a carved tree I came across. Have any of you seen it?"

Wilbur groaned. His mother answered quickly. "Oh yes. 'Wilbur Lee Weaver loves Betty Ann Dupree'—you mean that one?"

"Uh-huh. He wouldn't tell me much about her. Who is she?"

"That's the girl he was suppose to marry," blurted Sarah.

"Oh. I had no idea. I'm sorry—"

"Don't be," interrupted Wilbur.

"She asked. I don't see no good reason not to tell her," said Sarah, and then she directed her speech back to Marilyn. "Betty Ann's a sweet hometown girl who's waited for him since grade school. Up until last week, until Punk told me about your dilemma, they were betrothed."

"Not officially," said Wilbur. He and his mother began a heated argument over Betty Ann, Marilyn, the pregnancy, and the future. Marilyn had opened a can of worms, and no matter how hard she tried, she couldn't put the lid back on. She excused herself from the table, went to her room to lie down, and stayed until the next morning.

Wilbur came to her bedside at six o'clock. "Good morning," he said, getting a smile in return. "I wanted to talk to you about yesterday. Don't waste another thought on old girlfriends, okay? The past is where it should be. We're together now, and well, I can't see waiting. I mean, what are we waiting for? Let's settle everything. Today."

"What do you mean?"

"I'm asking you to marry me. Will you marry me? Today?" He knelt beside her bed and held her hand. "I've planned it all: we'll get married, go on a little honeymoon this weekend, get your military discharge, and then move as a family to North Carolina."

She felt as if she'd caused all the trouble yesterday, not him. Yet there he stood, fulfilling all her hopes, rescuing her, as if he were to blame. She did love him. Her face beamed happiness and love as she looked at him and replied, "Yes, Wilbur. I'd love to be your wife."

She wore a light blue suit that matched Wilbur's dress uniform as they exchanged vows given by a Catholic priest. The priest had been her only condition about the ceremony. Sarah and Jesse were witnesses, reserved in attitude. Afterward, Marilyn called her parents in Missouri. They apparently received the news with little interest, their main concern being whether or not she'd had a Catholic ceremony.

After two days of honeymooning at a cheap lodge, Wilbur and Marilyn returned home to pack, planning to leave the next morning for North Carolina so they'd have enough time to find an apartment before he reported for duty.

Between them, they'd saved $300, despite Wilbur giving his mother $100 a month in financial support. Minus the $175 they spent on a used 1948 Chevy Bel Air (which had seventy-five thousand miles on it and was on its second engine) and the $50 spent on their honeymoon, they had $75, a car, one suitcase full of clothes, and a baby on the way when they began their lives together.

Chapter 7

For thirty-five dollars a month, the newlyweds rented a one-bedroom apartment in New Bern, North Carolina, twenty miles from Cherry Point. Wilbur had hoped to save money by living on base but had learned with disappointment that privates were expected to live in the barracks. The marine corps didn't give a damn whether he had a wife or not; wives weren't military issue. They had no option but to rent while they waited—up to a year—for available base housing.

The fact that pregnancy was grounds for discharge embittered Marilyn, so she wanted to distance herself from all things military, and she persuaded Wilbur to commute. *More expense,* he thought. They'd have to watch every penny to make ends meet. At Wilbur's insistence, they'd slept in the car for two days prior to signing the rental agreement, living off the turkey and ham sandwiches Sarah had packed for their journey. But despite his worry, they were happy. Their new home sat across the street from the Tryon Palace: a grand eighteenth-century estate and the historic home of North Carolina's colonial governor, William Tryon. Its sweeping formal gardens of boxwood mazes, apple espaliers, rose arbors, and statuary covered several acres of lawn, ending at the banks of the Neuse River, and lay in full view from the balcony of their second-story apartment. Thankfully, the bedroom came furnished with a bed and one dresser. The ten-foot square living and eating area held a Formica table and two chairs, a sink, and a two-burner electric stove. They had no living room furniture, and a telephone was beyond their budget. Marilyn's first task was somehow to accumulate for pennies all the necessities, such as dishes and linens.

They spent three days settling in and buying staples, including toothpaste, soap, toilet paper, and a minimum of pantry supplies: beans, rice, butter, sugar, and tea. Marilyn questioned his purchase of a ten-cent bamboo fishing pole. "We're only a block from the river. I can catch fish for supper," he replied.

When Wilbur reported to work Monday morning, he stopped for gas and fretted over deciding whether to fill the tank or just pump a few gallons. After paying the rent and security deposit, purchasing supplies, and giving five dollars to Marilyn to buy everything else they needed, he had ten dollars to his name until payday—which was one month away.

Christmas came and went without Wilbur and Marilyn spending an extra cent. They took delight in the holiday decorations provided by the palace and in listening to the carolers as their songs drifted through the night air, reaching their balcony. They didn't have a tree or exchange gifts but were content to have a home to share and food, sparse though it was, to eat.

Wilbur came home one evening and found Marilyn looking a little happier than usual. When he asked what was going on, she said, "Oh, I got us an invitation for New Year's Eve."

"Really? Where?"

"At Cindy and Jack's house. They need some people to play gin rummy. I met Cindy on my walk through town today. She invited me in for a Coke. Can you believe they live just up the street? Jack's a master sergeant. I told her all about you."

"Huh," said Wilbur. He didn't know a master sergeant named Jack and decided he would have to look him up. "Sounds fun. Maybe they'll serve food too."

On the day before payday, they were broke. They'd emptied their last bag of beans the night before, and if the fish didn't bite for supper, they'd go to bed hungry. Wilbur and Marilyn decided to take their chances and forego fishing, hoping their night out would provide an evening meal.

While playing gin rummy, Wilbur found Jack annoying. Flaunting his rank by referring to Wilbur as PFC, Jack would say, "Nice play, PFC," and "Shoulda held that one, PFC," instead of calling him by name. Marilyn took offense too but remained polite for the sake of the popcorn and Coke they served; as disappointing as the food was, it was still supper.

Wilbur looked forward to cashing his paycheck, and then, with dread, he immediately sent two-thirds of it home to his mother via Western Union. Still, he had twice as much to live off this month as last. It was a tenuous existence, he knew. If anything major happened, such as the car breaking down, he didn't know how they'd make it.

But somehow, they did.

As they limped along through the winter, time passed quickly. Their love for each other grew as frugality united them in a common cause, laying a marital foundation based on trust, need, and dreams of their future.

Spring came, and Wilbur looked forward even more to coming home. His fishing had rewarded them abundantly since the April thaw. Now in her seventh month, Marilyn's ravenous appetite kept him busy with providing enough food to stave off her cravings. His usual supper bounty consisted of wilted dandelion greens picked from the yard, bread purchased at the day-old store, four to six good-sized brim, and two or more blue crabs he could scoop up with a small net. Wilbur did not have frequent access to poultry scraps (the usual bait), but his supposition about the crabs' indiscriminate appetites bore true; he caught crabs with fish heads.

Though it provided good fishing, springtime in the South proved a lot warmer than anywhere else they'd been. Already, temperatures hit eighty degrees. The apartment had no cooling system, and Marilyn began to complain about the midday heat when the inside temperature neared ninety degrees. By the first of May and through the end of her pregnancy, she'd take walks down the frozen-food aisles in the supermarkets for relief, pretending to shop but rarely buying anything, and at night, she'd lie in the bathtub filled with cool water.

On Saturday afternoon, June 5, Wilbur walked with her in the local A&P for what seemed like miles as she stood in the freezer doors, "examining food." Her back had ached all day, and walking provided the only relief. An elderly woman passed as Marilyn grimaced through a particularly strong cramp. "You all right, darling?" said the old lady.

"Oh yes. I think so. My back just won't stop aching."

"Sounds to me like you'd better go on to the hospital," she said, turning to Wilbur.

"But she's not due for another month," he replied. Another cramp gripped Marilyn, causing her to scream out in pain.

"I know a bit about childbirth, young man, and this girl's in labor."

"What do you think, Marilyn?"

"I think we should go. Now."

In a panic, he managed to get her home and then drove her to the naval hospital at Cherry Point. As the nurses wheeled her into the delivery room, he hurriedly explained to the doctor that her due date was more than a month away. "Don't worry. We'll check her out and let you know what we find," replied the doctor, and then he left Wilbur alone with his fears, pacing in the fathers' waiting room.

Eight hours later, a nurse appeared, surprising Wilbur with a small bundle held in her arms. "Would you like to meet your new son?"

"What? She had the baby? I have a son? Is he okay?"

"You certainly do. A healthy six pounds and three ounces."

He stood at a distance, looking at the bundle. The nurse walked closer and placed the baby in his arms, familiar with a new father's timidity. "He won't break. You can hold him."

Calm and alert, the infant opened his eyes, searching, trying to come to terms with his new surroundings while melting Wilbur's heart. "Hey, little fella. I'm your daddy. Yes, I know; it's a cold, cruel world. Shhh," he said, cradling him closer as the infant started to cry.

"Your wife is doing fine, Mr. Weaver. You can go back when the ether wears off; she's still quite anesthetized. I'd better get him back to the nursery." She took the baby from Wilbur, leaving him to ruminate on his new role of fatherhood.

Five days later, the three returned home. Since neither Wilbur nor Marilyn had had positive role models, they named their son Paul Edward in honor of no one, free to blaze his own trail in life, though having the initials spell PEW almost made them change their choice. Wilbur had rejected his wife's offer of a namesake, concluding that the name Wilbur hadn't brought him any luck.

Marilyn called her parents from the hospital to give them the news but hung up feeling disappointed by their bland reaction. She'd thought news of their first grandchild would evoke joy, congratulations, and excitement, but they'd only said, "Well, take care of yourself."

Newborn Paul Edward slept in the bottom dresser drawer for a month. They hadn't prepared for his arrival, but he didn't seem to mind. The young couple thrived on watching his daily activities, taking turns warming his bottles and changing his diapers. Wilbur was a natural father. He'd come home from work and relieve Marilyn of the baby, and then Wilbur would take Paul Edward fishing, setting him in a laundry basket and watching over him as he caught their supper.

At the time, nursing mothers weren't in vogue, and without asking, the hospital had injected Marilyn with droperidol, a drug used to stop the production of breast milk. The added expense of formula and diapers began knocking big holes in their already-fragile budget. Near the end of Paul's second month, Wilbur came home from work to a frantic household.

"We're out of milk, and I didn't have money to buy more!" Marilyn cried above the baby's wail.

Wilbur searched his pockets for money out of habit but knew he'd find nothing. "Did you try to give him some water?"

"He's had nothing but since noon. I even walked to the store and asked for credit, but they said no. How can anyone refuse a baby milk?"

Wilbur looked around for something to sell, and his watch caught his eye, offering him a solution to their problems. "Take his clothes off."

"What? That won't help."

"I'm taking him with me to pawn my watch. It's a Bulova, you know, worth at least a hundred dollars. We'll get more sympathy and maybe more money if I bring him along. He's gotta look the part of the poor, starving child."

"Look—hell, he is." She agreed with his plan. Wilbur's willingness to pawn his most-prized possession for the baby's milk touched her heart.

Wilbur, now a lance corporal, wore his uniform and carried his squalling, diapered son to the nearest pawn shop. Charming its owner with extreme humility and politeness, he got five dollars by hocking the watch, which would feed them until his next payday.

His first stop upon cashing his next check was to get his watch back. Two more times, he pawned it when they found themselves in dire straits between paydays. But when the Bel Air's transmission gave out, they owned nothing valuable enough to pawn as a means of rescue.

Chapter 8

In a heart-wrenching decision, Wilbur moved into the barracks and sent his wife and son home to live with his mother in West Virginia until base housing became available.

Marilyn balked every step of the way. She thought they could stay in New Bern if he stopped sending his mother money, and she tried to convince him to do so, but he resisted the idea as if she'd suggested he rob a bank. "You're asking me to abandon my own mother, Marilyn. She'd lose the house and be out on the street in a month."

"What about Jesse? He could shoulder some responsibility too."

"I made her a promise when I enlisted—that she'd never worry about money again—and I won't break it. A man's only as good as his word; I intend to keep my word. Besides, even if I did stop, we still wouldn't have enough to fix the car and pay rent." She agreed out of necessity.

Paul Edward was sixteen weeks old when Wilbur kissed him good-bye and put him and Marilyn on a bus, his sorrow directed more at the pain of not seeing his son every day than at missing his wife. Though he'd miss her too, she'd look the same upon their reunion. How much would Paul Edward have changed when he got to hold him again?

Wilbur waved as the bus departed, feeling sorry for himself and alone in the world but comforted in knowing that his family would be safe and well cared for. He was unconsciously blind to the underlying conflict between the women.

He had four days' leave and originally planned to stay in North Carolina, working odd jobs to earn money. Then, one evening, his mother called.

"Hi, Mom. What's up?"

"Oh, Punk. I need to talk to you."

"You already are. What about?" Something was wrong. She sounded angry.

"It's Marilyn, Punk. Today we had a little fight with her over nothing in particular. But she told us the truth—what I've always suspected about her."

"Spit it out, Mom. What is it?"

"She said that Paul Edward isn't your son, Punk."

"Why would she say a thing like that? It can't be true."

"It's true, Son."

"It can't be true! Put Marilyn on the line. Let me talk to her."

But Marilyn refused to come to the phone. It was as good as an admission, blowing his world apart. She'd tricked him into marriage.

With the Bel Air up and running, his thoughts ran from outrage to confusion as he drove the five hundred miles home, hoping and, for the first time, praying. *Maybe it's all just one big misunderstanding.*

He arrived at three o'clock in the morning and went directly to Marilyn's room after stopping to relish the last few moments of his sleeping child before he knew for certain that another man had fathered the son he'd grown to love.

"Marilyn, wake up. It's me—Wilbur."

"Wilbur?"

"Yes, it's me. Can we go outside and talk?" She followed him through the falling snow until he stopped at the door of his first home. "I want to go in here," he said. He opened the door, and they entered the chicken house, which was ravaged by time, filthy, full of chickens and manure, and cold. He sat at the old kitchen table and chairs that remained from his childhood. "Do you know what this place is?"

"Since there's chickens in here, I'd say it's a chicken coop."

"We used to live here. All of us—Dad, Mom, me, and Jesse. Before we built the house. Can you imagine living in such a place?"

"Well, no. Not if I had a choice."

"That's right. No one would, given a choice. Funny how, when we moved, once we finally had better options—a nicer home, running water, better clothes—Mom quit working for others, and my life spiraled downward. All my choices were shot down by other people and circumstances. I think it's sad that my happiest memories come from this rickety piece-of-shit building where chickens live."

"Do you want to move in here?"

"No. That's not my point." Wilbur paused to gather his words and keep his anger quelled.

Marilyn knew to be patient. His words would decide her future. However, her frozen hands and feet made her curter than she meant to be. "What is your point, Wilbur? I'm freezing out here."

"I don't give a damn how uncomfortable you are. I've suffered through hell since Mom called. The least you can do is hear me out."

"I'm sorry. You're right. Go on."

"My point is this: having the right to make choices. My mother chose that I would not go to college. My father chose to drink himself to death and made me responsible for everyone. And now you. You stole my right to choose who and when I'd marry. Now I'm forced to make a horrible choice about what I'm going to do. Do I choose divorce? Walk away from you and our precious boy—even though he's not mine? In my heart, he is. I couldn't love him any more if he was. Do I choose to stay married with the knowledge of your deception and lies? And what about Betty Ann and the devastation I put her through? What about the life she and I were supposed to share? Then there's my mother. She wants me to choose between you and her. Says I can't have both. You tell me, Marilyn—what should I do in my situation?" He looked up from the table and glared at her for an answer. He'd spoken calmly, but his face registered rage.

She placed her hand over his. "I can't tell you what to do. I won't take another choice from you. All I can do is tell you everything and tell you how I feel. Maybe after that, you can decide."

He allowed her hand to stay and listened while she said her piece. She began by telling him about her childhood, including her parents' loveless marriage and her struggle to stay out of the convent after her sisters joined. She told him of her discovery and loss of love and explained how the endless search to find it again had led her to Lenny. He'd told her he loved her, and she'd believed him.

They'd met in boot camp, where he was her drill sergeant, and he had transferred to Olathe after she got her orders, just to be with her—proving his love, she believed. She'd thought she loved him too. "The night you saw us arguing was the night I told him about my pregnancy. I thought he'd be happy, but he reacted all wrong—accused me of lying and said the baby wasn't his. Wilbur, I hadn't even talked to another man until you. We were together all the time. He knew what he said was lies. He wanted to hurt me, to get me and my baby far away from him. The last words he ever said to me were 'Get an abortion, or give it away.' He called me a whore," she said, barely able to say the last word. "You came to me in my worst moment, trying to help. I swear I didn't have a plan. It just happened between us—you were there. You know it's true. Up until the day I told you about the baby, I hadn't thought to trick you. But in the gazebo, I did lie. It was selfish and cruel, and I'm so sorry, because I can see and feel your pain.

"But most importantly, I want to remind you of what's come out of this. We were happy in New Bern, weren't we? In our own little chicken-house apartment. That's the happiest I've been in my whole life. I do love you—a deeper, stronger love than I've ever known. I think you loved me. I'm hoping you still do. Paul Edward *is* your child. Lenny knows nothing about him—or me—since the day you saw us argue. You and our baby love each other as father and son, and right now, you're the only one who could change that. Please don't. I'm begging you to give me another chance. I promise to be a loving and faithful wife to you for as long as I live." She faced Wilbur while saying these words, gripping his hand for dear life, speaking with conviction as tears rolled down her cheeks.

Her speech softened his face. "I believe you," he said. An eternity passed in silence before he stood up, taking Marilyn with him, and walked back to her bedroom. She followed him, not daring to speak. It was five thirty in the morning when he undressed and slid into bed beside his wife. "You are freezing," he whispered.

"I told you so, Punk," she replied, making Wilbur laugh.

"I always hated that name." They held each other and drifted off to sleep. Though it was unspoken, he'd made his decision.

They slept in late and arrived downstairs to find Sarah having lunch with Vance Sanderling, a lifelong neighbor who owned all the property surrounding Sarah's home and who had been a widower since last year. He began courting her after Jesse moved out, having finally become tired of Sarah's nagging him to get a job and to stop drinking. Vance had made a habit of coming over every morning at eight to eat breakfast; he would leave by nine to tend his cattle. He'd return around three and spend the afternoon either running errands with Sarah or just sitting in conversation until ten at night, when he'd leave to go home and sleep.

"I'm surprised your baby let you sleep, Marilyn," said Sarah, not looking up from the table. They all noticed to whom she assigned Paul Edward.

"I got in quite late and woke her up," said Wilbur, taking his mother by surprise.

"Why, Punk, it's you. I didn't expect you till today." Nor had she expected to see him and Marilyn come down together. Sarah looked them over. "Have you two talked?"

"Yes, we have."

"You're awful calm, considering."

"Well, Mom, nothing's changed, really."

"What do you mean? Everything's different now. Now that you know what kind of woman you've got yourself tangled up with."

"Hi, Mr. Sanderling. You know about all this?" asked Wilbur. Marilyn had told Wilbur about their relationship over the last weeks, and having known Vance all his life, he thought them a good match.

"Yes." Obviously on Sarah's side but judicious with age, he chose his words diplomatically.

"Then I reckon you're entitled to hear the rest. Mom, you have every right to resent Marilyn. She's sorry and knows what she did was wrong, but the fact is, Paul Edward could have just as easily been mine, and I love him. I can't imagine living without him." He took the child from Marilyn's arms and held him close. Paul Edward grinned at his granny, drool spilling over two new bottom teeth, and then squealed with delight as he spread his arms out, reaching for her. "Can you?"

"I'm sure that was part of her plan. Get us hooked in 'fore the truth came out," she said.

"Maybe so. But you don't know everything. Put in the same position, you'd have done desperate things too," said Wilbur. His mother started to argue, but he continued. "Like I said, he could have been mine. Despite the truth, I love him, and I love her. And she does love me. We have something good, and we're gonna work through this together."

"You're staying with that Jezebel?"

Marilyn came forward with tears of pain and hurt, took Paul Edward, and said, "I never meant to hurt anyone. I'm sorry," and she went back to her room.

Thanksgiving dinner passed uncomfortably. Wilbur and Vance tried to make pleasant conversation, but no one could escape the tension between the women. Both wanted the other gone. They took great pains to ignore each other, thus making their individual presence more noticeable. Afterward, Marilyn pleaded to return to North Carolina.

"We'll even live in the car. Anywhere but here."

"I realize you can't stay. What about going home to Missouri?"

"I guess I could. But I want—I need—to be with you. Maybe I can find a job where I can keep Paul Edward with me. Just take me back, and we'll work out something."

"I'll make some phone calls tomorrow and see what I can do."

On Friday afternoon, Wilbur received his return phone call from the base housing authority. He'd spent the morning placing calls to everyone he knew and had found success only after a long chain of called-in favors. Starting with his barracks supervisor, who regarded Wilbur as an intelligent and rare young man, Wilbur had explained his housing dilemma as a conflict between wife and mother-in-law. The supervisor had then made a call to their unit commander, winning his favor because of Wilbur's exemplary character. The commander had offered to speak on Wilbur's behalf to the husband of the BHA secretary, who was a personal friend, Gunnery Sergeant Price. Gunnery Sergeant Price had told Wilbur to wait by the phone until he talked to his wife. She'd call him back with an answer.

"We got a house," he said to Marilyn after hanging up the phone.

"You always come through, darling."

66

She'd already packed their bags that morning and was ready to leave within minutes. As they left, Wilbur kissed his mother good-bye and promised to continue his financial support, and then he shook Vance's hand. Vance finished his good-byes to the baby and handed him to Sarah. She affectionately kissed and squeezed Paul Edward before handing him to Marilyn, who sat in the car waiting, offering Sarah a timid smile of gratitude. Sarah forced a smile in return

The years 1954 through 1956 passed in contentment. Wilbur never dwelled on Paul Edward's paternity and found a comfortable rhythm as a husband, father, and marine.

Though living in Slocum Village freed them from paying rent and utilities, meaning they had enough money to live without worrying about where their next meal came from, they still lived frugally, saving every extra penny as a down payment on a better life. Most of Wilbur's peers lived hand to mouth, spending their money on souped-up cars and drunken weekends, but Wilbur kept repairing the old Chevy and fed his family by hunting, fishing, and gardening. Even married families on base were spendthrifts. The wives and children sported new clothes as Marilyn mended neighborhood hand-me-downs and shopped at thrift stores and the Salvation Army. Impoverished by circumstance, their lean first year together had instilled such a fear of spending that their greatest pleasure came from seeing their bank account grow.

Slocum Village, an overflow community of base housing at Cherry Point Marine Corps Air Station, sat in the center of Havelock, a civilian town surrounding Cherry Point. The majority of the military base was used to house aircraft, hangars, airfields, control towers, barracks, and government offices. Aside from its central purpose as an air base, it had two (one for officers and one for those enlisted) self-contained hamlets of housing and entertainment complexes, complete with swimming pools, bowling alleys, restaurants, movie theaters, a commissary, nightclubs, and a hospital. Cherry Point had outgrown its available space and recently built Slocum Village to handle the unexpected influx of new recruits.

Marilyn felt she had the best of both worlds: she had the benefits of free base housing but did not have to live on base. Their neighbors liked it too but for a different reason: they had more freedom among the civilians, out of sight of the ever-present military police. Slocum Village could get rowdy with young marines partying at all hours of the night.

Stability at home afforded Wilbur the time and energy to concentrate on his career. He rose quickly through the ranks, making corporal in June 1955. After news of his hunting skills got around, he earned a spot as captain of the armed forces' skeet-shooting team. In August 1956, he led them to a second-place finish at the national competition in Colorado, shooting a perfect score of 100 out of 100. The victory earned him his promotion to sergeant in January 1957.

By winter, Wilbur and Marilyn had $3,000 in savings. Havelock—as well as the entire nation—was in the midst of an economic boom. For the first time in his life, Wilbur felt financially secure and optimistic about the future.

"What do you think about buying a house?" he asked Marilyn one night over dinner.

"Why not ask me what I think about diamond rings and fur coats? I think it would be absolutely wonderful. And the timing couldn't be better."

"I agree. Interest rates are low; prices are good. Everywhere you look, there's another subdivision going up."

"That too. And we'll need more room for the new baby." She smiled lovingly at him, happy to be giving him the gift of biological fatherhood.

He choked on her words, swallowing a chunk of venison too soon. "A baby? You're pregnant?" he croaked. Marilyn nodded. He gulped his tea, dislodging the meat, and broke into a huge smile as he leaped up from the table and ran to smother his wife with kisses.

In February, for $16,000, they bought a three-bedroom brick house on a large corner lot in town. Budgeting to the dollar, they figured they could pay the bills, including the mortgage, utilities, food, gas, and Sarah's allotment, and still put away fifty dollars a month, all on a year's salary of less than $5,000. Most people would've found their prudence bitterly constraining, but Wilbur and Marilyn celebrated their accomplishment twelve months later not with lavish expenditure but by relishing the knowledge that together they could do anything.

Elizabeth Louise Weaver was born on September 20. Paul Edward, now a beautiful, loving, and charming three-year-old, welcomed the baby into their new home, along with his parents, as the glue cementing their family; they felt complete.

Since the last four years had proven prosperous and life no longer seemed to have a predetermined destiny to screw him, Wilbur felt that his history of bad luck had changed. Influenced by his friends' recent financial victories, he intrepidly sought to promote his fortune.

Working the night shift in April 1959, he and his coworkers passed hours of downtime, as only a small number of planes flew, by playing the board game Risk. They'd sit in the darkened control tower, illuminated only by the neon blue cast of the radar screens, jawboning through the wee morning hours, often talking about their investments and attracting Wilbur's interest.

"Hey, Wilbur, why don't you stop sleeping on your mattress full of money and invest it?" said Smitty, a fellow sergeant.

"I just haven't found the right one yet."

"I've got just the thing—shopping malls. I know a guy—a lawyer and a real estate developer, Larry Dinkins. He's made tens of thousands building strip malls. It's the wave of the future."

Wilbur had noticed the new malls going up around town. It seemed all the stores were now banding together under one roof. "How well do you know him?"

"I know him well enough to mortgage my house and invest five thousand dollars of my own money."

"Five thousand dollars?" The amount floored him. Smitty went on to explain how once Larry got twenty people to front $5,000 each, he and his partner, a local builder, planned to construct a mall in the center of Havelock.

"They built the first one over by the bank, and their investors tripled their money within six months. This one would be only the second one on the north side of town and in a better location. We've got seventeen people already. Once we get twenty, the deal's closed."

Wilbur thought about it for two days and, after finding no good reason not to, convinced his wife to take out a second mortgage. The proposal sounded so lucrative that they coaxed their neighbors, the Bishops, into investing too. Within a week, the twenty shareholders met with Mr. Dinkins in his law office, signed papers, and handed over $100,000.

Wilbur and Marilyn drove home in a state of euphoria. Marilyn rattled on. "I'm thinking we could use some new clothing. We need it. And we'll definitely need it for the vacation that the Bishops suggested. Do you think the kids will like Disneyland?"

"I don't see why not," said Wilbur. "I think I'll get a new car when the money comes in. It might be fun to take a vacation without the kids. What do you think of Las Vegas?"

"I love it. We could fly in at night with everything all lit up."

The next night, Marilyn sizzled deer burgers while the kids played outside and Wilbur flipped through the paper. Out of the blue, she said, "You know, I'm awfully tired of eating deer and fish every day."

"What's wrong with deer?"

"It's just that we eat it every day. I never even had it before I met you."

"So? It's good."

"It's good, yeah. But for once, I'd like some good old-fashioned beef like everybody else has."

"Okay then."

That was how things went for them now. Everything felt okay. They spent the next two months dreaming of ways to spend their riches. They hungered for the money. When June passed and construction of the strip mall still hadn't begun, the investors started to grow anxious. They'd expected to see ground breaking or some evidence of progress since early May. The Bishops asked Wilbur almost daily for answers, holding him personally responsible for the deal. He'd question Smitty at work, but also clueless, Smitty would reply, "These things take time."

In the middle of July, the Bishops invited Wilbur and Marilyn to dinner and demanded a meeting with Larry Dinkins. Agreeing it was time to get some answers, Wilbur offered to call his office Monday morning.

When he arrived at work, he informed Smitty of their discontent, and the two placed the call; the phone rang unanswered. They double-checked the phone number. By now, Smitty had also become concerned. After calling the given number all morning and getting no one, they drove to Larry's office during lunch. Smitty reached the door first and tried to open it. "The damn door's locked."

"What about his secretary? I know he has one. She was here when we signed the papers," said Wilbur.

"Maybe they're both out to lunch."

Wilbur cupped his hand over his eyes and pressed his face against the glass, looking through the door. His heart began to pound as he surveyed the empty room. "Oh my God, Smitty. The office is empty."

"What?" Smitty looked for himself, confirming the same. They frantically searched for indications of Larry's existence. "Where's his sign?"

"It's gone too." His placard over the door had been removed. They called information and searched the phone directory for any number remotely connected to Larry Dinkins, to no avail. Never having met the builder, they didn't even know the builder's name. They returned to work empty-handed and confused. After calling the other investors, they called the police.

A month-long investigation uncovered the facts: Larry Dinkins had a record of embezzling. He'd been convicted five years ago in another state and had served three years in prison. He didn't even have a valid license to practice law. They later found him living under an assumed name, pulling the same scam in Florida.

"But what about that first mall?" Wilbur asked Smitty after hearing of his record. "I thought you knew the previous investors."

"I met Larry when I bought my house. The Realtor recommended him for the closing—he did the legal work. That's when he told me about the first mall. Gave me names and everything. But no, I didn't personally check them out. I thought since my Realtor knew him, since he was a lawyer, he had a credible reputation." Smitty's closing had turned out to be the first and last time the Realtor had used Larry. Larry had henceforth declined his services to them, feeling he had enough investors hooked to soon reach his goal. When Smitty had reeled in Wilbur, who'd then convinced the Bishops, they'd made twenty, and Larry's scam had been complete. The first mall, used to bait the investors, was a legitimate deal, and the names given for reference were the actual names of its happy shareholders. But

Larry had no connection to the deal whatsoever, other than using his knowledge of it to claim the deal as his.

"You'd better make sure you really own your house," said Wilbur.

The swindled investors endured Larry Dinkins's trial, finding a small measure of consolation when the jury sentenced him to ten years in prison. However, every one of them lost his or her full investment. In addition to their life savings and their home's equity, Marilyn and Wilbur's toughest loss was the loss of their dreams, and as a result, they succumbed to dismay.

Wilbur lost his unseasoned belief in optimism and his hope in humanity, himself, and life in general. The scam had served as a reminder that every time he dared to dream, he got inversely and disproportionately rewarded. By any measure, Wilbur had risked the most and lost the most.

Chapter 9

Victimized and ashamed for allowing himself to be conned, Wilbur vowed never again to trust anyone or anything but himself. He concluded that getting ahead required hard work and dedicated saving; other means were only get-rich-quick schemes for fools. He'd been fooled once, and in his mind, that was one time too many.

He made staff sergeant in the beginning of 1959 and continued working in the control tower at Cherry Point. Usually, marines were relocated every few years, so he felt lucky to remain in one place. His commanding officer took a special liking to Wilbur and assured him he'd stay at least another three years, revealing that the officer had already diverted two transfer orders.

Knowing he had time, Wilbur decided to pursue his dream of going to college, not only for the personal satisfaction but also to advance in his career. As an E-6 staff sergeant, at his current rate of promotion, he'd soon top out in the enlisted ranks—E-9 sergeant major and master gunnery sergeant were the highest obtainable levels for the enlisted.

Wilbur wanted to be one of the rare ones to make officer, to be a so-called mustanger. A true mustanger began as a private and, within three years of exemplary service, got selected for Officer Candidate School. He or she then graduated directly to the status of an unrestricted officer, eligible to serve in any field and eventually able to make general. Wilbur saw his destiny as a mustanger.

His specialized training as an air traffic controller made Wilbur ineligible for unrestricted duty. He'd have to stay in his field as a limited duty officer, but he could make officer. Undeterred by this distinction, he set his sights on the highest rank obtainable by a marine in his position: full-bird colonel. Even though realizing the dream might take another thirty years, he felt that man was rewarded only by his hard work and effort. Having a college degree guaranteed him the first step.

After evaluating his high school transcripts and meeting with the college guidance counselor, he felt his goal would prove easier to reach than he'd thought. The advanced classes he'd taken and his remarkable grades counted for credit toward the first eighteen months of college. With an overloaded schedule, he could get his bachelor's degree in a mere two years. But earning the degree alone wasn't enough. His perfectionist attitude demanded the best. Simply getting credit for a class counted toward his degree but not his GPA, or grade point average. Though he needed only fifty hours to graduate, sixty hours of attended class qualified one for the distinction of graduating with honors if the student had at least a 3.5 GPA. To Wilbur, having a Latin phrase on the bottom of his diploma—graduating cum laude, magna cum laude, or summa cum laude—meant as much as the degree itself.

He kept these details in mind when he started classes in the fall.

For two years, Wilbur managed his days down to the minute: waking at six in the morning to work in the control tower until three and then coming home and running three miles to stay in shape for his required physical-fitness training tests. He ate dinner with his family at five in the afternoon and then went to school three nights a week from six to nine, only to return and study in bed until midnight. He spent his free nights writing papers and studying. Saturdays were for chores, but on Sundays, he'd finally relax. Marilyn, having reestablished her Catholic ties, took the children to church while her husband slept in.

Wilbur didn't care much for organized religion—or religion in any form. Believing in a higher power and having someone else to blame for one's failure was, to him, a sign of weakness, a flaw in man's ability to take and accept responsibility for his own actions. Pride made him decline his wife's repeated invitations to attend church, and after six months, she stopped asking.

Six-year-old Paul Edward and Elizabeth, now three, relished every Sunday as if it were Christmas. They'd come home from church; find Daddy in bed, reading the paper; change out of their

Sunday clothes; and jump into his bed with him. Hours passed as Wilbur read the comics to them. Paul Edward learned to tell time and tie his shoes there, and Wilbur delighted in listening to Elizabeth jabber along, trying to include her thoughts in their conversations.

Paul Edward once asked Wilbur why he didn't go to church with the family. Wilbur carefully considered his answer, debating whether to instill his own views in his son and when to begin laying the foundation toward manhood. Like all parents, he wanted to make his son's life journey easier than his own. He wanted Paul Edward to reap the benefits of learning from his daddy's mistakes without having to experience life's cruelty firsthand. Gaining a strong character and a somewhat pessimistic view of life had served Wilbur, as he avoided the emotional pitfalls of disappointment, embracing the credo "Hope for the best, but prepare for the worst." Wilbur decided to answer his son with the hard truths as he knew them. "Son, I think it's great you like to go to church with Mom, and she enjoys taking you and your sister, but I don't share her beliefs in God."

"You don't believe in God? In Jesus?"

"Well, I do believe there was man named Jesus and that he was a great person who helped a lot of people. But he was still just a man who lived and died like everyone else. As his story got told over the centuries, people embellished"—he digressed by explaining what that new word meant—"upon his life and created the fantastic story you hear in church today."

"But what about God?"

"Science tells us how the world was really created: eons ago, there was a big bang." He continued his lecture, explaining the big bang theory and what the word *eon* meant.

"Are you what they call an atheist? The priest says those people are going to hell."

"No, sweetie. I'm an agnostic—someone who's unsure about God. People today are too quick to ask God to solve their problems instead of going to work and helping themselves. When you grow up, you have to get a job and keep your family fed and safe. Do you see God bringing home the money or buying groceries for us?"

"No. But I sure wish you weren't going to hell."

"Don't worry. Good people like me, who don't lie, cheat, or steal, are safe. I'm not going to hell."

Wilbur thought their talk went well. He chose subconsciously to ignore the troubled look on Paul Edward's face.

In May of 1961, young Elizabeth sat on her mother's lap in Wright Auditorium at East Carolina College. They sat near the center aisle, halfway to the stage. Elizabeth's pink chiffon dress matched her mother's, both of which Marilyn had made just for the occasion. Marilyn held Paul Edward's hand as he sat next to her, his thick, curly black hair trying to escape from its forced part.

"Where's Daddy? Why's he not here?" asked Paul Edward as the auditorium filled to capacity. "There sure is a lot of people."

"You'll see him soon, dear. He'll be on the stage."

"You mean everyone's here to see him?"

"These people are here for their family members. A bunch of people will be on stage, not just Daddy."

"Oh. Why?"

"Because they went to a hard school, and now they're done. Remember how hard Daddy's been studying? Well, this is his reward."

"Why?"

"Because I said so. That's why. Now, hush." They sat watching while 140 graduates walked quickly across the stage, barely glancing at the dignitary as he handed them their degrees. Elizabeth fidgeted with the bows on her dress, tying and untying them. They had been sitting there for hours, as far as she could tell, and it seemed as if they'd never get to stand up. Her mother kept telling her to keep still, and every few moments, she had to move Elizabeth's head out of the way.

"Stop it," Elizabeth whispered. Her mother only shushed her and moved her head again. "I don't see why we couldn't just come when it's Daddy's turn. I'm bored."

Someone with the last name of Wallace walked off stage, and Marilyn said, "The Ws. Thank goodness." Elizabeth followed her mother's gaze and saw Wilbur standing ready in the wings, his smile a mile wide.

"Receiving a bachelor's degree in general studies and our only graduate earning the distinction of summa cum laude, Mr. Wilbur Lee Weaver," said the dean.

One by one, the entire audience stood, clapping and cheering enthusiastically. "Mommy, what does 'sooma coom lowdy' mean?" She noticed some tears dripping down her mother's cheek.

"It means Daddy was the best of the best, dear."

Elizabeth's father took his time walking toward the dean. The dean vigorously shook Wilbur's hand, patting him on the back with the other, saying something they couldn't hear.

Wilbur said, "Thank you," unable to suppress the smile breaking across his face. He exited the stage, and the last three students followed almost invisibly as the audience remained astonished that anyone had earned a perfect GPA of 4.0.

"Why'd everyone holler for Daddy?" asked Paul Edward.

"Because your daddy is an incredible man," said Marilyn.

Even as a college graduate, Wilbur waited three more years until his next promotion to an E-7 gunnery sergeant, still among the enlisted ranks. Apparently, the marine corps had all the officers it needed at that time.

In 1964, rumblings about deployment to Vietnam became pervasive among the units at Cherry Point. Though no formal declarations had been made, marines bustled about their duties in an anxious and hurried manner. The base buzzed with unspoken orders of "Hurry up and wait" as soldiers went on special combat training missions and mechanics worked day and night, fine-tuning hundreds of aircraft. As supervisor of the air traffic control unit aboard the base, Wilbur spent sixteen hours a day manning the radars, keeping up to a dozen F-100 Super Sabre fighter planes practicing their maneuvers out of each other's airspace, and forcing his men to take their mandatory midshift naps in the back room of the control tower.

The world was a much more frightening place, especially after November 22, 1963, when Wilbur and Marilyn sat together watching television and crying in horror as they witnessed the aftermath of President Kennedy's assassination. As young adults of twenty-six and twenty-seven, Wilbur and Marilyn believed in Camelot, a new world of sustained peace and prosperity heralded by the young, charismatic president. He'd surely keep America's young men safe, containing Vietnam's problems overseas before war's ugly realities consumed the lives of American families. But Kennedy's assassination squashed such hopes. In the minds of most military families, war now seemed inevitable.

The nation limped along, negotiating and sending advisers and small, specialized combat missions to Southeast Asia but avoiding full engagement until March of 1965. In his fatalistic view, Wilbur thought the end of civilization was coming near and began preparing his family for the worst.

After recovering from their financial losses from the real estate scam eight years ago, Wilbur jumped on a young private's offer to sell his 1965 Chevrolet Super Sport at cost. Wilbur sold his Bel Air to a junkyard for parts after its eighteen total years of service and nearly 250,000 miles and paid the private $1,600 cash.

"Now you won't have to worry about transportation," he said to Marilyn while making arrangements for his overseas tour.

"We don't even know if you're going or not."

"It's just a matter of time. And you know it."

"No, and I don't want to deal with it until the orders come."

"Just humor me then. I need to know you can manage without me."

Marilyn had never handled the finances, and he struggled to teach her how to pay the mortgage, deposit paychecks, budget for necessities, and save. (Saving was a new possibility since his mother's marriage last year, as she'd forgiven his monthly "debt.") However, with more than $5,000 in savings, he felt uncomfortable leaving such a sum to her management. "I want to buy gold stocks with our savings," said Wilbur.

"What for? I'd feel better knowing it's there if I need it."

"You'll have at least a hundred dollars a month for emergencies. The world's going to hell in a handbasket, and gold is the safest place to invest. Every fool I know keeps sticking his money in the stock market, believing its rise from seven hundred to a thousand marks the beginning of a new age. It's ludicrous to think it will continue—crazy it's even gone that high. New age, my ass. What goes up must come down; it's a simple law of physics. Inflation's tripled since we bought the house—meaning our dollars are worth less every day. Just look at history, my dear: gold is the only thing of proven lasting value. Why do you think the government banned owning it? Because there isn't enough to go around, and they want it all. If we own its stock, we may not make a fortune, but at least it'll be worth something when nothing else will be. I'll feel much better in Vietnam knowing our money's safe."

His financial tirade was beyond her comprehension, and she agreed. The following Monday, Wilbur converted their savings into shares of ownership in several Canadian and South African mines. As a brilliant afterthought, he then scoured local coin dealers and bought all the collectible twenty-dollar gold pieces he could find, netting 182 coins by the end of the week. He showed Marilyn their treasure before stowing it away in old ammunition boxes and hiding them in the attic. "Don't ever tell anyone about this. Do you understand? Even one casual remark would be an invitation to thieves," he warned.

After twelve years of service, Gunnery Sergeant Wilbur Weaver was selected as a limited duty officer and became a mustang second lieutenant. His promotion wasn't purely meritorious. As the marine corps' commanding chiefs prepared for war, they surveyed the ranks and found a need for more officers to send with the troops. Wilbur's career advancement came concurrently with deployment orders to the Marine Amphibious Unit in Chu Lai, Vietnam. Come December 1, he'd depart as the commanding officer of a small air traffic control unit at the base of Marble Mountain—only thirty miles from battle lines.

Wilbur had ninety days to savor his home and family before leaving. After two months, thoughts of West Virginia and his mother and brother kept coming to his mind. He'd kept in touch with them through phone calls and letters. Jesse had spent a year in Germany after completing boot camp but had returned home following a dishonorable discharge for assaulting an officer while drunk. Sarah had taken him back, allowing him to freeload while he worked just enough to support his alcoholic habit. He tried to hide his alcoholism by sleeping in the basement whenever he came home drunk, and because he was the son she lovingly favored, she chose to ignore the truth by living in denial and making excuses for his laziness: "He's never gotten over his father's death. Nobody appreciates his charming personality. He just hasn't found the right girl to straighten him out. If only someone would give him a chance."

When she'd married Vance, Vance had seen Jesse for the shiftless drunk he'd become and had forbidden his wife from continuing to enable him. Vance had given Jesse a job working in one of his coal mines but had later booted him out, as Jesse had rarely shown up for work. Now twenty-eight years old, Jesse slept wherever he could, living off odd jobs he kept just long enough to buy his liquor. He was like a sad carbon copy of his uncle Ned.

Wilbur longed for home. He hadn't seen his mother for eleven years, and now, about to leave for Vietnam, Wilbur worried he might not ever see his mother and Jesse again. "Marilyn, what do you think about spending Thanksgiving in West Virginia?" he asked one Sunday morning after church, hoping to catch her in her most charitable mood.

"Must we? I'd rather not spend our last few weeks together arguing, and you know that's likely if we go."

Wilbur listed his reasons for wanting to go, and his last one won her over. "After all, they're my family. And family is all we really have."

Thanksgiving 1965 was memorable.

Sarah had never before met her eight-year-old granddaughter, Elizabeth. Instantly upon their arrival, the child's curly brown hair, infectious smile, and endearing ways touched Sarah's heart as no one else had ever done. Sarah wanted to hold her constantly and showered her with hugs and kisses while Elizabeth sat in her lap. Whenever Sarah had to stand up, Elizabeth would jump from her grandmother's lap into Vance's lap and then begin inventorying the contents of Vance's shirt pocket. After she found his Goody comb, a favorite pastime became getting paid a quarter for scratching his scaly scalp. She liked to jiggle the folds of skin under his chin and ask, "What's this?"

Vance would chuckle and reply, "That's my turkey neck." The question and answer became a game of ritual between them. Often, the three just sat in silence until Vance decided to strike up conversation again by asking, "So whaddya know?" expecting no particular reply.

Paul Edward most enjoyed spending time with Vance, especially riding beside him in his big truck to survey the cattle, the unfamiliar farm equipment piquing his interest. Vance patiently waited behind the wheel for what seemed like hours as the boy pretended to drive the tractors. Then, when Paul Edward finished his imaginary travels, he ran wildly through the barn, exploring the hayloft. Left on his own, he'd roam through the attics and storage sheds of all the old buildings, discovering their ancient hidden treasures. A rusted Radio Flyer wagon invited his invention of new games, and a tomboy at heart, Elizabeth eventually left her lap perches and joined her brother in playing outside.

Sarah's backyard leveled off eight feet before sharply swooping downhill to three large willow trees that delineated the property's edge. After parking the wagon at the top of the hill, facing the slope, Paul Edward made his sister sit inside and bent the handle back for her to hold. "Just hold on, and steer the wagon by turning the handle," he said. She followed his orders without a care in the world, wiggling her bottom as she firmly seated herself in the old wagon, smearing her ruffled pale yellow dress (newly made by Grandma) with rust. "One. Two. Three!" yelled Paul as he took a running start and shoved Elizabeth down the hill.

She let loose an ear-piercing scream, speeding straight ahead (not understanding what her brother had meant by "steering"), and crashed headlong into the large trunk of a willow tree. The noise brought the others outside, where they found her lying on the ground, dumped from the now-sideways wagon. Wagon and child were entangled in torn willow branches and covered in red dirt, grass stains, and rust. The adults rushed to her aid, helped her up, and upbraided Paul Edward for injuring his sister. When righted, Elizabeth stood smiling and said, "Wow. That was fun. Let's do it again." Everyone laughed except Sarah, who stood aside, disgusted by the ruination of her dress.

"No, honey. I think that's enough for today," said Marilyn.

Elizabeth wiped her dirty hands on her dress and then stopped to sniff them. "Daddy, why does the dirt smell different here?"

Paul Edward had noticed it too. Not just the dirt but also the air, the grass, the trees—everything smelled different. "Because West Virginia's full of magic. That's why," he replied.

Deer season opened during the two weeks surrounding the holiday. Wilbur spent his days in the woods, reliving happy childhood memories as he walked silently through the morning dew. He wore full hunting gear, including a camouflage ski mask, and scouted a spot of concealment—an aboriginal intruder belonging to the wilderness yet lethal to its inhabitants. He preferred to find a comfortable old stump as close as possible to a large tree trunk before stopping to prepare mentally for the hunt, knowing he'd probably wait for hours until the perfect shot presented itself.

At first, he'd meditate, listening to the language of the forest— the whippoorwills' last calls, warning of dawn's imminence; the squirrels' footsteps as they scurried from their nests, chattering to their comrades in the distance; the creaks and moans of the trees, as if they too stretched in waking. He'd then let his mind wander, its train of thought carrying him wherever it chose. He relived his life as young boy, recalling his awe of his father, Webb. Alert and wide awake at five o'clock in the morning, Wilbur had mentally catalogued every detail as Webb taught him the secrets of the wild. He romanticized the man he'd loved before the drinking had begun. Enjoying the memories of his and Jesse's escapades most, Wilbur made a conscious effort to savor those moments, such as the time the boys had thrown rotten tomatoes at Henry Straley's truck windshield—with Straley in it.

That incident had started when the boys were trying out a new route to school. The mean old codger had looked out his kitchen window and seen them cutting through his backyard. He had run out the back door with a smile on his face and hollered at them, "Wait right there a minute!" They had. Since he'd been smiling, they'd thought they'd exchange pleasantries. But when he'd gotten closer, he'd grabbed their arms and whooped them for trespassing, accusing them of trying to steal the milk off his porch. A week later, as they'd ridden in the bed of their father's truck (filled with donated bushels of spoiled fruit intended for slopping their hogs), Mr. Straley's truck had suddenly appeared behind them. With the recent and, in their opinion, unjust punishment at his hands still fresh in their minds, they had been unable to resist the opportunity.

Wilbur chuckled out loud, forgetting where he was and the need to keep silent. He remembered the look on Henry Straley's face. That had been more than worth the spanking Webb had given them afterward.

As his musings progressed, so did his mood. Remorse and worry replaced his feelings of happiness, security, and comfort. Forcing his mind out of the past, he'd begin hunting in earnest, keeping the woods his private sanctuary for introspection.

The familiar sounds of softly crunching leaves broke in on his musings: a deer, ten or so yards away, headed toward him. He removed his gun's safety and raised the gun to eye level, bracing the butt against his shoulder, and then he looked through the scope, pointing it in the direction of the footsteps, all in one easy, silent motion. Wilbur appeared as one with the tree while he waited for the target to appear mystically within the small lens. A ten-point buck walked unsuspectingly into his crosshairs. Wilbur exhaled completely, held his breath, and slowly squeezed the trigger as if stroking a loved one, firing a single bullet directly behind the animal's shoulders and hitting the heart dead center.

At his wife's insistence, he brought their son with him the next two times he went hunting. When Wilbur woke his six-year-old son, he expected at least a little enthusiasm, but he could tell Paul Edward came along only because his parents forced him to, and the boy spent his time fidgeting around restlessly. Still, that morning before dawn, Wilbur woke Paul Edward, dressed quickly, and grabbed his gun with a look of pride on his face. They stalked through the dark woods, the boy behind, his gaze shifting left to right, up to the trees, and down to the bracken. After an hour or so, Wilbur held up a hand, the signal to freeze and keep quiet. "Watch closely, Son. Watch how it's done."

Wilbur followed the squirrel by sound for another thirty seconds, until it poked its head from the far side of a tree trunk. Wilbur didn't waste a second, and the report echoed through the woods. He stalked around the tree and picked up his prize.

"There it is. A clean shot. Think you can do that?"

Paul Edward kept quiet. He stared at the ground.

"What's wrong, Son?"

"I just—I don't know. Can we just go back?"

"Not a chance. Your mother wants you to hunt. So you're going to hunt." Wilbur bagged the squirrel and walked on. Paul Edward followed, sulking. The next squirrel was long in coming. It was sitting on a branch, opening an acorn—the easiest shot in the world. Wilbur motioned Paul Edward up next to him and pointed. "Okay, this one's tailor made. Let's see you take aim."

Paul Edward shouldered the gun, but he couldn't bring himself to raise it to get the squirrel in his sights.

"Come on, Paul Edward. Before he gets spooked." He noticed that Paul Edward was blinking, and then he saw the tears coming down his cheeks. "Now what—" He didn't even bother to finish his question. He brought up his own weapon, but it was too late. The squirrel had vanished.

They walked around for another hour or two. When Wilbur felt he'd done his duty, around noon, he purposely cut their outing short. The next time they went out—also at Marilyn's insistence—he didn't even bother to get Paul Edward to take aim. He shot the squirrels himself and again came home early. Other times, he offered to take Elizabeth. She jumped up and down at the idea, but Marilyn and Sarah said it wasn't fitting for little girls and wouldn't allow it.

Wilbur gradually began to hear other telling remarks by Paul Edward—such as the time Paul Edward caught Elizabeth squashing ants on the sidewalk and said, "Don't kill them. They won't hurt you if you don't hurt them." Upon hearing this, Wilbur knew he'd never share the special hunting bond with his son. Wilbur learned to accept his son's differences, loving him for his sweetness and caring sensitivity, but deep down, he feared that Paul Edward's life promised disappointment.

Elizabeth's temperament gave him hope. With her curious nature and fearless attitude, he saw himself in her. When he came home with game to clean, she eagerly helped him skin and gut the animals. Hunting equaled food, and that required killing. It all made sense to her. She eventually took possession of her brother's guns and frequently went outside to shoot the BB gun under her father's supervision, first practicing with cardboard boxes as targets and then shooting birds. Only once did she misjudge her capabilities, when, on a windy March day, she made a mistake that almost caused her to quit shooting forever.

"Hey, Daddy. Can I go shoot the BB gun?" she asked, already dressed to go outside and holding the gun in her hand. Wilbur would have preferred to sit on the porch steps and watch over her, but he and his wife were entertaining company at the time, so Wilbur let Elizabeth go alone.

She went into the front yard and placed an open cardboard box against a bush for a target. The bush outlined the border of their driveway, and their car sat parked directly behind it, but that didn't enter her mind. She shot twice, but the wind kept blowing the cardboard away. On her third shot, she chased the blowing box with the scope and fired, shattering the driver's-side window of Wilbur's car. She was overcome with fear, and her fight-or-flight response took charge; she chose to hide and then lie if she had to, hoping someone or something else could take the blame. She went back inside. Her parents sat in the living room, talking with the Bishops. "Back so soon?" asked her mother.

"Yeah. It's too windy." *They didn't hear it.* She put the gun away and crawled to the farthest corner under her bed, hiding, and she stayed there for nearly three hours. When her parents said good-bye to their friends and walked them to the door, they saw what she'd done.

Wilbur found her (in her usual hiding place) and, to her surprise, didn't scold or spank her, as she'd feared. Not wishing to dampen her enthusiasm for guns, he said that he understood how accidents could happen and that hopefully, she'd learned her lesson.

Wilbur came in from the woods one day to find Marilyn cleaning up the kitchen. "Any luck?" she asked.

"You seem like you're in a good mood," he said.

"You know, I am. I'm having a nice time here. I'm getting more time with the kids than I usually do. Although ..." She was going to say that she was hoping Wilbur would spend more time inside, socializing with everyone, but she was in such a good mood that she didn't want to spark any conflict. He didn't even notice that she'd cut herself off.

"You and Mom getting along?"

"We are. No complaints here." She and Sarah had compromised with a tacit agreement to speak only about neutral issues: cooking, television, and housekeeping. Their deepest remarks centered on their shared fears of Wilbur's deployment.

Jesse's daily presence helped ease the burden of conversation. Visiting his brother gave reason for Vance and Sarah to overlook his drinking, and they welcomed him back into the house without reservation. Wilbur looked forward to spending their days together hunting, as they had as boys, but Jesse repeatedly declined. "The last time I went hunting was with you, Wilbur, and I only did then because you made me. I just don't care much for it," he explained. Getting up early to sit in the woods for hours didn't fit Jesse's partying lifestyle of socializing and sleeping late. Jesse did love to talk. Marilyn thought she'd have gone stir-crazy if it weren't for the entertainment he provided. Paul Edward and Elizabeth were charmed by him too, awed by his complete contrast to their father: his laid-back attitude; his jeans (they'd never seen their father in jeans) and white T-shirts, with a pack of Lucky Strikes always rolled up in his short sleeve; and his thick, slicked-back black hair. In their opinion, Jesse was cool. They couldn't see his immaturity; they didn't know he hadn't changed a bit in dress or sophistication since high school.

He'd show up sometime in the early afternoon, whenever he woke, and stay for supper. Afterward, the whole family sat at the kitchen table, talking for hours. The kids enjoyed that time the most, joining in to offer silly jokes of their own and receiving laughter as a reward. Their nine o'clock bedtime came much too soon; they'd beg and plead unsuccessfully to stay up. By the third night, they figured out to agree, go upstairs, and then later sneak out of bed and hide on the top steps, where they could listen to the grown-ups talk, deciding on their own when to sleep.

The only interruption of contentment came when fragments of Jesse's party-animal life came home with him. Twice, he invited a girlfriend, Jean, to the family's nightly chats. The first time she came knocking was after dark, and expecting her, Jesse rushed to open the door first and let her in. "Everyone, this is my girl, Jean. You don't mind if she sits down?" he asked, but he didn't wait for an answer as he sat her down at the table.

"Hey, y'all. Howzit hanging?" she said, smiling, exposing a mouthful of blackened teeth. Older than Jesse, maybe thirty, she looked fifty, and she had frazzled hair and wrinkled, unkempt skin. She also stank. A cloud of tobacco, liquor, and body odor hung over her. They learned that Jesse often slept at her house, one of those teetering hillside shacks surrounded by junkyard paraphernalia down the hollow. The children had never seen anyone like her and enjoyed her company. She added to the magic of West Virginia. Wilbur reluctantly accepted his brother's friend and treated her kindly, but Sarah and Vance were less than hospitable, knowing her as one of the many ignorant ne'er-do-wells who mooched off the state and spent her welfare checks on alcohol and tobacco.

Jean came over a second time, staying just long enough to gather Jesse and leave for a night out. The next morning, Sarah went to the basement pantry for a new jar of apple butter and came back raving mad, yelling as everyone sat for breakfast. "Jesse brought that good-for-nothing whore home to my house last night! They're both downstairs, sleeping in the basement."

Vance left to investigate and found them curled up together on an old tarp laid out on the concrete floor, still wearing yesterday's clothes and their coats. He woke Jesse, demanding an explanation. "What the hell's wrong with you, boy?"

"We just needed a place to sleep. We ain't bothering no one."

"Well, your mother's upstairs pitching a fit—disrespecting her like this. Why didn't you two go home to her place?"

"We tried, but Eddie showed up."

"Who the hell's Eddie?"

"My husband," replied Jean groggily from her drunken stupor.

"Your husband? Get the hell out of here. Both of you. Before you bring more of your kind here looking for you."

"Can you give us a ride, Vance? Her old man took the car."

"Hell no. Get your things, and leave the way you came!" shouted Vance before going back upstairs to finish his breakfast. Jesse and Jean took off walking down the hollow, cold and hungover.

Wilbur's visit came to an end after ten days. He and Marilyn packed their suitcases in the trunk, along with a cooler full of processed venison from the two deer he'd killed, and prodded the kids to get in the car early on a Sunday morning as they said their good-byes. Sarah couldn't hold back the tears pouring down her face as she hugged her grandchildren, not wanting to let go. Paul Edward and Elizabeth bawled too. Grandma's house seemed a world away, and they didn't know when they'd ever return. "Come on, kids. We'll come back soon. Maybe even next year," said Wilbur.

"Oh, please do. Don't keep these precious babies away so long again. You all come next Thanksgiving," said Sarah.

"Okay, plan on seeing us every Thanksgiving after I come back from Vietnam. I love you, Mom."

"I love you too, Son. Please keep safe over there."

"I'll be miles away from danger. Don't you worry."

The promise pleased everyone and made leaving easier. Vance offered hugs, shook Wilbur's hand, and watched them back out until the car disappeared from view. The children wiped away tears for hours, until the pain of separation subsided—somewhere along the Virginia border.

Wilbur had three days of family time in North Carolina before he shipped out on December 1, enduring a second heartbreaking farewell within a week.

He left his wife and children at their front door. Giving her father as big a hug as she was able to, Elizabeth asked, "Why do you have to go, Daddy?"

"To tell you the truth, I'm needed. The country needs men with my skills to go across the ocean and control the airplanes over there."

Elizabeth scrunched up her face. "The country? You mean the president?"

"You could say that," Wilbur answered.

The next morning, while Marilyn was loading the children into the car, Elizabeth suddenly pointed upward. "There he is, Mommy. There he is."

Marilyn looked up but couldn't fathom what her daughter meant. "There who is, sweetheart?"

"It's Daddy. He's up in the plane."

Sure enough, an airplane was crossing the sky right above them. Elizabeth waved to the plane. Marilyn almost explained that Wilbur didn't control every plane in the sky, but then she thought better of it. After a few seconds, Paul Edward joined her. Marilyn's heart melted with sweet sympathy. After that, they would run outside whenever they heard a plane flying overhead (living near an air base made this frequent), yelling and waving at their daddy.

Chapter 10

Paul Edward spent his most-formative years without a father around, though he knew it wasn't by choice; a lot of his friends' dads were in Vietnam too.

Marilyn had her hands full with her precocious daughter, going head-to-head with her almost daily. Elizabeth never accepted no for an answer to her barrage of social requests: she wanted at least one, preferably two or three, of her friends to spend the night every weekend, or she would run off into the neighborhood without telling her mother and stay out until dark. Parenting her was like caging a wild animal. Elizabeth had an independent streak Marilyn could not confine.

Thank God Paul Edward's not like her, Marilyn often thought. His quiet nature lessened her burden of rearing two children alone, allowing her to channel most of her energy into Elizabeth. As a result, she unintentionally ignored Paul Edward. Finding his sister always at the center of attention, he began to withdraw into himself for comfort, love, and company, existing on the edges of life. Eventually labeled an outsider in school, he didn't make any close friends.

He got in trouble only twice—and both times were results of his efforts to gain affection.

On Mother's Day in 1966, the first year of his father's absence, he presented Marilyn with a beautiful bouquet of roses and a card he'd made himself. Being twelve at the time, he thought she'd lovingly accept his perfect gift from the man of the house. Filled with excitement over his brilliant idea, he went out at sunrise and picked all the roses in the neighborhood: he took them from every front-yard bush, climbed into Mrs. Moses's prized flower garden (which was gated for protection against animals and intruders), and came home with more than forty roses in hand before anyone awoke. *She's going to be so happy*, he thought as he crammed the bundle into a vase, pricking his fingers on the thorny stems. They wouldn't all fit, so he wrapped them with masking tape, and then he waited for her to rise. Since it was only seven o'clock, he had at least another hour and decided to make a card too. On a piece of ruled paper folded twice, he wrote,

> These roses are red and yellow and pink.
> From the man of the house,
> You're terrific—I think!
> Happy Mother's Day.
> Love, Paul Edward

He felt proud after finishing the card; he couldn't stand waiting any longer and woke her up by presenting his gift.

"How beautiful, Son. Thank you so much. I guess you are my man around here." She covered him in hugs and kisses.

At ten o'clock, Mr. Moses knocked on their front door and spoke to Marilyn. He'd tracked Paul Edward's muddy footprints from his wife's garden across the street to their house. Apparently, Mrs. Moses had gone out for her morning inspection ritual shortly after Paul Edward's thievery and thrown a fit upon realizing the butchering of her roses. She was still throwing it two hours later.

Marilyn apologized profusely and made her son apologize too. She tried giving the roses back, but Mr. Moses refused them. He'd only come because his wife had made him, and he empathized with the boy. However, by noon, when three other neighbors came over fuming, his gift's loving intention quickly wore off. Marilyn spent the whole day, Mother's Day, trying to make amends and apologizing to her friends, confining her son to his room in punishment.

The second time he got in trouble, he had a crush on a high-ranking colonel's daughter, Kimberly Fletcher, the most-popular, prettiest girl in school. She was also the most spoiled and selfish, but Paul Edward didn't see her ugly qualities. To him, she was a beautiful angel sent just for him to gaze upon. He had liked her for years and couldn't remember ever liking anyone else. He yearned for her to look his way, smile at him, or offer any acknowledgment of his existence. She never did. Peons like him didn't warrant her notice.

Three years ago, on the first day of school in December, his teacher introduced Kimberly to the class as the new girl from Arizona. Military families moved often, so children often suffered when changing schools midyear. At one time or another, almost everyone had been a new student somewhere. The designation was generally no big deal, but her arrival created a big deal for Paul Edward.

He loved her from afar that first year, too afraid to approach her in any manner. The next year, when he saw her sitting in his class on their first day of school, he made it his seventh-grade goal to make contact. After a week of cogitating, he found the words to express his feelings and courageously set them to paper, secretly planning to slip the note into her book bag for her to find later and read privately. It read,

> Dear Kimberly,
> You are so beautiful. If you knew
> how much I love you, you would love me too.
> Your Secret Admirer

He held the note in his hand for hours, working up the nerve to follow through with his plan, until his sweaty palms soaked the paper and finally shredded it into pieces. He wrote the same note over and over for a month but never gave it to her. His obsession caught the attention of David Nelms, a bully who sat beside him and who later found out what Paul Edward secretly wrote. Having the ammunition, David began to tease him relentlessly, threatening to tell everyone unless Paul paid him to keep quiet.

Quiet, shy, introverted Paul Edward went without lunch for the rest of the year, his money extorted by David and his goal of reaching Kimberly thwarted in fear of class ridicule. David's bullying didn't end with extortion. Getting his pleasure at the expense of others had no boundaries, and he took his powerful information further. Unbeknownst to Paul Edward, David began writing different versions of Paul Edward's love note, all signed "Your Secret Admirer," and slipped them to Kimberly all year long. Some notes were innocent, sweet copies of the original, but others were ugly, nasty, and even threatening versions, such as the following:

Dear Hot Mama,
You smell so sweet. Good enough to eat.
Watch out for me. I just might bite,
Cuz if you're alone, you'll be dead meat.
Your Secret Admirer

The notes frightened Kimberly, and she showed them to her parents. After Colonel Fletcher called the school, demanding that her principal and teacher find the perpetrator, they decided the best chance of catching him was to keep quiet, watch, and catch him in the act. But nothing happened that year.

Eighth grade started as the year before had. Paul Edward still longed for Kimberly, who, luckily, sat in his class again. In a stroke of luck, the bully, David, did not, as he'd moved away over the summer. With renewed optimism, Paul Edward decided to make his move on Kimberly on their first day of school. He wrote the same note he'd first written and, not waiting to lose his nerve, placed it on top of her desk when she got up to sharpen her pencil. The whole class, except Kimberly, saw him do it. When she returned to her desk and read it, she screamed and cried, "Not again! I can't take this another year!" She ran to the teacher, asking to call her parents.

Paul Edward sat in the principal's office, confused and scared out of his mind as Kimberly, her parents, his mother, and a truant officer bombarded him with questions and accusations, crediting him for all the terrible notes David had written the year before. Denying everything only increased their anger.

Never getting a confession, the adults concluded that Paul Edward suffered from some sort of mental illness. Marilyn blamed it on stress due to his father's duty in Vietnam. The school officials agreed that Paul Edward could remain in school as long as he underwent counseling and didn't act out again.

The boy never understood why he spent the next six months talking to a stranger about his so-called problems, when all he'd done was write one nice little love note to the girl of his dreams.

The Weaver family reunited for Christmas in 1969. Wilbur came home on December 10 to his wife, who was just as beautiful as when he'd left her; a tall, gangly, strange young man it took him a few moments to recognize as his son; and Elizabeth, who was now twelve and on the crest of budding into a twin of her mother. Marilyn greeted him warmly, and he was excited to see everyone, but there was something a little off about his demeanor. She wanted to ask him about it, but the moment never seemed right.

They had one month to readjust to each other before the family moved to Hawaii for the next three years; Wilbur's new duty orders also came with his promotion to first lieutenant.

Chapter 11

The Weavers learned a whole new way of life in the South Pacific. Everything they'd grown accustomed to was different in Hawaii: the waters of the Atlantic paled in comparison to the violent deep blue waves of the rocky Pacific coast; the children walked to school in cut-off shorts, bathing suits, and flip-flops. They cut through backyards; picked bananas, kiwis, and mangoes; and ate them for breakfast along the way.

Living on the Kaneohe Bay military base on the island of Oahu, the children likened the experience to the popular children's game Candy Land. Paul Edward and Elizabeth were living pieces advancing along its board as they passed houses painted in bright colors of alternating pink, yellow, blue, brown, green, and purple and walked the meandering sidewalks up and down, curving around vine-covered hills. The coconuts, plumeria, hibiscuses, and abundance of fruit, free for the picking, were the candy. None of the houses had glass windows, just screened openings with canvas awnings to be rolled up and down in case of rain. Lying in bed at night, they heard the roar of ocean waves crashing in the distance.

Elizabeth, who was pretty, tall, and tanned to a dark brown and had long, thick, straight brown hair with sun-streaked strands of blonde and dark brown eyes, fit right in among the locals. But her gangly, white, green-eyed brother, with his head full of curly black hair, brightly contrasted with the native Samoans. This was unfortunate for Paul Edward since both children attended the public schools off base, where Caucasians were, by far, the minority, and the locals barely tolerated Americans—a lesson learned painfully just months after they arrived.

"You make sure and come to school tomorrow, Paul. It's a national holiday, and you don't want to miss out," said Akaida, a native Hawaiian classmate of his.

"What's the holiday?"

"It's Killahaule Day."

"What's that mean?"

"Just come tomorrow. You'll see."

Paul Edward and Elizabeth had a thirty-minute walk home. They took the same route and occasionally caught up to each other, as they left separately. Elizabeth was always with her crowd of four or five of the popular girls, and her brother was usually alone. They attended class the next day, and all day long, the locals taunted them with the word *killahaule*: "Don't you know it's Killahaule Day?" They'd say to Paul, "Killahaule Day'd be no fun without you." No one would explain what they celebrated on that day or what the word meant. Paul Edward and Elizabeth noted the absence of most of the other Caucasian students, which struck them as odd and ominously foreboding.

The dismissal bell rang, and everyone left to walk home. When they thought they were safely off school grounds, a crowd of frenzied students formed, standing in a circle, watching some event taking place in the middle. Elizabeth went to investigate and, pushing her way to the front, found three local boys beating her brother to a pulp. The crowd encouraged the assailants, chanting, "Kill the haule," over and over.

"Get off my brother!" Elizabeth charged in, screaming. She jumped on one guy's back and pulled his hair.

"He shows up on Killahaule Day—he asks for it," said the guy, peeling Elizabeth off him. She screamed, kicked, and pinched enough to break up the fight and went crying to Paul Edward, who lay bruised and bloodied on the ground. A pencil stuck out from his kneecap, its lead stabbed deep into the cartilage. The sight of her crying, holding his head in her lap, and lambasting the crowd must have made the attackers remorseful, for they quietly dispersed. One sympathetic onlooker stayed behind.

"Don't let him come to school on Killahaule Day again."

"What does that mean?" she asked.

"*Haule* is Hawaiian for 'white'—for 'white man.' *Kill-a-haule* means just what it says: 'kill a white man.'"

As newcomers, they learned the hard way how the native islanders took out their smoldering anger—passed down from generation to generation—over being forcefully made part of the United States. In their hearts, many Hawaiians believed they were an independent nation and resented all things American.

Elizabeth had escaped persecution because of her native looks, because apparently, discrimination only went skin deep. Although it wasn't an officially recognized holiday, everyone—the students, teachers, and administrators—knew what happened on the last day of school, and everyone chose to turn a blind eye.

Elizabeth got her brother home, and Marilyn nursed his wounds. He had to have surgery to remove the imbedded lead from his knee. Refusing to believe their children's story of Killahaule Day, Wilbur and Marilyn met with the school principal, who blamed the incident on typical teenage aggression. Wilbur and Marilyn felt vindicated when the perpetrator got a ten-day school suspension—unfortunately for him, the attacker had miscalculated the end of school property, and the assault had taken place on school property.

In Hawaii, Wilbur's duties changed from air traffic controller to college adviser. He had applied for the transfer to a desk job because he wanted to encourage other young men to go to college. Now in his midthirties, the nine-to-five office hours allowed him to live a normal life of dinners with his family and weekends off and to take full advantage of what felt like a three-year tropical vacation with his wife. But Marilyn still wondered what he wasn't telling her. She knew he'd gone through a lot while in the war, but his letters had mentioned nothing particularly traumatizing. She asked him about it several times once they were settled, but he shrugged off her questions.

The islands offered so much to see and do that Wilbur seemed to come back to his old self while he kept busy. Even after three years, they hadn't done everything. At least twice a month, Wilbur took the family sightseeing, including trips to Diamondhead Crater, Waimea Falls, Polynesian Park, Waikiki Beach, Kailua Bay, the North Shore, and Moana Loa. For twenty-five cents each, Paul

Valedictorian

Edward and Elizabeth would ride the city bus and traverse the whole island in one day. Elizabeth often went alone.

Wilbur's boss, Captain Maxi, flew a biplane as his hobby, and after they'd seen all of Oahu, he took Wilbur and Marilyn island hopping to Maui, Molokai, and the Big Island.

For the first time in their marriage, they spent weekends socializing with friends and going to neighborhood barbecues. Another couple introduced them to bridge, and Wilbur and Marilyn became hooked, finding a lifelong passion they both shared.

It was this comfort, Marilyn figured, that finally allowed Wilbur to talk to her about what had bothered him. It started simply enough, when Wilbur was taking out the garbage. He paused with the briefest of hesitations as he tied the bag shut, but Marilyn noticed. She didn't say anything, waiting for him, knowing that one wrong word would shut him down for who knew how long.

"Sorry," he said, looking over at her as if he'd done something wrong. "It's just this reminded me of something that happened in-country."

"What is it?"

"It was October of '68. I was making a trash run with this guy, Garland. Friend of mine. We had all this rejected office equipment— chairs, desks, old file cabinets, things like that—and the mess hall trash. We headed to the one and only landfill in South Vietnam. I asked him if he couldn't get some grunts to do the work. 'Nah,' he said. 'You can't leave Vietnam without seeing this place.' Said I wouldn't believe it even when I saw it.

"It was a few miles past Marble Mountain, which is actually a free-standing piece of pure marble maybe six hundred feet high jutting out of the ground. There's this open landfill spreading out as far as you can see. Next thing I know, everything was shaking. The truck was vibrating more than usual. Felt like an earthquake.

"Garland says, 'It's not an earthquake. Just look closer.' Then I saw it: an ocean of Vietnamese people stood shoulder to shoulder on the mountains of trash, combing the garbage for anything worth keeping. Like thousands of earthworms wiggling on a dinner plate, they made the hills of trash look alive. Everywhere and in every direction—for miles—that's all I could see.

97

"I was about to get out to unload, but Garland warned me not to. He drove closer and said, 'We just have to stay out of their way. They'll do the rest.' He drove along this narrow path and turned off the ignition. In seconds, people—men, women, old and young, mothers with babies—swarmed the truck like locusts. He told me to lock the door. We rocked back and forth inside as they took everything from the bed. The whole process took less than five minutes.

"The worst was seeing how happy they were about all the leftover mess hall slop, like they'd been given caviar. There were all these kids, naked from the waist down, peeing and pooping right where they stood, not a diaper to be seen. I tell you—I had to choke back tears. No human being deserves to live like these people did. If ever I believed in God, that ended that day. Now I come here and see all this stuff, and I can't help but think—"

"Think what, Wilbur?"

He smiled. It was the most genuine smile she'd seen on his face in quite a while. "Nothing," he said. "I've got to take out the trash."

The three years passed seemingly overnight. August 10, 1973, marked Wilbur's twentieth year of service in the USMC. When his tour of duty in Hawaii ended on January 10, 1972, the marine corps gave him a choice: he could accept one final deployment to Japan and then retire with partial benefits, or he could re-up for another ten years, be immediately promoted to captain, choose his next place of duty and its term, and receive a $5,000 bonus. He and Marilyn discussed their options.

"We've finally gotten to a place in our marriage where we can enjoy each other. I really don't want you to leave me again. Not now," said Marilyn.

"I don't either. But it'd be only a year, and then I'll be home forever."

"And then what? You've always wanted to make colonel, and becoming a captain's not far from it."

"Yes, that's true. So shall I re-up, and we go back home to North Carolina?"

"Was it ever undecided?"

It wasn't. He had wanted to reenlist all along but asked his wife for her opinion mostly as a formality.

From a legal standpoint, he didn't have to make his decision for another eighteen months, but then he'd be forced to go to Japan. They wanted the security and stability offered now and chose to return home to their little three-bedroom house in Havelock.

On January 9, the day before they left Hawaii, Wilbur signed up to remain in the USMC. His next chance to opt out would be August 10, 1983.

By the middle of January 1972, the Weavers had settled back into their home in North Carolina. Wilbur wrote to Sarah, telling her about their move and letting her know that, as promised, he had made captain and gotten the $5,000 bonus.

The money prompted him to take stock of his finances, particularly the gold investments he'd had since 1965, and compare them to the returns his friends had made. Being 100 percent in gold, he'd made a profit of 20 percent. The Bishops and his friend Smitty had made more than 40 percent playing the highs and lows of the Dow Jones Industrials. Looking back, he realized gold hadn't risen above forty-five dollars for decades; inflation had returned to a comfortable 3.5 percent; and with the Vietnam War behind them, Wilbur concluded that gold would likely stay at or near its present level for decades. Besides, everyone was putting his or her money in the stock market. After factoring in every economic aspect, he decided once again to try his hand at improving their finances.

On January 22, 1972, without consulting his wife, he sold all his gold stocks at forty-five dollars, bought a factory-new 1972 Toyota Corolla station wagon for his family (a gift of guilt), and used the rest of his bonus and the gold proceeds to buy into the Dow at 800.

Two months later, retaining his position of college and continuing-education adviser, Wilbur sat in his office on a Monday and questioned a memo that came across his desk offering a $20,000 reenlistment bonus to all marines ranking E-6 and up. He called his commanding officer, Major Frank Reynolds. "Good morning, Major Reynolds. This is Captain Wilbur Weaver. I'm calling in regards to a memo I received today offering a re-upping bonus."

"That's correct, Captain. You're to encourage every man who comes through your door to reenlist. And with that kind of bonus, it shouldn't be hard."

"I think they've made a typographical error, because this offer is for twenty thousand dollars."

"No, it's not a typo. General Rawlings approved it last month. Is there anything else, Captain?"

"Well, uh, I was wondering, Major. Seeing as how I just re-upped, well, I—"

"The bonus is effective as of today, March 1. Sorry, Captain. Sometimes timing is everything."

"But, Major Reynolds, I wasn't even due to re-up until this August. I signed early. Doesn't that count for something?"

"Listen, Wilbur. You're a great guy, and I think the world of you, but there isn't anything I can do about it. The directive came down after you signed. I'm sorry."

Wilbur accepted his sincerity, but the injustice he felt made him weak in the knees and nauseated—he'd been punished again for doing nothing wrong. He told Marilyn about it after supper; she responded with outrage.

"Let's sue. Call the general himself. This just isn't right."

"Nobody sues the government. You know, Marilyn, if it wasn't for bad luck, I'd have no luck at all."

His depression only worsened when he read in the newspaper that the price of gold had broken through its ceiling, closing at fifty dollars.

Paul Edward graduated from high school in May. Wilbur, Marilyn, and Elizabeth got dressed in their finest to attend the ceremony. As they drove to the school, Elizabeth sat in the backseat, as usual, staring out the window and generally ignoring her parents' conversation in the front. Then something changed in their voices—they got quieter, which drew her attention. She caught the tail end of something her mother was saying: " ... him a break. So he needed some help—so what?"

"Nobody ever helped me," said her father. "And I never had to repeat third grade. Not even with an alcoholic wife beater for a father."

"Everybody's different," said Marilyn. "You sound disappointed, but this is a big day for him."

"Of course it is. I'm just saying—" He caught Elizabeth's eye in the rearview mirror and kept to himself whatever he'd been about to say.

That didn't stop her mother, though. "Paul Edward's sensitive—that's all. I think he needed more than we could give him, what with your service and everything."

Another glance in the rearview mirror kept Wilbur silent again. They got to the school and applauded when Paul Edward crossed the stage. But there was still tension afterward.

"What are you going to do now?" Wilbur asked his son two days later.

"I don't know."

"Well, you'll be eighteen next month. Can't live here; you gotta come up with something. Your grades don't support college as a wise investment."

"But I want to go to college."

"Then prove it. You can take the first two years at Craven Community College. Then, if you make good grades, we'll talk about transferring to a university."

Paul Edward agreed but felt his 3.0 GPA would be good enough to start at any university now. Too timid to argue, he accepted his father's suggestion with bitterness.

Paul Edward inherited the '65 Chevrolet Super Sport with the understanding that he'd get a job and pay for his own gas and liability insurance. Foremost, he had to take summer classes at the community college in order to live at home—or choose to emancipate himself and strike out on his own. He enrolled in basic first-year college requirements, taking math, English, and humanities. However, working two part-time jobs interfered with his studying, and when he tried to concentrate at home, he found his mother's constant requests—"Empty the garbage. Clean your room. Mow the grass"—impossible to work around. He needed a quiet place to study and began going to the local library before and after his working hours.

One day Elizabeth met up with him there, and they walked home together.

"I've got a secret," he told her.

"What?"

"I'm joining the air force. I'm going to sign the forms tomorrow."

"No way! What did Mom and Dad say?"

"Nothing yet," he mumbled. "I haven't told them. Do you think they'll be mad?"

"I don't know," she said. "I don't think Mom will want you to be away anymore, at least not for long. As for Dad, he could do anything."

His parents took his increased absence for loafing. No matter what he did or where he went, Paul Edward felt them breathing down his neck. They tried to pin him down about his intentions for his future but he didn't know himself. As their constant questions turned increasingly into arguments, he made the same desperate decision his father once had.

"I quit my jobs today," he informed everyone the next day at dinner.

"Why would you do that?" asked his father.

"Because I joined the air force today."

Silence filled the room. Elizabeth's heart went out to her brother; she knew he felt lost and alone, as always. "That's great, Paul Edward. I'm proud of you," she said, hoping that would prompt her parents to say something encouraging.

Marilyn put down her fork and stared at him, saying nothing aloud. Her look said plenty: *How could you be so ungrateful?*

Wilbur took his time, thinking, and then said, "That's your choice, Son. Let's hope it's a good one."

Elizabeth finished eating, quietly crying at the same time, and then excused herself from the table to wait for her brother. She wanted to be alone with him to say her good-byes. He'd be leaving the next day.

On the steps of their front porch the next morning, Wilbur shook Paul Edward's hand—a man-to-man gesture of farewell without any evidence of love or support.

Paul Edward headed off for air force basic training.

Chapter 12

Seven years had passed since their last visit to West Virginia; his years in Vietnam and Hawaii had usurped the promise of spending every Thanksgiving together. Wilbur called his mother to tell her of their intended trip.

"Hi, Mom. It's your long-lost son Wilbur. How are you?"

"Well, I'll be. How are you?"

"We're fine. Nothing much new since my last letter—you know Paul Edward joined the air force."

"Yeah, that was the last I heard."

"We thought we'd come next month for Thanksgiving."

"We'd love that. I reckon it's about time you met everyone else."

"What do you mean?"

"Well, Vance and I—it's been a few years." Sarah hesitated.

"What is it, Mom? Is everything all right?"

"Oh, sure. You remember Darly Baker? No? Well, anyway, she's a good-for-nothing piece of trash that kept having babies and didn't care for any of them. Had six in all, and left them to fend for themselves, running around town, begging and stealing for food. Why, the littlest one, Danny, wasn't yet two years old and running the streets, soiled with old waste caked on his fanny. Anyway, the state came and took all the kids from her and put 'em in foster care."

"Sounds like they did the right thing," he said, wondering why she went on with the tale.

"Yes. They had to take them. But then they had to find a place for them. We took in three of them."

"You're raising three little kids? Now? At your age?"

"They ain't so little anymore. We took in the oldest ones—had 'em six years now. They're seventeen, sixteen, and fifteen. Two boys and a girl."

"Why didn't you tell me before?"

"I wanted to, but I wanted you to meet them first. Just writing to you about them didn't seem good enough. Oh, Wilbur, you just come on up and meet them yourself. It's been a good thing for everyone. The boys help Vance with the farm, and Mary—she's sixteen—helps me around the house. They're just plain happy to have a roof over their heads and food in their bellies. The state even pays me to keep them. Can you believe that? I get one hundred and seventy-five dollars a month."

"Okay, Mom. I can tell how excited you are. Marilyn, Elizabeth, and I—is there enough room?"

"We'll make room. Just come on."

They agreed on plans for Thanksgiving week and hung up. Marilyn came into the room and asked if they'd coordinated things.

"Yes, we're going as planned."

"So what's that look on your face then?"

Wilbur said, "You won't believe it, but Mom adopted three kids."

"What?"

"I know. Three teenagers. They're living with them now in my house."

"But why?"

"Something to do with them being homeless. I hate to say it, but she seems really happy with the whole thing."

"Oh," said Marilyn. When Wilbur didn't continue, she shook her head and started on dinner. Wilbur just sat at the table, lost in thought.

When Wilbur and his wife and daughter arrived shortly before six on Wednesday morning—Wilbur had left straight from work the night before for the twelve-hour drive—his mother and her new family were already awake and had breakfast waiting as they came inside.

"Welcome. Welcome. You all sit down and have something to eat," said Sarah as she hugged them one by one as they entered. "Gracious, Elizabeth, you're a full-grown woman."

"Whaddya expect? The same girl with curly brown hair from seven years ago?" said Vance, standing in line to offer his hugs.

Around the table sat three wide-eyed strangers warily looking back. Elizabeth's parents had told her about them, of course, so she had known what to expect, but somehow, it still felt odd to her. Maybe it was because her father looked so uncomfortable, as if he would rather have been anywhere else than in that kitchen at that moment.

"I suppose these are yours?" said Wilbur, addressing his mother but smiling at the others.

"Get up, children. Introduce yourselves to everyone," said Sarah.

The oldest rose first and stood at his seat, greeting them collectively with a formal "Hello. I'm Bob," and then he sat back down. Mary followed suit with the same, followed by Danny. They acted on cue and then, Elizabeth thought, somehow disappeared into the background, becoming invisible even though they sat right in front of them. They only spoke when spoken to, and their answers were short and direct. It was as if she forgot about them unless they were talking.

The three looked alike. Bob and Danny had light brown hair and eyes, both had buzz cuts, and their sharp features made them appear wise beyond their years. They wore navy work pants and matching collared shirts like uniforms. Mary was a female version of the same, only with longer hair cut to her shoulders. She wore a plaid dress belted at the waist and sensible, generic shoes. All three were groomed and squeaky clean, with every hair in place and their clothes ironed to perfection.

As they finished eating, one by one, the kids were excused and began cleaning, silently going about their chores, unnoticed. Elizabeth wondered if she should be helping them. "How's Jesse doing?" asked Wilbur.

Sarah became somber. "I haven't seen him for—must be eighteen months. That was when I got a call from the hospital. Turns out Jesse had been there a week after being found unconscious in an alley. He'd almost died from alcoholic liver failure. He didn't even have any ID on him, so they didn't know to call me until he woke up and told them his name. I could hardly recognize him. I thought there had been some mistake, right up until he called me Mama."

She was on the verge of tears, and when it was clear she couldn't continue, Vance said, "He was discharged, and sometime later, we got a letter from Texas, saying he'd found a good job and would come home after getting himself straightened out. That was the last we heard of him."

Wilbur didn't say anything. The small talk that followed got them through dinner, but that was all it was—small talk. Vance and Sarah later showed them to their rooms, offering rest after their long journey.

"Where'd the others go?" asked Elizabeth as they walked through the house. She thought she'd heard a vacuum cleaner running earlier.

"Bob and Danny are off to check on the cattle before walking to school. Mary's outside waiting for them. School's not out until tomorrow," said Sarah.

Elizabeth looked at the wall clock, pitifully amazed. Before seven o'clock in the morning, those kids (she didn't know what to call them—aunts, uncles, cousins?) had fixed breakfast, washed the dishes, cleaned the kitchen, swept, dusted and vacuumed the entire house, and left without a peep—the boys off to complete even more chores before beginning their day. Considering the time it took to dress and groom, she wondered what time they got out of bed.

"Punk, you and Marilyn can take Mary's room, and she and Elizabeth can share Bob and Danny's hall bed—they'll sleep downstairs on the floor while you're here," said Sarah.

"I hate for them to do that. Are you sure?" asked Marilyn.

"Well, they wanted to sleep in the barn, but I wouldn't let them. Don't fret about them; they've slept in a lot worse places than on a living room floor," said Vance.

"How'd our bags get up here?' asked Wilbur, noticing them once they reached the upstairs.

"The boys got them out while we were talking. They don't miss a lick," said Vance.

As the days passed, Wilbur enjoyed hunting every morning, but otherwise, he and his family grew restive. He felt unneeded and in the way, as his offers to help went refused. "I think I'll change the oil in your car, Mom. It's probably been awhile," said Wilbur.

"Don't bother yourself. Bob keeps it changed—just did so last week," said Vance.

"How about I check the fence posts? I'll replace any railings that need it," he offered a day later.

"Oh, they're just fine. Bob and Danny check 'em most every day when they feed the cattle, and they make repairs as needed," said Sarah.

Sarah and her foster children attended Duck Creek Baptist Church every Sunday—another surprising change in his mother's life. Not once did Sarah ever take Wilbur to church or discuss religion. While they were gone on the Sunday following Thanksgiving, he took it upon himself to scrape and paint the old chicken house before anyone could tell him not to. He bought the supplies and was an hour into scraping the boards, when Vance came outside. "Hey, Wilbur. What're you doing?"

"Frankly, I'm getting a little stir-crazy and thought I'd give this a new paint job. I thought you'd be at church with the rest."

"I'm not much of a churchgoer. But the Good Lord knows it, and I think he'll forgive me. And by the by, we take it serious about not working on Sundays. Besides, the weather's about to turn. There's no way you'll get that done before it gets too cold."

"Well, maybe the Good Lord will forgive me too."

"He might. But your mother won't. I suggest you pack all that up before she gets home."

"I'm only trying to be helpful."

"Why don't you just enjoy yourself? All the work's well taken care of—you can see that. You're company now," said Vance, politely telling Wilbur to back off.

"Sure. I see everything clearly."

Vance left after making sure Wilbur understood, seeing him begin putting away his scraper, sandpaper, and cans of paint. Dejected, Wilbur tried to identify what ate at him. Was it the kids, Vance, his mother's happiness? Was he himself being selfish? Though he might have outwardly grumbled in annoyance over the years, he liked doing the repairs and chores his mother asked of him. He liked that she needed him. Tending to the property had been his job as far back as he could remember, and now he didn't know his place in her house or in her heart.

Wilbur finally asked Marilyn to join him on his morning hunts, and feeling unneeded anywhere else, she accepted. Marilyn had done nothing over the last four days but sit in the house and listen to Vance and Sarah brag about Bob, Mary, and Danny. She couldn't take it anymore and looked at the morning hunt as an opportunity to vent some of her frustrations. As soon as they were fully surrounded by trees, she subtly brought up the thing that was bothering her the most. "Your mother really seems taken with the new kids."

"Mhmm," said Wilbur. He kept his eyes straight ahead, cocking his head as if to listen to something other than Marilyn.

She went on. "And Elizabeth seems to be having fun." When he didn't respond, she said, "But I'm concerned about what Sarah and Vance think of her." She still received no reply. "Haven't you noticed that they only seem interested in her when they're saying something like 'We don't let Mary wear jeans. Young ladies should wear only dresses'?"

"You think?" said Wilbur.

His response wasn't much, but at least it was something. She continued. "Just yesterday, Sarah said, 'Mary tells us all about the loose girls in school who wear jeans.' I held my tongue, but that just sounds so judgmental."

"Hmm."

Marilyn decided to cut off the conversation. It was clearly going nowhere, and so far, Elizabeth was enjoying the visit, spending her time soaking in her grandmother's stories and looking through old photos.

Being the same age, she and Mary got along, staying up late at night and talking in their bed, but Vance and Sarah kept Mary busy. To Marilyn, it looked planned that Mary didn't have much time to spend visiting with Elizabeth.

Later, when they took a break from hunting to eat some jerked venison, Wilbur did share his feelings, just not on the topic Marilyn had hoped.

"I'll tell you, Marilyn, this visit hasn't been easy for me."

"I can tell. For me neither. The weird thing is, I like those kids, but shoving them down our throats and ignoring their own blood is hard to understand."

"Exactly. That's exactly how I feel. But what do I do about it?"

"I don't think there's anything to do. We just move on with our own lives and accept it as it is. What else?"

Wilbur sadly agreed. All he had left of his childhood home were a few precious memories. Hunting in these woods, smelling this air, and walking the same trails revived the feelings, but the idea that his only brother was lost somewhere in the world nagged at Wilbur.

Late Monday afternoon, Wilbur stood in the barn, checking the oil in his car as Marilyn gathered their bags for the journey home. They were planning to leave within the hour, when his mother and Vance approached, making small talk about the weather. Wilbur wanted to say something relevant, to express his feelings or gain some measure of loving reassurance from his mother, when Vance started talking about the future. "I'm only bringing this up because I have to," said Vance.

"I'm not following you," said Wilbur.

"It may look like I've got a lot, but I don't. All the land I own was my first wife's, and when she died, she left it to our girls. Sure, I get to use it to my own benefit as long as I'm alive, but after that, it all goes to my girls."

"I didn't know. But what does it have to do with me?"

"I want you to think about your mother's welfare—that's what. If I die first, she gets nothing. And now we've got these fine kids to think of."

Enough already. "Mom, what do you need?"

Sarah had stood quietly up until now, too afraid to broach the subject.

"Go on, Sarah. Tell him," prodded Vance.

"When your father died, he left me with nothing but this house and its bills. You know that, right?" she said, and Wilbur nodded. "Well, it seems he didn't even leave me that. The house ain't mine legally. It's yours."

"What?"

"The deed to the house is in your and Jesse's names. I'm asking you to sign your half over to me."

"What about Jesse?"

"He's already given me his part. Punk, I know you had a hard life growing up, and I'm sorry for it. You know I done the best I could.

But I'm happy now. For the first time in my whole life, I'm happy, except for having the insecurity of not owning my own damn house."

The news shocked Wilbur. Sarah had known all these years and never said a word. When he was sure he could talk without losing his composure, he said, "Are you really afraid I'd take your house?"

"Well, no. Not exactly. But sometimes you can be kind of hard to read."

"What kind of thing is that to say? I can't believe you'd think for even a second that your own son would put you out on the street!"

Sarah clung to Vance for protection. "I didn't think you would. I just, well, I know you've had some hard feelings about how things went for you. In school and whatnot."

"Of course there were hard feelings," said Wilbur. "You and Dad basically forced me to go it alone. I had to learn everything on my own because you were too drunk most of the time to help me."

Vance stepped in. "Now, take it easy, Wilbur. This doesn't have to turn into something ugly."

Wilbur glared at him, and if he had been about to say anything further, he thought better of it. His mother suddenly looked small to Wilbur, her alleged happiness only a thin veneer covering her deception and greed. "Gimme the paper," he said.

"You'll sign it?" asked Sarah.

"Whatever makes you happy, Mother." He took the document, freshly prepared for his arrival, and signed away his only inheritance. He smiled as he handed it back.

"Will you come next year?" she asked.

"As long as there's woods to hunt in, I'll be back."

When Thanksgiving came around the next year, he planned to return—not only to hunt but also to make a statement: he had a right to be there. Protesting in anger about his signing over the house, Marilyn refused to go and pleaded with him to wait a few years, pointing out how unfairly his mother had treated him—not just then but all his life. He'd gotten himself through school, decided not to go to college, faithfully supported his mother for years only to be replaced by foster kids, and then signed away his inheritance. After debating with Marilyn, he felt drained and emotionally conflicted. Why should he open himself up to repeated disappointment? They could go later, once his wounds weren't so fresh. He decided she was right and agreed to wait. He called his mother the next day and made work-related excuses that prevented him from traveling. He did so again the following year. He made phone calls on Mother's Day, her birthday, Thanksgiving, and Christmas. Years passed, and the longer he waited, the harder it became for him to consider returning.

In the spring of 1974, Elizabeth graduated from high school and found herself in the same position her brother had been in two years earlier: put on the spot to decide her future—but without any prior guidance. The few years she'd spent at the foot of her grandmother had created a bond (at least for Elizabeth) of admiration and a desire to please the older woman. Sarah had repeatedly expounded the virtues of nursing, saying she'd always wanted to be one and planned on Mary going to nursing school. Marilyn had never discussed Elizabeth's future or planted any seeds of desire, so on the day her parents sat her down and asked her, "What now?" Elizabeth only heard her grandmother's voice, and she said she wanted to become a nurse.

She applied for the associate-degree nursing program at the same community college Paul Edward had attended, but due to heavy enrollment, the school put her on its waiting list until next year.

"I'd expected as much, seeing as how you barely made it through high school," said Wilbur after Elizabeth showed him the letter.

She had been ranked in the middle of her graduating class of 220 students and could have done better if she'd been expected to, but she'd gone through school on her own, choosing her own classes and doing the minimum to get by, because she didn't know any better. She had once asked her father if it was better to take American literature or statistics, and he'd grunted that he didn't have any idea. That was the last time she'd asked. Her parents had accepted her report cards without discussion; they had been strict and hadn't allowed her to join the kinds of extracurricular activities where all the smart kids hung out. She remembered asking if she could try out for cheerleading over dinner one night.

"No way," her father had said.

Elizabeth had looked to her mother, hoping for a different opinion. She hadn't gotten it.

"What your father means, Elizabeth, is that it's better to stay focused on your studies."

"But that's what you said when I wanted to join forensics. This is totally different."

"It's all a waste of time," Wilbur had said. It had been clear the conversation was over.

"That's not fair," Elizabeth had said in parting.

She felt suffocated by their micromanagement and confused by their parenting logic: she was to go to school, come home, and do nothing. Having a social life of her own caused too much tension in the family, so she suppressed any desires of achieving and droned through school like a prisoner serving her sentence, known to the other students as a beautiful wallflower growing up on the outskirts of their teenage activity.

She was so frustrated that she called Paul Edward at the air force base, hoping to commiserate with him, but she got little out of him. He told her about training but didn't seem interested in hearing about her high school troubles. She gave up after a few minutes without venting her frustration and knowing virtually nothing more about his situation.

Elizabeth got a summer job as a waitress at the local pizza parlor while she waited for her name to reach the top of the community college's waiting list, an event that came one year later.

After three years at Cherry Point, Wilbur got orders in the fall of 1975 to Willow Grove, Pennsylvania. Since Elizabeth was due to start the nursing program, her parents arranged for her to stay behind in North Carolina and attend school while they moved up north. They found a ten-year-old trailer for sale in an established park only one town away from her nursing school. They paid cash for it and supplied her with their old pots, pans, dishes, utensils, and linens— all the living essentials she'd need—and then drew up a contract for her to sign. She'd get seventy-five dollars a month to pay for tuition, books, and her living expenses, including utilities, food, and lot rent, and Wilbur would return every six months to inspect her grades, her finances, and her trailer.

Their support money didn't come close to meeting her needs, and her parents knew it. As they'd planned, she'd need to find a roommate and continue working to make up the difference. But it all sounded wonderful to Elizabeth. Getting her freedom and a place to live felt like receiving the keys to her own kingdom, and meeting their demands seemed a small price to pay.

Nursing school turned out to be a two-year-long boot camp. The schedule was heavily loaded to weed out the weak, and by the end of the first quarter, fifteen of the sixty students had dropped out. Another ten flunked out by the second. Finding the academics so grueling, none of the remaining students worked while attending school, except Elizabeth. However, she'd always had the academic ability to succeed; it had just lain dormant in high school. Once she engaged herself and actually tried, she became one of those rare students who could sit in class, listen without taking notes, and confidently absorb the material. When working late as a cocktail waitress (a new job she'd found that paid far more than waiting restaurant tables), she wouldn't get home before one o'clock in the morning, but she would still be sitting in class, a forty-minute-drive away, by eight o'clock the next morning. She did not mind carrying a full class load or having to work, but her father's biyearly inspections caused her stress and anxiety.

Weeks before he came, she'd exhaust herself cleaning—renting carpet cleaners to shampoo the wall-to-wall carpet, power-washing the outside of the trailer herself, and scrubbing and detailing so he'd find nothing to criticize—which added significantly to her already-burdened schedule.

She thought herself ready when he arrived in February 1976 for a two-day visit. He'd kept a key to the door, so he let himself in early Saturday morning, and he found her sleeping in bed. Her roommate, Sandy, a fellow nursing student, slept in the second bedroom at the opposite end of the trailer.

Elizabeth awakened as he went to her bathroom to wash up. As he surveyed his trailer, she spent the day talking with him before reporting to work. "School's going fine. I'm taking biology, English, some dumb required class called family dynamics, and psychology. The worst grade I expect is a B in English, but I'm trying for the A."

"That's a full schedule—you have to study hard," he warned, opening the refrigerator door and examining its rubber insulation strip. "See this?" He pointed out a grape jelly stain. "You need to wash down this strip sometimes. Stains like that cause the door to seal improperly."

Elizabeth stood beside him as he peered at his found flaw as if he'd discovered gold, and she nodded in acceptance of his advice. "And another thing," he added, leading her to the kitchen cabinet doors and opening one for her display. "These screw hinges become loose over time. You need to tighten them with a screwdriver. It's what you'd call 'oil can maintenance'—going through the whole house oiling squeaks and tightening screws."

"Sure, Dad, I'll remember to do that."

He left the next day, never having said one positive word to her.

Constant knocking on the trailer door at two o'clock in the morning in July awoke Elizabeth and Sandy. "Are you expecting anyone?" asked Elizabeth.

"No, not tonight. David left hours ago," said Sandy, explaining that it couldn't be her boyfriend. They peered through the curtains, trying to identify the stranger, a little frightened by the event. The knocking continued. "Who's there?" asked Sandy.

"Elizabeth, it's me—Paul. Your brother."

"Paul Edward?" said Elizabeth as she opened the door.

"Hey, Sis." He held out his arms and offered his embrace. She led him inside and hugged him back.

"What are you doing here?"

"Well, I got out of the air force and wanted to see you."

Sandy greeted him before returning to bed, and he and Elizabeth sat and talked for a while. He revealed that the air force had discharged him—for not being military material, according to his superiors. Over his eighteen months in service, he'd received twenty-seven demerits for minor offenses: never learning to make his bed right, reporting to a dental appointment late, defacing government property (he'd written "Jesus loves you" on the wall inside of an aircraft), and more. His lack of conformity had resulted in his general discharge three months ago.

"What are you going to do now, Paul?"

"I guess I'm searching for an answer. I really don't know. I wanted to come home and figure it out. Can I stay with you awhile?"

"Sure you can," she agreed, seeing the pain and confusion he felt. "Do Mom and Dad know?"

"No, I haven't talked to them in almost a year. I want to call them with only good news, ya know?"

"Oh yes. I know."

For two weeks, Paul Edward slept on her couch, and over time, Elizabeth noticed the drawings he left out: a shapeless figure in squiggly lines, saying, "Who am I?"; Gothic-lettered words asking God to show him the way; and small dead bodies drawn with questions about death surrounding them. Her brother's innermost thoughts written down denied his outward appearance of constant smiles and optimism as he laughed and spent his time fruitlessly looking up old friends, hoping to meet with them to socialize. Throughout high school, he'd only had one true friend, Noel—another isolated loner who'd been in trouble with the law. When Paul discovered that Noel's current address was the Raleigh State Penitentiary, Elizabeth watched with sympathetic pity as her brother reached out to old acquaintances for friendship and support, people who didn't even remember him in person or name.

"Paul, forget about making friends, and go get yourself a job. That will keep you busy, and you'll feel better having some purpose," she suggested after ten days.

"If God wants me to have a job, I'll find one. I just need time."

"Well, God only helps those who help themselves." Her remarks sounded terser than she'd intended, and they offended him, but his actions frustrated Elizabeth and had begun wearing on her hospitality. "Besides, Dad's supposed to come down in a few weeks for his routine visit. What are you gonna do then?"

"I don't know."

Over the next few weeks, Elizabeth worried constantly about her brother. She feared his drawings indicated thoughts of suicide, yet his foolish need to find old friends and his refusal to get a job ate at her sympathies, telling her instincts that a good kick in the ass would serve him best. Feeding and housing Paul also put a strain on her budget, and for the first time, she looked forward to her father's visit, hoping it would bring an end to this burden.

Wilbur arrived around four in the afternoon, shocked when Paul Edward answered the door. "I thought I drove to North Carolina, not Arkansas," said Wilbur.

"Hey, Dad."

"What are you doing here?"

"It's kind of a long story."

After settling in and briefly exchanging pleasantries with Elizabeth before she left for work, he put Paul Edward under scrutiny, listening to his story and his explanations about God directing his future. "Well, you can't stay here," Wilbur concluded. "You're twenty-three years old, and it's time to be a man: get a job, keep it, and pay your own way. It's not my responsibility, nor your sister's, to look out for you—not even God's. I love you, Son, but you can't keep floating through life with your abstract views and then hope to make anything of yourself. I'm leaving in two days—and so are you."

"Okay, Dad." *No big deal*, he thought, as he'd expected nothing less than what he'd heard. He already felt lonesome, homeless, and directionless. Actually being so didn't feel any worse.

On Saturday, Elizabeth cried as she said good-bye again to her brother, feeling a guilty déjà vu. The scene was similar to when he'd left home two years ago, but this time, she'd been instrumental in this latest separation. Wilbur handed him $200 in cash, shook his hand, and said, "Come back when you've made your mark." Paul Edward meekly took the money and hugged his father over the offered handshake, blew a kiss toward the window where Elizabeth stood watching, and left for parts unknown.

In May 1977, Elizabeth graduated and earned her associate's degree in nursing as one of the thirty students left from a class of sixty. Her parents came for her pinning ceremony, and a week later, she started as a floor nurse at Craven County Hospital. Before her parents returned to Pennsylvania, they had a new agreement prepared for her to sign, asking her to pay seventy-five dollars per month in rent. Still young and lacking the strength to oppose them, she agreed, dreadfully knowing her father's inspections would continue, but having earned the title of registered nurse, she had the security and means to get out from under them.

Somehow. Someday.

Chapter 13

On Sunday, October 28, the phone rang in the late afternoon as Sarah and Vance sat in their armchairs, watching television. "You want me to get that?" asked Vance.

"Nah, I'll get it," Sarah replied, answering the phone. Vance sat listening to the one-sided conversation and watched his wife as her voice faltered. She began crying. "Are you sure it's him? Yes, he's thirty-eight years old. Good-looking man. You say you've identified the body by fingerprints?"

"Who are you talking to?" Vance's interruption went ignored.

"Yes, I'll go to the morgue when he arrives." Sarah hung up.

"What in the dickens was that all about?" asked Vance.

"That was a coroner from Texas. Said the police had found a John Doe dead, frozen in an alley. His fingerprints identified him as ..." She couldn't bring herself to say the words out loud. She sat, dazed, staring at her husband, waiting for him to reverse time and make the phone call go away.

"What, Sarah? Why did they call you?'

"They said it was Jesse. Oh my God, my Jesse. My sweet, dear boy. Dead. Sleeping outside in the cold. Alone. Drunk. Oh, Vance, he froze to death." Affirming the news stung deeper than hearing it spoken to her. Vance stared back in disbelief.

"Are they sure it's him?"

"I need a drink of water." She rose from the chair and saw the room spin around as she fell to the floor.

"Sarah! Sarah, are you okay?" Vance held her head in his lap, trying to rouse her. She came around and cried out in horror, feeling the awful truth all over again. "It's all right, darling. They've just made a mistake. You'll see. When we see the body, it'll be someone else—not Jesse."

But Sarah knew in her heart that the coroner had spoken the truth. Her beloved son had fallen just as his father had—another victim claimed by alcohol.

The body arrived at the county morgue in Clarksburg early the next morning. Sarah and Vance were there by nine o'clock to identify him. "Why don't I go look, Sarah? You don't need to do this," said Vance.

"I want to go. He's been away from his family long enough. My boy needs his mama." No longer weighed down by shock and grief, Sarah mustered her strength to mother her son one last time. She went to view the body, steeled with a purpose: *My son needs me.* Vance spoke with the attendant at the morgue, who went unnoticed by Sarah—to her, he was just a faceless employee doing his awful job as he led them to a form laid out on a cold metal table. He pulled away the white sheet, revealing the naked body underneath. Vance broke down crying, his hopes of it being someone else crushed, though if it weren't for the memories of Jesse's childhood innocence, Vance wouldn't have known the unkempt, malnourished, haggard man before him. Through the long, greasy black hair, thickened nails, and sallow skin, he saw, in death, Jesse's long-lost expression of comfort and his easygoing nature, released by the burden of living.

Sarah caressed his face, asked for a cloth, and then began wiping the lingering grime of street life away from his cheeks and forehead.

"Is this your son, Mrs. Sanderling?"

"Yes, sir. His name is Jesse Raymond Weaver."

"What do we do now?" asked Vance, regaining control of his emotions.

"We've got to do an autopsy to determine the exact cause of death before releasing the body. You can claim him tomorrow, barring any homicidal findings."

"He may have been killed?" Vance asked.

"No, I doubt it. It's just standard procedure to do an autopsy on these kinds of deaths."

Vance and Sarah left to make the funeral arrangements and to call Wilbur. As they drove home, Sarah's calmness surprised Vance. Seeing Jesse had unnerved him, the ugly truth wiping away all his delusions of a case of mistaken identity. He now felt what she had the day before and struggled to accept reality. However, through the last eighteen hours, Sarah had felt every emotion possible and had embraced each one to its depth, wearing shock and grief like garments until she felt comfortable in her new clothes.

"I'm real sorry, Sarah. It's all such a shame. I can't get the picture of him when he was still a boy out of my head. His sweetness and good looks—so full of promise."

"You know, this may sound crazy, but I finally feel like I can rest. I've worried about him for so long—where he was and if he was okay. Now I know exactly where he is: home, where he belongs, and at peace with the Lord. And I don't have to wonder anymore. It's Punk I'm worried about now."

"What do you mean?"

"How's he gonna react? When Webb died, I never saw him shed a tear. He turned inward, feeling like he had to be strong and take care of us, and didn't let himself grieve. It ain't right to hold those feelings in. Jesse's death might open his stored-up grief, and I'm fearing for him."

"Wilbur's always been the stronger one. He'll be all right."

Once home, they made phone calls to the funeral home and to their pastor and then realized how exhausted they were from the emotional toll. They decided to nap before calling Wilbur.

As empty nesters, Wilbur and Marilyn enjoyed their last two years alone in Pennsylvania, rediscovering the individual traits that had brought them together before the birth of Paul Edward. Marilyn dabbled in classes in cosmetology and fashion design before gaining full-time employment on the base at Willow Grove as a supply secretary. Wilbur returned to air traffic control, advancing his career with exemplary performance as the commanding officer of the small base, and in March of 1977, he proudly received his promotion to major, two ranks below his coveted full-bird colonel. Now forty-one years old, with twenty-four years of service behind him, he knew he could put in another nine years and then retire as a colonel at the young age of fifty, having achieved all of his career goals.

Wilbur and Marilyn found a social life among like-minded friends, playing bridge together and joining supper clubs.

"How about going out for dinner?" Wilbur asked once he and Marilyn returned home from work.

"Oh, great. I'm beat." She went upstairs to freshen up in the two-story stucco house they'd rented in affluent Bucks County, when the phone rang.

"I'll get it," said Wilbur.

"Hey, Punk. It's Mom."

"Hi, Mom. What a surprise. I've been thinking about calling you. Thanksgiving's right around the corner."

"Listen, Son. I've got some terrible news." She hesitated, and Wilbur thought he heard her stifle a sob.

"What is it, Mom? Are you okay? Is it Vance?"

"No, it's your brother. Punk, Jesse's dead."

"What did you say?"

"I saw his body this morning. He was found dead after a cold spell in Texas. Froze to death because he'd been living in an alley, like a homeless drunk." She paused, and when Wilbur didn't respond, she said, "Are you there? Punk?"

"I'm here, Mom."

"I'm sorry, Son. You know we did all we could for him, but he was too much like his dad—couldn't stay away from alcohol. I'm just so grateful you chose a different path."

"Jesse couldn't have chosen differently if he'd wanted to, Mom. When's the funeral?"

"Probably Wednesday. Can you come home, Punk?"

"Sure, Mom. We'll all be there as soon as possible—before tomorrow night."

"Good. Marilyn and the kids will come too? I don't want you to drive alone."

"Yes. We'll see you then."

Marilyn came downstairs as he hung up. "Who was that?"

"My mother. She said Jesse's dead."

"He's really dead?"

"She said she saw his body this morning." Wilbur related the details of his death, feeling their weight increase with the telling. He didn't cry or feel sorry. Somehow, he felt Jesse's destiny had lain in tragedy all along—since those early days when Wilbur had first recognized his brother's insecurities. He recalled how Jesse had clung like a shadow to Wilbur for guidance and protection and had lived in the background of their home life, staying hidden yet watching and yearning for happiness, connecting happiness to the drunken laughter of their father and concluding that alcohol created happiness. Jesse had chosen his path of self-destruction by the time he'd turned ten years old. No, Wilbur didn't want to cry, at least not for Jesse. If he cried, it would be for himself, because he'd never felt more alone in his entire life.

"Are you okay?" asked Marilyn.

"No. But I will be. I need to be in West Virginia by tomorrow night. What about you and the kids?"

"I'll go if you want me to. But I just started this new job; I'd hate to take off already. I'm sure Elizabeth will go with you."

Wilbur didn't have an opinion as to whether his wife went or not, and he replied apathetically, "I'll call Elizabeth and Paul Edward." He picked up the phone but hesitated.

"What is it, Wilbur?"

"It just occurred to me that I don't even know how to find Paul Edward."

Hearing of the first death of a close relative, Elizabeth cried, and she agreed to ride with her father to the funeral. She offered to meet him halfway, somewhere in Virginia, but he declined, saying he'd rather take the whole week off to come get her and then make the trip from North Carolina.

"You'll add nearly twenty hours to your driving."

"I know. I don't mind; the extra time will do me good."

She noted his strange tone of voice, almost pleading with her, but for what, she didn't know. Elizabeth agreed to whatever he suggested and prepared for his early morning arrival. Afterward, she thought about Paul Edward and decided to call him with the news, not sure if her parents were going to call him.

No one had seen him since his visit the summer before last, but she'd kept in touch by phone after he called her from his apartment in Little Rock, Arkansas, a few months later.

He told her he'd driven away that fateful day without a set destination and kept driving for two days, spending all but ten of the $200 their father had given him. As he'd held the last bill in his hand, he'd finally realized that his options were few. His journey had unknowingly landed him back in Arkansas, on the doorstep of a girl named Sherry, who had befriended him when she briefly dated a fellow air force recruit. She had taken him in and, being the manager, gotten him a job waiting tables at the Capitol Hotel, an upscale restaurant and historic building in Little Rock. Though he'd spent less than two years there, he felt more at home in Arkansas than anywhere else and decided to stay among the few friends he'd made. After six weeks of sleeping on Sherry's couch, he'd proudly called Elizabeth the day he'd rented his own apartment. They'd kept in touch ever since. Their conversations brought them closer as they delved into their childhoods, each interpreting his or her own views about how their parents had reared them, the reasons behind their parents' actions, and, most revealing, why Paul Edward felt so lost. She had been shocked when he'd told her about it.

"I used to stay up late," he'd told her over the phone. "I never could sleep well. I think that's one reason I didn't hack it in the air force. So I'd crawl to the door and open it a crack, and I'd listen to Mom and Dad talk. This one night, I heard Dad say, 'The boy's not even mine.'"

"Wait," Elizabeth had said. "'The boy's not mine?' What did he mean?"

"It means exactly what you think it means. I didn't understand at the time. But about a year later maybe, I did the math. Mom and Dad got married, and I was born just a few months later. Wilbur's not my dad."

Elizabeth had had no idea what to say. "Paul Edward, I'm so sorry. I never knew."

"You don't have to apologize. To tell you the truth, it was sort of helpful. It made sense—why I never felt like I belonged. But it also made things even worse, you know? Like, who am I?"

"Did you ever talk to Mom and Dad? Tell them that you know?"

"Are you kidding? When I first figured it out, I thought for sure I'd be punished for staying up too late and eavesdropping. And as I got older, I don't think I ever got over that. Somehow, I'd still get in trouble. I was scared. Still am, I guess. Now, though, the whole thing just makes me sad."

"Well, why didn't you at least tell me?"

"Are you kidding? After what I heard him say to you?"

"What do you mean?"

"Gosh, this must have been ten years ago now. You came home late from something. School maybe? I can't remember. I was in the yard out back, but the window was open. I heard him say, 'You know you're my favorite. Why do you do this to me?' After that, I don't know. I just couldn't tell you."

Elizabeth had racked her brain, but she couldn't remember that conversation. She'd told him as much, but it didn't matter

"You were little," he'd said. "It figures you wouldn't remember. And besides, it wasn't something that you'd care about if it was said to you. But if you were in my position, you'd remember. I remember being so angry at you."

"At me?" She had been unable to believe it. She hadn't done anything to him.

"Yeah, it sounds silly now, doesn't it? I should have been angry at him. But at the time, all I could see was that you fit in perfectly, and I didn't."

It had become obvious to Elizabeth that her brother had lived in shame. Blaming himself for their parents' circumstance, he'd felt unwanted, unloved, and undeserving. The last eighteen months of independence had given him the strength and clarity to confront all these issues. Talking with Elizabeth about them would, she hoped, though she dared not say it, become the prelude to confronting his parents in an honest, adult manner in hopes of reaching a relationship based on respect and trust.

He had to be included in mourning Jesse's death.

She made the call to his apartment after midnight, waiting until he'd assuredly be home, and as she'd thought, he wanted to attend the funeral. He needed to feel like part of his family.

The sound of loud snoring woke her at seven. Elizabeth got out of bed and smiled at the sight of her father flat on his back, his head extended over a cushion twisted under his neck, slack-jawed and mouth open, snoring loudly enough to shake the walls. She knew he'd be ready to go the minute he awoke, so she hurriedly dressed, brought her suitcase to the door, and then began preparing a big breakfast of bacon and eggs. She'd force him to eat before they left.

The smell of frying bacon aroused him. *Where am I?* he wondered upon awakening, taking a few minutes to register recent events. *Oh yeah. Jesse died.* He smiled, seeing his daughter in the kitchen, grateful for her thoughtful foresight in fixing breakfast. "Now, that's the way I like to wake up—to the smell of bacon."

"Good morning, Dad. How are you?"

"Oh, I'm just fine. The drive was surprisingly quick. Are you ready to go soon?"

"I'm already packed," she said, pointing to her suitcase. "By the way, I called Paul Edward, and he's coming too. Said he'd arrive at Grandma's about the same time we will."

"That's good. He can get off work?"

"Oh yes. He said it wasn't a problem. You know, you ought to take a little time with him while we're together."

"We'll see. It may be hectic. I don't have any idea how many people will be there. Jesse used to have a lot of friends—before he left. And not the kind of friends your grandmother cares for either." Elizabeth laughed, and he added, "Remember Jean?"

After breakfast, Wilbur washed up, and they headed to West Virginia. The morning hours passed quietly with neither of them talking much. About halfway, they stopped for lunch, and afterward, Elizabeth insisted on driving. Wilbur preferred to listen to the car's engine as they drove, its dull roar music to his ears, rather than the garbled interruptions of the radio, and he soon fell asleep. Five hours later, he awakened as Elizabeth turned onto his mother's street. "What time is it?" asked Wilbur. As the lavender of dusk gave way to the darkness of nightfall, he struggled to orient himself to time and place. He could smell the scent of bluegrass and knew they were close to home.

"It's almost seven. We're on Duck Creek Road."

"Already? I thought you'd wake me up for directions at some point. I didn't know you knew the way."

"Well, I can read and follow the signs," she replied, relishing the opportunity to impress him. She pulled into the drive and parked in front of the barn. The kitchen lights shone through the windows. Shadows of people moving inside broke the light's steady stream as Sarah and Vance came out to meet them in the cool night air.

"Hey, Wilbur," said Sarah, embracing him long and hard. He returned the hug, sharing grief. She let go, wiped her eyes, and then turned to Elizabeth in greeting. "I can't believe he let you drive. Give me a hug, child."

"Come on in. We've got supper on the table, waiting for you all," said Vance.

"Where's Marilyn?" asked Sarah.

"She started a new job and couldn't get off work," said Wilbur.

"Oh. Just as well," replied Sarah sharply.

"Is Paul Edward here, Grandma?" asked Elizabeth.

"He's coming too? No, he ain't here yet."

"Maybe he had a delay. He'll be coming, though. He told me he was," she said, mostly to her father.

The Baker clan had already eaten, but they stayed long enough to help serve Wilbur and Elizabeth and greet them from a safe distance before excusing themselves to go to their rooms. Only then did Wilbur notice the change in the house. "I see you've built on, Mom." There was a new first-floor bedroom next to Sarah's room, off the bath.

"Not me. Bob and Danny paid for the new room and had it built last year. I guess they got tired of being pushed out of their own room when company came. It's come in handy more than once, I must say. You'll sleep there, and Elizabeth can share Mary's bed again."

They sat around the table, listening as Sarah talked about everything except Jesse while Vance added the occasional obligatory "Uh-huh" and "Yes, that's right," beginning with the farm, church, and local friends and moving on to Bob, Mary, and Danny. Bob had gotten a job with the electric company after high school and hadn't missed a single day in four years; the funeral was causing him to miss his first one.

"I thought he'd want to go to college after high school. Lord knows he's smart enough—graduated second in his class. Why, I just grinned when his teachers said, 'Looks like you've raised another valedictorian, Mrs. Sanderling.' But he liked his job too much, and they pay him real good. And they just love him—promised him a good future if he stayed. So he went against me and decided not to go."

Wilbur kept his mouth shut, though the sneer on his face left no doubt as to what he thought about Sarah's statement.

"Even though Mary's not as bright as Bob—she graduated tenth in her class—I made sure she went to college. She wanted to become a physical education teacher, but I told her there weren't no future in teaching physical education and that I wasn't paying for anything but nursing school. Well, that helped make up her mind, and she got her registered nursing license last year—an associate's degree, like you, Elizabeth. Now I'm trying to convince her to go back and get her bachelor's degree."

Sarah moved on to Danny's work status, another proud litany, as Wilbur fumed in his chair. In the middle of Sarah telling about Danny's security of working for Vance in the coal mines (Danny was not college material), Wilbur interrupted, saying, "I think I'll go to bed now."

"So soon? It's just after nine."

"Yeah, Mom. I'm really tired. Elizabeth will stay up and chat with you. Good night, all." After kissing only Elizabeth on the cheek, he walked to the newly built bedroom and shut the door.

"Well, I'll be. What's wrong with him?"

"I'm sure he's just tired. And sad about Uncle Jesse," said Elizabeth, mentioning for the first time the reason they had come.

"Oh yeah. I almost forgot," said Sarah.

"Shall we go sit in the living room, Grandma?"

Sarah and Elizabeth ended up talking until two o'clock in the morning. They related more like long-lost girlfriends as Elizabeth listened to her grandmother talk about things she hadn't spoken of in forty years.

"The Lord never intended for parents to outlive their children. Did you know that, Elizabeth?"

"No. I can't imagine he did," she said, nodding in agreement.

"To bury your parents is to let go of the past. To bury your spouse is to let go of your present. But if you bury a child, then you bury your future, and there's nothing worse than that." Sarah paused in thought and then continued. "Jesse ain't the first child I've buried."

"He's not?"

She told Elizabeth about her first child, Stewart. She spoke his name with reverence, as if in telling his story, she'd finally given

126

this child life. He did exist. His memory deserved words. When she finished, she turned to her granddaughter, who sat beside her with tears rolling down her face, shocked by the revelation. "Now, don't you cry, dear. Life goes on. And we'd best get ourselves to bed before sunrise."

"I love you, Grandma."

"I love you too, Elizabeth."

At six o'clock in the morning, Paul Edward's arrival woke everyone up except Bob and Danny, who were busy laying out eggs and bacon, getting ready to fix breakfast. Having never met him before, they wondered who the dark-haired stranger was; he walked in as if he knew someone. "Hi. I'm Paul—Paul Edward Weaver. Wilbur's son," he explained to their confused looks. "Who are you guys?"

Bob and Danny laughed, finding his affectionate and awkward yet uninhibited demeanor comical as he shook their hands. He got himself a glass of water and then sat down at the kitchen table.

"What's all the ruckus?" asked Sarah, walking into the kitchen. She stared at Paul Edward, trying to place him.

"Hey, Grandma." He gave her a hug.

"Why, hey there. Paul Edward?"

He didn't catch her tone of questioning and sat back down, chattering away about his drive, saying how nice it was to meet Bob and Danny, and asking how his dad was. "Sure is sad about Uncle Jesse," he said.

Vance and the boys ate and then went to check the herd, leaving Mary and Sarah to entertain and update Wilbur, Elizabeth, and Paul Edward, before returning to get dressed. Jesse's funeral was scheduled for that afternoon, and Duck Creek Baptist Church's pastor came over before lunch to mourn and prepare the family. He gathered them together in the living room. "Now, bereavement can be one of the most-difficult things to endure, and when it happens to one so young and vibrant, it's worse. I'm here to see how we at the church can best serve your needs. Would anyone like to say something?"

No one did.

"I understand your silence," said the pastor. "I also understand that Jesse presented those who loved him with some difficulties along the way. Now is a good time to express yourself—unburden yourself about these things."

Apparently, no one had anything to unburden. Everyone sat in silence, not even looking at each other.

"Love for a family member is a complicated thing," said the pastor. "It ebbs and flows on its own tide. But it can be harnessed to ease our sorrows."

Sarah, visibly taken aback by the line of questioning, said, "Pastor, would you like something to drink?"

"No, thank you, ma'am."

"How about something to eat?"

"I'm not hungry, but thank you for your kindness."

"Some tea?"

Despite how obvious she was being, it took the pastor thirty minutes to take the hint. He settled for having them all join hands in a circle while he prayed for Jesse's soul and for God to bless the grieving family. Paul Edward was the only one to shout a hearty "Amen!" at the closing.

Living as a street bum, Jesse, of course, had died uninsured and, as far as anyone knew, unsaved, never having publicly professed his acceptance of Jesus Christ as his Lord and savior. As a favor to Sarah, a member of his flock, the pastor conducted the service at the funeral home instead of the church. They all arrived at the mortuary in the city of Jane Lew in their own vehicles (there was no need for the expense of a limousine) to view his body and say their good-byes before guests arrived. Vance drove Sarah, Bob, Mary, and Danny; Wilbur followed separately with Elizabeth and Paul Edward. As they rode, Elizabeth thought it odd that as of yet, her father and grandmother hadn't talked of Jesse's death. She studied Wilbur, who was sitting behind the wheel, driving. He was dressed in a suit, and she wondered if she'd ever seen him wear one before. He knit his brows tightly together into one, and a deep line furrowing the middle of his forehead dissected his face to the bridge of his nose. The muscles running from his temple bulged as he clenched his jaw; faraway thoughts occupied his mind, distancing him from human interaction. Recognizing his inward agony, she wanted to reach out and comfort him. It seemed wrong for him to suffer in silence. Paul

Edward remained his cheerful self, making small talk from the backseat about how much he liked Bob and Danny.

"Hey, Dad? Dad?" she said.

"Yeah, honey? What is it?"

"Did you know that Grandma had a child before you and Uncle Jesse? He died too."

"No, she didn't. Wherever did you hear that?"

"She told me about him last night. When she was only fifteen years old, she got married after her mother died and then had a little boy named Stewart. But he died at seven weeks old."

"She's never told me that. Why would she tell you?"

"We stayed up late, and she just started talking about her life. I think Jesse's death made her want to share Stewart's memory. She said there's nothing worse than having to bury your child—that it was like burying your future—and doing it again hurts even worse. I just wanted you to know how truly hard this is for her," she said as she rubbed his shoulder and smiled, "as I'm sure it is for you."

"Thank you for telling me. For being here."

The mortuary, a once-grand old home now converted for commercial use, retained the features and elegance of bygone days. Red velvet drapes hung over the large windows, tapestries ran wall to wall, and chandeliers hung in every room. The family passed through a large foyer before Jesse's open casket, set in the center of what used to be a formal living room, confronted them. Its appearance seemed to come too abruptly, as if they needed to pass through several more rooms first to prepare their emotions as they approached the coffin.

Wilbur halted in the doorway, and Elizabeth saw how scared he was. She hung back with him. Vance and Sarah went directly to the body, posting themselves at Jesse's side and encouraging the family to speak to him. Sarah went first, stroking his hair and kissing his cheek before releasing her restrained tears as she tried to hold herself together. Vance gave her a tissue as she talked to her son. "May you rest in peace in the arms of Jesus, my sweet boy. I'm sorry your life was so hard. I look back and so wish things were different—that our home could have provided you with the love and support you needed to overcome your addiction and that you could have seen a brighter future and found happiness in a family of your own, in a career, in faith." Her tears flowed freely and fell onto his face, streaking the orange-hued makeup the morticians had applied.

Sarah stood and turned, holding out her hand in invitation to Wilbur. She said, "Won't you come closer?"

After a nudge from Elizabeth, which she hoped Sarah didn't notice, Wilbur automatically went to her and looked upon his brother's face for the first time in twelve years. "This doesn't look anything like him. Where's his mouth—his lips?" he asked Sarah.

"They had to wire his jaw shut after the autopsy. I guess they got pulled in a little too much."

They'd dyed his hair jet black, which starkly contrasted with the orange-hued makeup used on his face and hands. Elizabeth, standing next to her father, became fixated on Jesse's eyelashes: long, thick, and still coal black, as his hair used to be. They were the only thing that rang true about his appearance. He bent down closer and attempted to speak, but the words came out choked with sadness. A well of tears came pouring out as he falteringly said, "I love you, little brother," and then he quickly took a seat across the room, sitting by himself.

His display of emotion struck Elizabeth's heart. She'd never seen him cry, and seeing him wrenched with sadness moved her beyond words. Paul Edward was just as grief-stricken and took her hand. When they cried, their grief was in part for Wilbur.

Guests began arriving. Older people in the community who'd known Jesse since his childhood came to pay their respects to his family, as did friends of Sarah and Vance. Only one personal friend of his came: his toothless old girlfriend, Jean. In all, nineteen people, including the family, came for the short service. The pastor postponed his eulogy until all possible mourners had arrived, and then he spoke for fifteen minutes on the mercies of God, saying that maybe Jesse would have made it to heaven after all if, at some point, he'd humbled himself before the Lord in life. Then, as they stood in the cemetery, rain clouds gathered above them, enveloping the small crowd in mist and dampness on the cold Halloween day. It had begun raining during the eulogy, but now the rain slackened off, making umbrellas unnecessary; however, it was wet enough to muddy the steep roads leading to the gravesite. As the procession entered the gates, cars spun their wheels in trenches dug deeper by each one going before, making everyone feel sure that someone would eventually get stuck. But no one did. They all parked on the highest hill of the mountaintop graveyard and then walked half a mile, soiling their shoes with mud and water, to a hole in the ground dug beside the tombstone of Webb Weaver. No one talked. They had nothing to say during the minutes they waited for the pastor to arrive and assume his position.

Thirty minutes later, two workers shoveled the dirt atop Jesse's casket, and the rain poured down, sending the mourners to their cars and off to Sarah's house, where they gathered to eat for the rest of the day.

With the socializing over, Wilbur woke the next morning and told Elizabeth he wanted to leave. Through the night, the falling rain had turned to snow, covering the ground six inches deep.

"So soon? You haven't spent any time with Paul Edward or Grandma."

"Yes, I have. I've been here two days, and I've got a lot of driving ahead. Besides, we need to stay ahead of the weather."

Paul Edward awakened and said, "You're going to leave today? I cleared my schedule for another two days so we could spend some time together."

"Yeah. Your mother expects me home as soon as possible. And I don't see any reason for staying."

"Oh. Okay." Paul Edward's disappointment went unnoticed by Wilbur.

Elizabeth bargained to stay at least until after lunch, reminding her father that she hadn't seen her brother or grandmother in years.

The morning passed in angst. Elizabeth watched Paul Edward flit about the house until she couldn't take it any longer. "Talk to your father," she said.

"It's pointless," said Paul Edward. "Have you tried having a conversation with him lately?"

"You're not being fair—not to your father and not to yourself."

But he remained obstinate. Angry with both himself and Wilbur, Paul Edward said his good-byes and began the drive back to Arkansas.

His leaving further provoked Wilbur's desire. Elizabeth found herself doing nothing more than sitting in limbo while a bunch of silly adults refused to talk about the obvious. Her grandmother was just as bad as the rest of them—busying herself with kitchen chores and ignoring reality. *What exactly am I expecting?* Elizabeth asked herself. *Maybe there's nothing to be said.*

Chalking up her instincts to immature romanticism, she packed her bags, said her heartfelt good-byes with kisses, and left with her father—before lunch. Wilbur gave handshakes and hugs but nothing extra.

Huge snowflakes fell continuously, making the drive back to North Carolina slower and more dangerous as the hours passed. Wilbur and Elizabeth witnessed tractor trailers jackknifed on the highway and cars sliding over the icy roads into one another. A traffic jam on the interstate had cars backed up as far as they could see. Inching along, Wilbur spotted an old route he used to take before the interstate developed, and he turned out of traffic onto Old Route 309.

Luckily, they'd driven Elizabeth's Jeep, which had four-wheel drive. A record-breaking winter storm covered their entire route; the road they traveled hadn't been cleared or even driven on since the storm started, and they were forced to use power lines and trees as road markers for guidance. Frightening at first, the drive became an adventure once Wilbur got a feel for the roads. They stopped at unknown, out-of-the-way spots to get gas and to rest. At one place, three old farmers sat around a coal-fed stove inside an old-time wooden grocery store, drinking Nehi soda and talking about the weather as a bantam rooster paced the floor.

It seemed that the farther Wilbur drove from West Virginia, the more vivid his memories of Jesse became. Somewhere across the Virginia border, about four hours into the trip, he started to regale Elizabeth with childhood stories about himself and his brother. He released everything he had inside: discovering his love of the woods, learning to hunt and fish, taking care of Jesse when he was just a toddler, living in the chicken house, dealing with his parents' alcoholism and camping to escape it, taking refuge in school, and discovering girls and cars. He even revealed his anger about not going to college and about Sarah's adoption of the Baker kids.

Elizabeth laughed and empathized, fascinated. She replied with stories about what she found to be true in life and about Paul Edward's loneliness. She left out the part about Paul Edward's unknown parentage, though she offered hints, such as "He said he felt like he never belonged." She told him about the special bond she felt with her grandmother and retold all she'd revealed earlier, in greater detail.

They talked for eight hours straight, and when he pulled into her driveway in North Carolina, he came inside to talk some more. They finally exhausted all possible topics around dawn, and Elizabeth laid a blanket over her dozing father, whom had fallen asleep on the couch.

At noon, Wilbur got up and ate a big breakfast prepared by his daughter. He then showered, dressed, and called Marilyn to tell her of his expected arrival time.

"Well, dear, I guess I'd better be off."

"Okay. Drive careful, and thanks for the stories."

"Jesse's life may not have been worth much, but it made our trip home memorable. I love you."

"I love you too."

Chapter 14

By the end of 1978, the housing market in America had boomed. Though inflation had risen to almost 8 percent, Wilbur's scientific nature bent his confidence toward the numbers he gleaned through reading charts, and according to Fibonacci patterns and the Elliott wave theory, he felt inflation wouldn't reach beyond 10 percent—a ceiling of resistance set in 1975. Factoring in the government's use of oil prices for backing the dollar instead of gold and noting how the Dow apparently had found stability (it had traded between 600 and 1,000 for more than a decade), he reevaluated his investments, wondering which path would prove most profitable: conservative gold or speculative stocks.

Gold's rise to 180 frustrated him. If he'd kept the shares he'd bought at forty-five dollars, he would have made a 400 percent profit. Instead, his stock investments remained the same as they had six years ago—earning nothing. *Hell, I could buy T-bills and make 15 percent,* he thought, lambasting himself for his poor record. His gut told him to buy back into gold, especially now, since owning the bullion itself had become legal in 1974. But with the post-Vietnam housing, optimism prevailed as the general rule among society; it was just a matter of time before Wall Street exploded. The Dow would soon break out of its sustaining baseline levels and then soar to record highs.

After much analysis, Wilbur concluded that his past decisions had cost him substantial earnings. Desperate to make up these perceived losses, he went with the conventional wisdom of the times and decided to leave his money in stocks, waiting for the big payoff, but he'd watch carefully for any developing trends over the next year. If Wall Street didn't show promise by the end of 1979, he'd buy back into gold. He gave a brief thought to what Marilyn would think about all this but decided it was his decision. She didn't have anything to do with it.

Elizabeth returned to the trailer one Wednesday morning in May to take a last look around and see if she'd left anything behind.

Sandy had sublet the place from her for the last six months, ever since she'd moved in with Michael. Her father had decided to forego his biyearly inspections after she graduated from nursing school, allowing her the privacy and respect of an adult paying rent. He didn't know about her current living arrangement.

She'd met Dr. Michael Armstrong at the hospital a year ago, after he'd finished his training as a thoracic surgeon at Duke University Medical Center in Durham and then moved to New Bern on the heels of divorcing his wife of eleven years. His wife had been the one who wanted the divorce. His long hours at the hospital had proven too much for her, and she'd taken refuge from her loneliness in the arms of another man. They hadn't had children. He'd arrived in New Bern alone, putting together the pieces of his life in a new town and a new job.

While at the trailer, Elizabeth took her time, pausing in thought, reliving the night before, when Michael had asked her to be his wife. She'd never dreamed such happiness would come so soon in her life. Loving him and knowing how much he loved her made her feel whole and strong—invincible. She couldn't wait to call her parents with the news.

"Hi, Dad. It's Elizabeth."

"Hey, dear. How are you?"

"I'm great, actually. Just wondering if you and Mom would like some company next week. I want to bring your future son-in-law home for Christmas."

"What?"

"I'm engaged. But don't worry—you'll love him. Tell Mom he's a doctor—that ought to make her happy." She laughed.

"You're just full of surprises."

She and Michael spent three days with them in Pennsylvania. Her parents' immediate fondness for her catch surpassed the excitement of the holidays. Wilbur and Marilyn were glad to have her settle down with someone who could provide Elizabeth with a secure future. Marilyn fawned over Michael to the point of embarrassing Elizabeth: she wore mascara and lipstick every day—something Elizabeth had never seen her do before. Marilyn asked him what his favorite meals were and took great pains to prepare them. She even found occasion to remonstrate her daughter in front of Michael one night. Marilyn was at the stove, testing a batch of barley stew, when she said, "You know, Elizabeth, that old saw about the way to a man's heart being through his stomach? That's true."

"Yeah, I've heard that one," said Elizabeth.

"But it's also the key to keeping a marriage together."

Elizabeth looked over at Michael, who shrugged. "Okay," she said.

Marilyn wasn't done. "It's just that you seem to put so little effort into your dinners. I figured you'd want to make sure things are as good as possible."

"Okay, Mother." Elizabeth fumed inside. *Who are you to be telling me what to do and how to act? You've never taken the slightest interest in me. Now you want to give me advice.*

Elizabeth triumphed over her desire to tell her mother what she really thought by leaning on Michael for support and understanding. She held her feelings inside until that night. While getting ready for bed, she told him how angry Marilyn had made her. After he pointed out their happiness for her, Elizabeth couldn't hold her grudge long and let go of the minor injustices she had felt throughout her life. She then embraced a new relationship with her mother and father, based on equality rather than subordination.

Elizabeth and Michael left with plans made for their wedding in April. Despite Marilyn's insistence on a Catholic church ceremony, they planned to marry outside in the backyard of their home in New Bern. There were just two hitches in their plans. First, upon learning that her granddaughter was getting married, Sarah called Elizabeth and insisted that she make Elizabeth's dress. Elizabeth was so surprised by this that she couldn't think of a good reason not to accept the offer. Unfortunately, she wouldn't even be able to see the dress until the day before the wedding. The second difficulty had to do with Wilbur. Since Elizabeth's religious upbringing had been fraught with confusion, a magistrate would officiate the service. Though she went to church, her father's Sunday chats about Jesus being a vessel for the weak had instilled doubts, especially when Paul Edward's behavior bore out her father's theories. She remembered one of his tirades in particular. "All I'm saying," Wilbur had said, apropos of nothing, "is that it's awfully convenient that Jesus preached all that stuff about the meek inheriting the earth. He catered to people's feelings of weakness. It's no wonder people go for that stuff. It makes them feel nice and secure in this neat little world where there's eternal happiness waiting for them." Since there was little argument, his words had confused Elizabeth. He was contradicting the things she learned in church. But Elizabeth and Michael weren't going to let that stop them.

At five o'clock in the afternoon on Saturday, April 8, 1979, Wilbur stood beside his daughter in the living room of the home she shared with Michael. Thirty guests, with the noted exception of Paul Edward, who had been unable to come due to finances and work and had refused Elizabeth's offer of help, sat in their seats on the back lawn, overlooking the waters of the Neuse River. The water's tranquil depths shimmered with diamonds set aglow by the evening sun, and the sky was painted with a palette of pinks, oranges, and lavenders.

"You look beautiful."

"Thanks, Dad. Grandma did a nice job on my dress. Didn't she?"

Danny had driven her grandmother down the day before. Upon arriving, Sarah had unveiled the wedding gown she'd made herself. Elizabeth had been stunned. Though beautiful, it wasn't her dream gown. She'd watched with disappointment as Sarah had pointed out the hand-sewn pearls, the heavily laced full-length veil, and the empire waist of the dress Sarah had designed just for her. While Sarah had detailed her labor of love, Elizabeth had thought, *It's ivory! Why did you make my gown off-white?* But she had been unable to bring herself to refuse the gift and disappoint her beloved grandmother, even though she had brought her own gown with her in hopes that something would prevent her from wearing the one Sarah had made. "Thank you, Grandma. It's lovely," she'd said. Later that night, she'd secretly put away her original gown of white silk overlaid with white tulle. She'd run her fingers over its puffed, sheer short sleeves edged

137

in satin and envisioned how the satin-trimmed, square décolletage would have framed her slight bosom elegantly yet ever so seductively. Then she'd boxed up her dreams with the shoulder-length, simply designed veil.

When she'd donned the long-sleeved, beaded ivory lace dress of her grandmother's, she'd thought regretfully, *It's a beautiful dress for a winter wedding.* The Victorian maiden she had seen in the mirror had replaced the look of purity she'd wanted Michael to see as she walked down the aisle. Reminding herself that wearing a family heirloom, or would-be heirloom, meant more than wearing something bought off the rack, she'd worked to accept the image before her.

The guitarist outside started to play. After "The Wedding Song," Wilbur would walk Elizabeth down the grassy aisle.

"You'd be beautiful in a potato sack," he said. "I guess we're on soon. You ready?"

"More than ready."

"In an hour, you won't be my little girl anymore." He smiled, blushing slightly in his attempt at sentimentality.

She met his eyes and smiled back, inwardly giggling at him but touched by his words. "I haven't been a helpless little girl since high school, Daddy. But I'll always be yours." She kissed his cheek and then took his arm tightly as they headed down the aisle.

Standing with Michael, she turned to face him, feeling peaceful, right, and strong as the magistrate began. When it came time to pledge their love, the way Michael repeated his vows shattered Elizabeth's veneer of strength. She hadn't wanted to cry, but when he stared into her eyes and held her with his gaze, he declared his love with the conviction of a dying man, and the full force of his emotions broke her heart with his intensity. She bawled like a baby. She said her return vows in broken sobs in between snorting sounds of snuffling back her runny nose. When it came time to kiss, Michael took her in his arms, dipping her slightly back. She fell limply into him, surrounded by the strength of his love. Then he sealed their marriage with a lengthy, full-bodied osculation. An eternity later, she came up for air. The tunnel-vision world where only she and Michael existed ended when she turned to face their family and friends and saw not one dry eye in the audience, not even her mother's. The magistrate pronounced them man and wife.

By October, Wilbur had nervously and anxiously watched the year pass as the nation's economy headed directly opposite his expectations, proving his chartist theories wrong. Inflation stood at nearly 12 percent, the Dow hadn't budged, and the worrisome fact of gold's meteoric rise pissed him off.

In his confusion, he began talking about various investment strategies to anyone and everyone who'd listen. All of these people—from the other officers at Willow Grove to their bridge-playing friends to the prosperous civilian businessmen in his supper club—said they too were holding stocks, waiting to cash out when the Dow made its inevitable move. Knowing others thought the same, he felt a little better—but not much. He started talking to a new face who turned up at the base—a young sergeant of Mexican descent, Lester Rivera. Rivera had joined his unit after transferring from the military base in Yuma, Arizona. He carried a record of reprimands for minor acts of insubordination and fighting with a bunkmate, but he kept quiet, and that made for a good audience as far as Wilbur was concerned.

"I've always thought gold was the key to securing your future, you know?" he said to Rivera one day. "I mean, they used to base the whole economy around it."

"If you say so," said Rivera.

Wilbur didn't hear the apathy in the sergeant's voice. He focused on his own train of thought. *The year's not over yet. I said I'd wait a year*, he told himself whenever he read disturbing evidence contrary to his holdings in the newspaper.

Marilyn grew tired of his constant obsessing; the subject held no interest for her. It seemed no matter where they went, whom they saw, or what they did, Wilbur always steered the conversation his way, and she couldn't escape it. In a desperate measure to reach her husband, she made him an offer he couldn't refuse, hoping to wrench his mind away from his world of numbers, charts, theories, and government conspiracies.

"Honey, why don't we go see your mother for Thanksgiving?"

"I'm sorry. I thought I heard you say something ridiculous, like you wanted to go visit my mother."

"That's what I said. You need to get away. Do some hunting, and see your mom. I bet Elizabeth would come, being able to travel before the baby arrives. Maybe even Paul Edward. What do you think?"

Now four months pregnant, Elizabeth had surprised everyone, including herself, by starting a family so soon after getting married. However accidental it might have been (so she said), she and Michael were ecstatic, as were her parents, over the news.

"I'd love to. Shall I plan on it?" said Wilbur.

"Go ahead. Give her a call tonight. I'll call Elizabeth afterward and convince her to bring Michael too. Then I'll call our son."

The Weavers all agreed to meet at Sarah's house for Thanksgiving. Having been promoted to maître d' from waiter, Paul Edward worked a busy schedule at the Capitol Hotel, making good money. As such, he could only come for the actual dinner and then had to return to Arkansas, as he was scheduled to work the next day.

Elizabeth and Michael arrived Wednesday night, and Wilbur and Marilyn arrived shortly after.

Sarah and Vance loved the company, but Bob, Mary, and Danny still lived at home, and they wouldn't finish the new addition they were building—a larger living room off the original—until spring. The house couldn't hold everyone, so Vance imposed on his daughters and sent Elizabeth, Michael, and Paul Edward up the road to sleep at his former residence.

Nothing controversial loomed during their visit this time. They ate Thanksgiving dinner together—ten in all—and enjoyed one another's conversation as adults bonded by the ties of blood, marriage, and family.

Elizabeth spent every available moment with her brother, making sure he felt he belonged and successfully enticing their parents into his life by congratulating him on his small successes. She'd say, "Did you hear that, Dad? Paul Edward bought a new car last year. Tell him what kind again, Paul," or "Uh-oh, Mom. Paul Edward's got a girlfriend. It sounds serious too. You might have a daughter-in-law before long. What did you say she does again?" Before long, she happily stood as the third-party outsider among his and their conversations.

After he left, she spent the remaining three days of their visit showing Michael the wonders of West Virginia she remembered from her childhood. She walked him down the dirt hollow, which was now covered in snow, to show him the house where her great-grandmother had once lived; the hollow's scenic beauty; and the smell of the air. They found the old beech tree carved with "WLW loves BAD" and conjectured that her father had certainly carved it. But when? Who was BAD? The answers didn't matter. The find simply added nostalgia to their walk.

Wilbur hunted in the woods all day every day he could, as if refilling an empty tank. Marilyn kept content by watching television, shopping, and helping with meal preparations in between chatting about politics and weather with Sarah and Vance, who finally included her in their conversations.

Elizabeth enjoyed the nights best, when the family came together to discuss their days. Bob's, Mary's, and Danny's arrivals home from work often brought news from the outside world and sent their group discussions into renewed and different directions. The last hour or so of the evening wound up with Bob at the piano while Sarah, Mary, and Danny sang Christmas carols and hymns—something they'd done regularly in church the last few years.

Sunday morning brought the visit to its end, prematurely so in everyone's heart. Marilyn and Elizabeth were packing up last-minute items. Elizabeth couldn't help noticing the satisfied look on her mother's face. "You seem happy," she said.

Marilyn sighed. "I am. This was all about Wilbur. I haven't seen him this relaxed in a long time. He's actually laughing—with his mother! Can you believe it?"

"Mission accomplished?" said Elizabeth.

They left with tears, kisses, hugs, and the promise of seeing each other next year.

"I'm going to make sure you know your great-grandchild," said Elizabeth, tearing herself away from Sarah's arms.

"Drive careful, Michael. You've got precious cargo with you— and be expecting us in March, when my grandchild arrives," said Wilbur. With all the farewells over, Elizabeth and Michael followed her parents out of the drive, leaving Sarah behind as she wiped away her customary river of tears.

Goddamn it. The hell with this. I'm buying gold.

On a Monday afternoon in January 1980, Wilbur was panicking. He regretted waiting a full year, as planned, when he saw the price of gold reach $800 an ounce. Before the end of business hours, he called his broker and ordered him to cash out his portfolio, netting a small profit of 15 percent over the last eight years—or, as he saw it, a meager and disgusting 2 percent per year. He arrived home fuming. He found Marilyn in the kitchen. It took less than a second for her to ask, "What's wrong, dear?"

"A measly two percent—that's what." She smiled and then went back to organizing the cupboard as he continued. "I knew I should have put everything in gold. Two percent—can you believe it? I could have made more in a savings account." He realized the truth of what he'd just said, and that made him so mad he couldn't even talk. With the interest in a savings account, he could have then bought more than $10,000 worth of gold in the form of Canadian Maple Leaf and South African Krugerrand coins. Buying at $780 meant his entire fund equaled a mere thirteen coins. He dug out an old magazine with an article by George Reisman, the famous US economist who also distrusted governments and believed in gold.

The next morning, when gold dropped to $750, he still felt good about his decision and took comfort in following Reisman's advice. Wilbur's purchase price, though high, would become tomorrow's greatest deal. However, as gold dropped throughout February and March, his forced optimism gave way to a deep depression. He blamed the government for conspiring against average Americans like himself, manipulating the commodity in order to drive the price down and deprive citizens of a free market. Coming to this realization, he waited for one last bounce in the gold market, which would enable him to get out and quit investing altogether. He'd return to the tried and true savings account or stick his money under a mattress. But months went by, and it seemed more and more as if the bounce were never going to happen. The price continued to fall. When he could take no more, he angrily stalked into the attic with his coins. He didn't even notice he was mumbling out loud: "It only counts as a loss whenever you sell. It's going to happen." He looked around, but no place seemed perfect. "It has to be perfect," he said. "Otherwise, what's the point? Besides, the dollar's not going to last, so owning gold is the only real insurance. Right?" It only occurred to him that he'd been talking out loud when no one answered. A worry flashed through his mind, but before he could figure out what it meant, he saw Marilyn standing at the door to the attic. "What?" he said.

"That was Michael on the phone," she said. "Aaron Michael Armstrong. That's the name of our grandson—Aaron Michael Armstrong."

A sense of peace came over Wilbur when he held his grandson in his arms for the first time. In the presence of the perfect little boy with an unmarred life of opportunity ahead of him, Wilbur felt renewed and optimistic. Maybe this child would escape the emotional scars of disappointment, failure, and crushed dreams.

"He has our nose, with the same bifid tip of yours, mine, and Grandma's. See?" said Elizabeth, sitting in her hospital bed.

"I do. He looks a lot like his grandpa. Why, you're a chip off the old block, aren't you?" He rubbed his nose against Aaron's, kissing him Eskimo-style. "Are you sure about naming him Aaron? I'll forgive you for not calling him Wilbur—it's a tough name to live with. But what about Lindy?"

"Lindy? Where'd you get that name?"

He told her about the uncle who'd died long before his own birth—the golden child full of promise and hope.

"How sad. I didn't know about him. But we like the name Aaron. It means 'mountain-like strength,' and it's biblical—Moses's brother. And Michael likes it because the initials are AMA."

"Yeah. Maybe it'll encourage him to become a doctor like his father," said Michael with a laugh.

"Well, it can't hurt," Wilbur agreed. "Keep Lindy in mind for the next one. Okay?"

Wilbur and Marilyn stayed with Michael, Elizabeth, and the new baby for three days before heading back to Pennsylvania. While in North Carolina, Marilyn helped around the house, cleaning and cooking the meals, allowing her daughter to regain strength and sleep as much as possible. Michael had taken off work the Tuesday his wife delivered, but he returned to work for the rest of the week. Wilbur happily performed his duty of holding Aaron every moment he could. In fact, the new mother had to pry the child from Wilbur's arms to nurse the baby. "The boy's got to eat. Let him go," said Marilyn when taking the crying baby to his mother. "What's got into you? You didn't act like this with our kids."

"Yes, I did. You don't remember how I held Paul Edward?" he replied defensively.

"Well, maybe. But I don't recall you fawning so."

As Wilbur and Marilyn drove home to Pennsylvania, Wilbur said, "I think we should move to North Carolina. When I retire, I mean. It'd be good to be near Elizabeth."

"Well, why not? You say that as if I might disagree," said Marilyn.

"I didn't mean to. I just want you to understand how much it means to me to be near Aaron and to be an influence in his life." Wilbur felt awkward in revealing this newfound mission and hoped his wife didn't think him silly. Then again, Aaron's birth had affected him in ways he hadn't expected: their grandson gave new meaning and purpose to his life. He had a reason to live. How could he convey this to her without her thinking him silly?

"Okay, dear. I always liked North Carolina," she said.

In June 1980, Wilbur got a letter from his superiors, informing him of their favorable evaluation of his performance and recommending his promotion to lieutenant colonel in January. The news brought him closer to reaching his retirement goal and elevated his spirits.

He found himself in the mood to celebrate. As Wilbur's fraternizing was severely limited, he unexpectedly found himself toasting with Lester Rivera, one of his subordinates, upon hearing the news of his upcoming promotion. Lester's Irish mother and immigrant father had created a good-looking man of fair skin and dark hair. He was cocky, intelligent, and short yet strong as a bull, and he possessed a proud work ethic. The twenty-year-old sergeant reminded Wilbur of a mix of himself and his brother, Jesse, and Wilbur took a fond liking to him. He felt that with some helpful guidance, Lester had a promising future, and he took it upon himself to become Lester's mentor. They started spending a little more time together than they should have.

Having spent two tours of duty in Pennsylvania, Wilbur knew his time could expire at any moment. It came as no surprise when the military transferred him back, as of January 1, 1981, to his home base in Cherry Point, North Carolina.

His men were sad when he told them the news in August. Hating to lose their friend and father figure, they got together and planned an end-of-summer barbecue in his honor.

On a hot Saturday morning, Wilbur and Marilyn joined ten other marines and their wives, children, and girlfriends at the small picnic grounds on base. Lynyrd Skynyrd, Led Zeppelin, and AC/DC blared from Lester's boom box as the men set up a volleyball net and horseshoe stakes and laid out a myriad of food: steaks, hot dogs, hamburgers, submarine sandwiches, brisket, beef barbecue, and chips. After taking up a collection, the enlisted men purchased three kegs of beer and tapped them in preparation for the celebration.

The party proved a rare occasion when Wilbur actually relaxed. He knew and liked everyone, his marriage was strong and healthy, a promotion lay ahead, and it was a beautiful, sunny day. Everything felt right—so much so that he eventually accepted the men's persistent offers to have a beer with them.

By one o'clock, Marilyn grew tired of the event and asked to go home. "I'd like to stay," he replied. "You can take the car, and I'll get a ride home later."

She agreed reluctantly. Not appreciating or approving of his drinking beer but seeing his happiness, she made an exception in this case.

The afternoon passed in revelry, and soon it was time for dinner. Not wanting the day to end, they decided enough food remained to eat supper, so they fired up the grills again and began draining the third keg of beer.

The wives and children grew tired after supper, exhausted from nine hours of endless activity, and began gathering their belongings, including their inebriated husbands. Once they packed up and left, Wilbur found himself alone—and very drunk—with Lester and his girlfriend, Theresa, who had stayed behind. "Hey, Major. It's still early. How about we go for a beer? Play a little pool or something."

"Sure, Lester. Why not?"

The alcohol was starting to affect Wilbur, and he decided to stay and party with Lester and Theresa. They piled into the sergeant's rusted Vega and headed to a pool hall.

They passed the next three hours at a dive called Tom's, a frequent haunt of Lester's. Wilbur played a few games before deciding he preferred to sit and watch his friend play, since Lester had beaten him every time. Theresa joined him at the bar while Lester shot pool with his acquaintances. "You don't mind if I sit here, do you?"

"Oh nooo," said Wilbur, his tongue thick in his mouth.

"Tell me, Major—how come your wife lets a good-looking man like you run around by himself?"

"Me? You think I'm good looking?"

"And sexy. Very sexy."

Flattered, Wilbur liked the attention of the pretty young blonde.

"Hey, Charlie, finish my game here, will ya?" Lester said, handing another guy his pool cue before walking over to the bar.

"Why, it's Lester. Finished already?" said Theresa.

"Yeah. We're done here. Let's blow this joint and go somewhere else, eh, Major?"

"Suuure." Wilbur swayed as he stood and took Theresa's proffered arm for support as they made their way to the car.

"You don't drink much, do you?" she said once they got inside.

"Nooo. In fact, this may be the first time," said Wilbur.

Lester said he needed some money and stopped at a grocery store to cash a check. Standing at the front of the store with the cashier, he saw Theresa get out of the car and into the backseat with his boss. *What's going on?* he wondered, and he watched them carefully through the glass.

In the car, Theresa snuggled close to Wilbur. "You poor thing—drunk and without a girl. I know what you need."

At the moment, all he knew was the bubble created around his drunken world, in which he was alone with a pretty young girl in his face, touching him and being so nice. He felt the urge to kiss her lips, and without thinking, he did.

Lester busted out of the store to take his revenge.

"What the hell?" shrieked Wilbur. Lester stood at the open car door with his hands wrenched around Wilbur's collar, jerking him out onto the pavement.

"You bastard! Who the fuck do you think you are?" shouted Lester as Wilbur scrambled to stand.

In his muddled head, Wilbur tried to make sense of things. He'd already forgotten about the kiss, and for the life of him, he didn't know why Lester was so furious.

Despite Lester's repeated questions, Lester didn't want or wait for answers, and before Wilbur got to his feet, Lester began attacking him. A forceful kick hit him in the stomach as he crouched on his hands and knees, trying to get up. The blow knocked his breath out, flattening him to the ground. Wilbur tried to speak but couldn't. Another kick—this time in his ribs—put fear in him. *He wants to beat the shit outta me.* The reality sobered him somewhat. He guessed the first two hits had been just a warm-up for Lester, as Lester lost control and began pummeling Wilbur with one blow after another. Visions of Lester taking a karate stance and dancing around appeared in a strobe-light effect as Wilbur opened and shut his eyes. Thinking Lester stood on his right, Wilbur protected his side with his hands. Then he felt a kick to his exposed left ribs and heard the sound of cracking bones. Before he had time to react to the pain, Lester punched him in the face—three, four, five times. Lester sat on his chest, bouncing his weight on his cracked ribs, repeatedly punching him in the mouth and eyes.

Chapter 15

The bedside phone rang, waking Marilyn from her slumber. When her husband failed to answer by the fourth ring, she picked up the receiver, annoyed by his apparent laziness. "Hello?"

"This is Hatboro General Hospital calling for a Mrs. Wilbur Weaver."

"This is she." Disoriented as to the time, she switched on the lamp to get her bearings and to awaken Wilbur, only then realizing she'd been sleeping alone; his side of the bed lay undisturbed.

"Ma'am, we have your husband in the emergency department. Can you come in?"

"What? Is he hurt?"

"He's been assaulted. He arrived by ambulance almost an hour ago, unconscious and pretty beaten up. But he looks worse than he really is. He should be fine eventually."

After saying she'd be right there, Marilyn hung up, threw on the first clothing she saw, and raced to the hospital. At three o'clock in the morning, the deserted streets allowed her to run red lights without pause, and she arrived at the civilian hospital within fifteen minutes. She identified herself to the triage nurse, who then led her to Wilbur's side in the main trauma room, where he lay among a crowd of doctors and nurses treating two other patients, apparently for injuries worse than his, since they seemed to be ignoring him. "We had a quiet night until your husband came in. Then everything fell all to hell. Gunshot wounds, crash victims—it's crazy right now," explained the nurse.

After being temporarily distracted by all the chaos, Marilyn finally noticed the man she stood beside as her husband. She wasn't prepared for his shocking appearance. "This isn't my husband," she declared.

"This is Wilbur Weaver. At least that's what his wallet says."

Oh my God. Nausea welled from the pit of her stomach, and she turned away to let out the rising vomit, spewing bile and supper remains onto the floor.

"It's okay, Mrs. Weaver. He's going to be fine. Have a seat, and let me get you a drink." Rolling a chair under her, the nurse handed her a soda and a wet cloth to wipe her face, and then she threw some towels over the mess on the floor. "He's already been seen by the doctor. We're just waiting to take him upstairs to his room. I'll get his doctor for you."

Marilyn appreciated the cool cloth and felt better after taking a few sips of the soda. Still, she couldn't bear to look at Wilbur's face. *Why? Who would beat you like this?* She sat wondering, certain in her assumption that he had been the victim of a mugging; only a stranger would commit such a heinous crime.

Finished with his assessment of the gunshot victim behind the curtain drawn next door, Dr. Harmon appeared. He introduced himself to Marilyn and began explaining Wilbur's injuries: "The x-rays and CAT scan revealed three broken ribs on his left side; he's also fractured his right orbit—the bones surrounding the eye. Though that eye looks pretty bad, his pupils react appropriately, and I didn't see any retinal damage; he should regain his vision once the swelling goes down. The nurse will put a dressing around his head and bandage that ear back down; it's been detached but should reconnect in time with applied pressure." She hadn't noticed that his swollen right ear dangled two inches lower than the left until the doctor pointed it out. "We'll have to do a hearing test later, after his ruptured drum heals and the blood in the inner ear dissolves; I suspect he'll sustain some loss. Otherwise, there's no internal bleeding or brain damage. Despite the way he looks, he'll be fine."

Wilbur came to as the doctor spoke, and his frail voice faintly yelled, "Stop! No more. Please."

"It's okay, Mr. Weaver. You're in the hospital," said Dr. Harmon.

"I'm right here, honey. It's me—Marilyn." Offering comfort, she leaned closer, trying to make sense out of his words as he rambled on incoherently and almost inaudibly, and the stench of dried blood and alcohol overcame her. "Is he drunk?" she asked the doctor incredulously.

"Well, yes. His blood alcohol level was quite high. The police said he was attacked by an acquaintance after being out drinking together. They'll come back tomorrow morning to get his statement."

Her sympathy for him lessened significantly after she heard the facts, and she was outraged. Knowing that his injuries had resulted from stupidity and that he'd recover, she couldn't stand the sight of him anymore and went home shortly after.

After two days in the hospital, Wilbur came home to recuperate and to face the consequences of his actions. Lester had been sent to the brig, where he was awaiting his court-martial—a just punishment, in Wilbur's opinion. However, the thought of having to endure Lester's trial, taking the stand to testify, and publicly telling his account of the most embarrassing and humiliating night of his life filled him with dread.

His injuries left him deaf in one ear, and the fractured orbit caused his right eye to sink back in its socket so that it healed out of position with the left. His vision eventually returned to normal, and his cracked ribs hurt for almost a year. Physically, he'd mend with few visible scars. He might have recovered as well emotionally, if only the episode had ended there, with painful injuries.

After twenty-seven years of exemplary duty, five months shy of promotion to lieutenant colonel, Wilbur stood before a panel of his superiors. Dressed in his finest, he held out hope that he could soon put the whole affair behind him. He was stunned when the judge said, "Major Weaver, this court has examined your case in detail, and we hereby inform you that your promotion to lieutenant colonel has been denied. Furthermore, your career in the military is ended, effective immediately. You've been granted a general discharge."

Wilbur's knees buckled. "Sir," he managed to say, "may I speak?"

The judge nodded.

"Sir, a general discharge is just one degree above a dishonorable discharge. I would ask more leniency. I've served for nearly three decades—exemplary service, if I may say so. Should one mistake discount twenty-seven years of work?"

The judge shook his head. "Major, you should count yourself lucky that we *are* being lenient. Your fraternization with enlisted men was a severe military infraction. It is only through this court's generosity that you have escaped your own court-martial."

There was no point in arguing any further. He soon left the room, the base, and his career. In his mind, a general discharge might as well have been dishonorable.

With his head hung low, Wilbur took a forced leave of absence until his retirement became effective on October 1. Every fiber of his being wanted to leave the state, to put distance between himself and the incident, but he had to stay until he testified at Lester's trial two months later. Until then, he purged his depression by packing up his house and making arrangements to leave. The day after giving his testimony, he and Marilyn moved to North Carolina.

He later learned by letter that Lester got twenty-five years in the brig after being found guilty of attempted manslaughter. *Poor bastard*, he thought with regret—about Lester and himself. Then he tore the letter into pieces and threw it away, along with his memories of his life of service.

At forty-five years old, he settled into his new life by pursuing only the activities he wanted. He and Marilyn bought a house on ten acres of woodlands in Jones County, where he dreamed of hunting to his heart's content and visiting Elizabeth, who lived only twenty minutes away. He set up an area in his garage for reloading and making his own rifle and shotgun ammunition, and the garage became his favorite spot of refuge and the place where he spent the majority of his time.

Wilbur practically lived there, tinkering, staying away from human interaction except when visiting his daughter and her family. Marilyn knew he'd eventually get restless sooner or later and find another career. After months of his self-imposed exile turned into years, he eventually became a hermetic, antisocial curmudgeon. Marilyn suggested he teach part-time at the local community college or, with his counseling background, become an academic adviser, but beaten down by past experiences, Wilbur adamantly opposed any suggestion to participate in the world around him.

"There's an ad in the paper for a part-time accountant. You're good with numbers, Wilbur. Why don't you apply?" she said one night while watching him sit in his recliner and gorge on potato chips and deer jerky. His daily routine consisted of a complete lack of exercise: he'd sit at his reloading station, only moving from the chair there to the recliner in the living room. He'd gained more than forty pounds since retiring two years ago.

"I don't want to."

"What about this one for an adult education teacher?"

"Marilyn, I followed orders for twenty-seven years. I'm enjoying doing what I want when I want. I don't want to go to work."

"Well, you need to do more than sit around the house getting fat. You won't go to church with me or make friends. The only people you see are me, Elizabeth, and her family. You're too young to do nothing."

"I do a lot—work with my guns, take care of the yard, hunt—and I like spending time with my grandson. Now, for the last time, get off my ass." He'd tried telling her before about his reasons for staying home, but she'd yet to stop nagging him. Maybe if he'd spoken the truth—if he'd told her that he felt safe at home, where no one could harm him, and that if he didn't try to succeed in anything, he'd never fail—then she would have left him alone. But admitting this truth to himself, let alone to her, hurt too much. The world he'd created around his guns and his family gave him all the stimulation he craved. The rest of society could kiss his butt. "Why don't *you* go get a job?"

"I think I will. You may not need socialization, but I do."

With her past experience as a secretary, she got a full-time job on the military base at Cherry Point within the month.

"Hi, Dad. What brings you by today?" said Elizabeth.

"It's a beautiful Saturday, and I wanted to see Aaron. Thought I'd take him to my place and show him how to catch a rabbit. The season opened last week."

"I'm sure he'd love to when he gets back in an hour or so. He's at a classmate's birthday party. His best friend, Kyle, turned five today." Three months pregnant with her second child, who was due in March 1987, Elizabeth looked the picture of contentment. She spent her days making her home a place of refuge for her busy husband, volunteering in Aaron's kindergarten class, and doting over her son.

"Then I'll wait, if it's all right. Where's Michael?"

"He's out on the dock, getting ready to winterize the boat and dreading the chore. I'm sure he'd be glad to see you and welcome the break."

Wilbur left to bend Michael's ear. It seemed only Michael willingly listened to the government conspiracy theories Wilbur loved to expound—Marilyn and Elizabeth had both previously told him to keep his predictions of doom and gloom to himself. Wilbur had replied, "Go ahead and stick your heads in the sand. Live your lives blissfully ignorant like the rest of the world while communism takes over."

Elizabeth loved Michael all the more for putting up with her father, especially since Wilbur resented doctors for being major players in conspiring for unnecessary surgeries, prescriptions, and tests, all for personal monetary gain. Given the chance, she felt her father would gladly tell Michael how to practice medicine and even how to operate.

Aaron came home and bounded into his grandfather's arms. Wilbur said, "Hey, champ. You wanna come play with me today?"

"Can we shoot arrows again?"

"Nah, not today. I want to show you how to trap a rabbit."

"Cool."

Wilbur took him home to spend the night with him and Marilyn. They worked hard for the rest of the day, building a plywood box with a trapdoor in front. After setting it in the field and hiding it among some brush, they propped half an apple against the door, inside the trap. "When the rabbit comes in to eat it, he'll trigger the door shut and be trapped inside."

"Then what?" asked Aaron. "Can I keep him as a pet?"

"No, then we can eat him—if you want. Wild animals aren't good pets. They'll just die if you try to keep them," he explained, somewhat worried about Aaron's attitude toward hunting. *Oh no. Please don't be one of those tree-hugging, animal-rights, plant-loving idiots.*

With the box in place, they went inside, where Marilyn had supper waiting. Aaron made cookies with her and enjoyed being with her. He enjoyed baking and being inside as much as he enjoyed being outside with Wilbur—who sat waiting impatiently for them to finish so that he and Aaron could get back to work. "Come on, Aaron—we better go check our trap before it gets too dark," he said once one batch of cookies had come out of the oven.

"Yeah. I almost forgot."

Wilbur grabbed the BB rifle in case they'd nabbed their prey, and they had. An adult rabbit stood scurrying inside the box when they approached. "We got one!" exclaimed Aaron, jumping up and down with excitement. After explaining the purpose of bringing the rifle, Wilbur prodded Aaron to shoot the rabbit.

"It won't hurt him. In fact, it's kinder to shoot him than to keep him and have him die slowly. I'll fry him up, and we'll eat him with biscuits and gravy. Mmm, good."

"Okay, gimme the gun." Now five years old, Aaron had been shooting the BB gun since the age of three, when he'd sat on Grandpa's back deck and targeted tin cans. With learned skill, he fired quickly and cleanly through the rabbit's head and then proudly carried off his quarry to show Grandma. Wilbur's heart filled with pride—and relief.

From the ages of three to ten, Aaron learned at the feet of his grandfather. Aaron could fish, trap, and hunt with equal skill; he'd inherited Wilbur's marksmanship abilities and coordination, plus skills that lent themselves to academics and musical talent. Aaron played the piano like a Mozart prodigy. He started lessons at age four and rose to playing as the grand finale in recitals throughout his school district. By the end of fifth grade, Aaron's achievements had earned him the title of class valedictorian.

"When did they start this?" asked Michael when Elizabeth showed him the graduation ceremony invitation sent home with their son, citing Aaron as the honored speaker. "Aren't valedictorians reserved for high school graduates?"

"Nowadays, they have elementary and middle school commencement ceremonies too. Some schools even celebrate kindergarten graduation—though I agree that seems to be a bit trivial."

Growing excitement replaced their reservations when Aaron's parents, grandparents, and little sister, Megan, sat in attendance among Jones County's dignitaries and observed the respect everyone had for the ceremony. Since Aaron was in kindergarten, Elizabeth had maintained a tradition of having Aaron give his teachers flowers on the last day of school. For this occasion, Elizabeth had picked a special bouquet of peonies, irises, and ivy for Aaron to give to the school's retiring principal, Ms. Duffy. Their finest hour came when Aaron, dressed in his Sunday suit, took his place at the podium. "Now I'd like to present our valedictorian, who's made nothing but As the entire year"—*He gets that from me*, thought Wilbur—"Aaron Michael Armstrong," said Ms. Duffy.

Standing front and center, holding his bouquet, he looked perfectly handsome, with his hair parted on the side and combed back and a white carnation boutonniere in his lapel. "First, I'd like to give these to our principal," he said, turning to Ms. Duffy and handing her the flowers. She accepted them with surprise and tearfully thanked him through the microphone, going on about the thousands of children who'd touched her heart throughout her thirty years in education. She cut her words off midsentence after suddenly remembering that the podium now belonged to Aaron, and she grabbed him in her arms as she stifled her tears.

He did that perfectly, thought Elizabeth as he returned the principal's embrace and began his speech.

"I'd like to read 'A Creed for Today and Every Day' by Anna Marie Edwards," he said, and he read the following:

> Think of the future as a wonderful door opening into a promised new land. Learn from the past; but do not let it determine your future. Forget about any past mistakes. Be glad you are living in a world that is so full of opportunity. Be optimistic. Appreciate the fact that you have God-given talents and abilities that are uniquely yours, and don't be afraid to use them. Be the best you can be. Seek the advice and help of others, but always remember that yours is the final word.
>
> Make your own decisions, explore your own self, and find your own dreams. Be persistent; try not to get discouraged when things don't go your way. Do all

that you can to make the world a better place to live. Be aware that life isn't always easy, but that given time and hard work, it can be everything you want it to be.

Most of all, be happy. The future awaits you, and it's a wonderful time to be alive.

Elizabeth broke down crying after the first paragraph and held Michael's hand in shared satisfaction. Wilbur sat with a wide smile on his face—until Marilyn elbowed him in the ribs. "Pay attention," she whispered. "This is some good advice."

Still, he hugged Aaron afterward and told him, "Great job," instead of shedding the tears he held back—and of course, he gave himself some credit for Aaron's achievement. *He must have been listening to me all along.*

Against Wilbur's objections, Elizabeth and Michael sent Aaron off to camp for the summer to learn how to sail and be independent, leaving Wilbur to entertain himself without the company of his grandson. He tried to bond with Megan, but something about the relationship wasn't the same. He loved her, but he couldn't think of anything to do with her. To occupy time, he decided to present Aaron a gift when he returned, and he spent weeks refurbishing an old 12-gauge shotgun. He completely outfitted it with accessories and dozens of custom reloaded shells and honed the trajectory to perfection. Wilbur gave Aaron the gun and spent the late summer and early fall teaching him how to shoot. Wilbur even built a tower for throwing clay targets, and he delighted in Aaron's accuracy. When the first day of hunting season arrived, Aaron killed his first deer.

Life settled into a happily predictable routine. Wilbur's world revolved around telling his government theories to Michael, indoctrinating Aaron (molding him into a wiser version of himself), and going on annual Thanksgiving hunting treks to West Virginia. Marilyn continued to work, content to let her husband live the way he pleased while she did the same. After finding her time wasted as she sat around bored and unneeded, she stopped going to West Virginia after the second year. There, hunting seemed to become Wilbur's sole purpose. He didn't visit with Sarah and Vance; instead, he spent every hour of daylight in the woods, only to come home and work late into the night in the basement, processing the deer he'd killed. Those first two years, Marilyn, Sarah, and Vance joined him downstairs after supper to help grind and package the meat, forming an assembly line to quicken the task. However, being a perfectionist, Wilbur criticized the way they worked. Sarah didn't weigh each package on the scale to measure exactly one pound; rather, she used her sixty-plus years of experience to eyeball the weight. Vance refused to suck the air out of each bag before tying it shut (Wilbur insisted on inserting a straw into the gathered top and then inhaling to remove the air—simply hand compressing the seal wasn't good enough). Marilyn put the wrapped and bagged meat in freezer paper, but her folds didn't conform to his specifications.

While Sarah and Vance had once welcomed his visits, his lack of congeniality and obsession with hunting soon felt obtrusive to them. Wilbur didn't notice how his butchering inconvenienced everybody, making it necessary for the family to park their cars outside in the cold for two weeks as he commandeered the garage basement. Whereas Sarah had once enjoyed cooking meals for Wilbur at the end of the day, she now resented her efforts when Wilbur would claim he was too busy to come upstairs to eat.

After the fifth year, Wilbur finally noticed that no one seemed enthused when he came. He complained about it to Marilyn when he got home and said, "Why can't they just sit back and enjoy the pleasure of my company?"

"Well, your company leaves a bit to be desired. You don't really talk to anyone."

He scoffed at her remarks. He felt they should see his mere presence as the gift it was. He ignored what she said, as well as the attitude of his mother's family, and looked forward to his Thanksgiving hunts with great joy—whether alone or not—because he always got what he needed: peace and renewal.

Except for the West Virginia trips, Wilbur refused to travel. Marilyn spent her vacation time apart from him, visiting acquaintances in exotic locales and rekindling old friendships.

Marilyn answered the phone when Paul Edward called home with surprising news in May 1993. "Hi, Mom. Guess what. I'm finally getting married." As he was thirty-nine years old, they'd concluded that his bachelorhood was permanent.

"You are? I'd have never guessed that. Who is she?"

"You remember Sherry?" He explained how the friend of a friend he'd moved in with upon his return to Arkansas had finally agreed to marry him. Paul Edward and Sherry had known each other for more than sixteen years and had watched each other's relationships. They had always been there for one another as friends, offering consolation. He'd been the first to recognize his feelings, but it had taken ten years of courtship to convince her that the man she needed had stood before her for all those years.

It all sounded romantic to Wilbur and Marilyn. They'd met Sherry once before, when Paul Edward had brought her home for a visit several years back, and they liked her fine. But he'd brought two other girls home since, and Wilbur and Marilyn hadn't thought any more about Sherry after that. They were happy for him and made plans to attend the wedding, which was six weeks away.

Elizabeth got a different feeling about it when he called to tell her. "Sherry? I thought you'd given up on her," she said. "That one time we talked on the phone, you kept telling me how frustrated you were after doing all that work on her house for her and getting nothing but a simple 'Thanks' in return. She barely even smiled at you."

"I know," he said. "But that was a long time ago."

"Yeah, but you took her to all those plays and everything. Sounded like you were wining and dining her."

"I know. But the only thing that really worries me is that we haven't consummated our relationship yet."

"You're going to marry a girl who's so far refused to have sex?"

"She says she will when we're married."

"Okay, if she was twenty years old, I'd think it sweet. But she's forty-three. Come on, Paul—even you've got to admit that's strange."

"Maybe. But I think it's cultural. Her mother's Chinese and barely speaks English after living in America forty years. Sherry's just different. That's why I love her."

"No, she's emotionally stunted. That's why you love her." With her reservations voiced, Elizabeth agreed to go to the wedding. On a

Friday in June, she and Michael flew to Arkansas and met her parents at the Capitol Hotel.

Wilbur and Marilyn arrived Thursday night at their son's apartment. The next day, Marilyn and Sherry headed out to finalize the wedding plans. Paul Edward found himself alone with his father for the first time he could remember since being a child.

"Happy belated birthday, Son," said Wilbur.

"Thanks, Dad. With all the wedding plans, I almost forgot my fortieth birthday." He laughed, but filling the silence with empty pleasantries proved uncomfortable for both. Paul Edward decided to bite the bullet and pour his heart out, wanting to begin this new chapter in his life without any emotional baggage. "Hey, Dad, I'd like to talk about some issues with my past. Can we?"

"Oh, sure. Why not?" Wilbur shifted in his chair. "What's on your mind?"

"I'd like to apologize for being so hard to get along with when I lived at home. And I want to thank you for being my father."

"Thank me?"

"Yes. I know you didn't have to." Paul Edward paused, wondering how much to reveal. He decided not to say bluntly what he knew; instead, he'd just talk about himself, leaving the door open for Wilbur to confirm or deny whatever he wished. Paul Edward continued. "But all my life, I've felt different from you. I think the religious issue really confused me. Maybe you shouldn't have told me, at four or five years old, about your agnostic beliefs."

"Uh-huh." *Okay, he's apologized and thanked me; now he's going to blame me.* Wilbur stared back, receptive but becoming defensive inside.

"It took a long time to figure out what I believed in, and you didn't, or couldn't, allow me that. Time, I mean. I felt forced to leave home because nobody understood or even loved me."

"Don't say that," interrupted Wilbur.

"I don't mean always," he said. "Just then. But growing up as an outsider in my own home, feeling like there was no one to turn to for guidance, support, and love, caused me to waste ten years of my life searching for myself. It wasn't just you. Mom's emotionally unable to have any kind of deep relationship, and Mom's the one who should have talked to me most."

"Son, if it makes you feel better to say these things, then I'm glad. I'm sorry you struggled in the past, but everything's fine now. We all make mistakes—parents, children. We can only do the best we can with what we have and go on from there. Okay? Now, let's go see your sister."

"Okay." *So that's it, huh?* Realizing his father's limitations, Paul Edward let go of his attempt to connect, finally accepted Wilbur for the man he was, and expected nothing more. Despite the disappointing results, Paul Edward felt relieved of the burden he'd been carrying all his life.

On Friday night, they held the rehearsal dinner. Paul Edward was the star of the night, directing the dinner party as he, his fiancée, and his family ate at his place of work. Sitting on the other side, he relished being waited on by his coworkers and ordered the most-expensive items on the menu, including the table-side preparation of bananas Foster. He enjoyed showing off his culinary knowledge and appreciation of life's finer offerings, even though Elizabeth and Michael had to pay the bill.

The next day, the family gathered for prewedding pictures at Sherry's house, where the ceremony would take place. Paul Edward confined himself to the guest bedroom so as not to see his bride. He looked radiant. Though a close-shaven ring of peppered stubble had long ago replaced his locks of curly black hair, his green eyes sparkled with joy as he assessed his finery in the mirror. "You look dashing," said Elizabeth, and she hugged him.

"Thanks, Sis. You wouldn't believe what all my friends are saying about you," he teased, knowing she understood. Even now, his friends were astonished upon learning that the gorgeous brunette was related to their awkward, nerdy friend, who looked nothing like her.

Chairs lined either side of the living room in the old Victorian house, leaving a center aisle. The guests were seated at three o'clock, and from behind, the vocalist began singing. Ushers escorted Elizabeth and Michael to their seats, followed by Wilbur and Marilyn. Paul Edward took his place, smiling front and center, looking more fulfilled than he'd ever been. A pianist played the wedding march, heralding Sherry's arrival.

As the preacher spoke of the necessary commitment required in marriage, Elizabeth became overwhelmed with sadness. She started crying and couldn't stop, making a spectacle of herself, for only she cried. Instinctively, she felt that the whole ceremony was wrong. While Paul Edward beamed with joy, his fiancée did not. She didn't appear to be a happy bride; in fact, it seemed she went through the motions like a lamb facing slaughter. She didn't smile or look at Paul Edward lovingly. *She doesn't love him. He's going to be hurt again.* Seeing the elaborate ceremony Sherry had planned, Elizabeth concluded that all Sherry wanted was a wedding, not the marriage. *My brother's marrying a forty-three-year-old Chinese virgin who only wants to have her bridal portrait made.*

She got herself together in time for the reception. The mother of the bride owned a restaurant and catered the event, serving a lavish Chinese buffet. Elizabeth jokingly asked if the dishes were lined up in numerical order and told Michael, "Get me another helping of the number four, the house special, will ya?"

Sherry milled around like a hostess and then called Paul Edward to the front to cut his groom's cake, which was chocolate and shaped like an aardvark.

Ninety minutes later, everyone had had his or her fill of food, both cakes had been cut and served, all the toasts and speeches had been made (one by Sherry's brother and another by a friend of Paul Edward's), and the newlyweds had finished their inaugural dance. The guests said their good-byes, anticipating the bridal couple's honeymoon departure, but another two hours passed, and still, Sherry sat deep in conversation with her guests. The groom tried unsuccessfully not to appear too eager to leave, but after waiting ten years to make love to her, his anticipation was obvious. After four hours, he announced their departure over the microphone, physically took hold of his bride's arm, and led her to the limo waiting outside. She stalled for another twenty minutes before getting in.

No one in the family heard from Paul Edward until ten months later, when he called Elizabeth, informing her of his impending annulment.

"Wow, Paul Edward. I wish things had worked out," said Elizabeth.

"Me too," he replied. "But I should have known. Even on our wedding night, she refused to give herself to me. She kept talking about these so-called physical disparities between us. She thought it would make sex too painful."

"Does that mean what I think it means?"

"I'm afraid so. I made do for as long as I could. We even went to couple's therapy. God, how didn't I see this coming?"

Elizabeth knew this wasn't the right time to mention her warnings.

Paul Edward said, "I even suggested surgery, but her heart wasn't in it. In the end, I threatened to get an annulment just to try to get her to react, but turns out it was just what she wanted. She agreed right away. She was happy about it even."

Elizabeth consoled him. "I'm sorry, Paul. I hate to say this, but I knew she was wrong for you. She didn't act like a woman in love. She just used you to get her wedding-day fantasy. I'd sue her for misrepresentation—she never planned on staying married."

"I don't think she's like that. In fact, she offered to keep trying if I'd just be patient."

"Paul, there comes a time when someone's got to say, 'What's wrong with you?' No man would take what you have—live like you have. Get real. Do you want a wife or a sister? Sex and intimacy are fundamentals of marriage. It's time you stop setting yourself up as a whipping boy."

He agreed reluctantly. As a small measure of pride, he refused the annulment and made Sherry divorce him. He moved back into the apartment building where he used to live. When he visited Elizabeth a year later, he summed up the experience by saying, "You know, I was engaged for one year and married one year, and now I've been divorced a year. And my life hasn't changed a bit."

"Well, hopefully you're wiser for it."

Chapter 16

Puberty hit Aaron with a vengeance. By age twelve, he stood eye-to-eye with his mother, and by age fourteen, he had grown to over six feet. His facial features developed into a strong Romanesque profile, with a beautiful, straight nose defining his thin face. A wide, full mouth always smiled over the dimpled, square chin. His yellow hair had turned dark, matching the rich coffee brown of his large, almond-shaped eyes. He was so handsome that his appearance stunned people, and academically, musically, and physically gifted, he acted more mature than his age. He was the tallest but youngest child in the ninth grade, and people frequently mistook him for being much older and viewed him as an oddity because he couldn't relate to his peers.

As he grew up in a small town where everyone knew each other, everything about Aaron caught the attention of the kids in high school. Elizabeth started worrying when sixteen-year-old girls began picking him up each morning and supposedly dropping him off at the middle school on their way to the high school. His interest in piano gave way to the electric guitar when Michael bought him one on his twelfth birthday. The guitar created a passion unrivaled to any other musical experience he'd had. After two years, he played the guitar exclusively, gaining an intimate knowledge of the instrument to the point of performing onstage with adult bands. Whatever anyone wanted to hear, he could play on demand: blues, jazz, rock, country, and gospel.

During the summer of 1994, Aaron and three older boys, ages sixteen, eighteen, and nineteen, formed a band. Elizabeth had never seen the other boys before. Though she didn't like their age differences, they seemed nice enough. They politely spoke to her whenever they came over, and they helped out with Aaron's chores so that he could play with them sooner. Then they'd hang out in the garage, honing their created music—a style Elizabeth and Michael hadn't heard before, which, in their opinions, left a lot to be desired. They tolerated it because of Aaron's history of good behavior. One day, as Aaron's bandmates arrived to practice, Elizabeth called them into the kitchen. She had let things go on for a while, but she'd gotten worried, so she directed her attention to the older two, Ryan and Nick. "Boys, I don't mind Aaron hanging out with you, but I need to know that you understand some things: he's only fourteen years old, and he's still in school. You must realize that school comes first with us. He has a curfew, chores, and obligations here, the same as any other young boy living at home. He's not like you, where he can come and go as he pleases and stay out all night. As long as you respect our rules, everything will be fine."

Her speech embarrassed and angered Aaron and shocked his friends. They looked at each other questioningly before agreeing and then collectively replied, "Yes, ma'am." They then went out to the garage. Aaron, however, remained where he stood. He stared at Elizabeth with a look of disbelief on his face.

"I can't believe you just said that to them. Why did you do that?"

"I know you don't understand, Aaron, but it's for your own good."

"How can embarrassing me in front of my friends be for my own good?"

The phone rang. Elizabeth took it as an opportunity to cut their conversation short. She answered, hearing her father's voice on the other end. Wilbur asked for Aaron, who was on his way to the garage. Aaron stopped to take the call.

Elizabeth knew that Wilbur hated Aaron's music. She'd heard him rant about how Aaron should play the piano if he wanted to be a musician. To him, the piano was in a different category—it was more respectable and intellectual. Aaron's guitar and new friends usurped his time, preventing him from doing things with his grandfather, which only made things worse. Elizabeth figured Wilbur was calling to invite Aaron over again. The half of the conversation she heard confirmed that. It ended, as it had often lately, with Aaron saying, "Sorry, Grandpa. The band's here. We've got to practice." Elizabeth could imagine Wilbur's reaction on the other end of the line.

At the end of ninth grade, Aaron earned a spot on the high school's skeet-shooting team, much to Wilbur's delight. Wilbur thought he'd win his grandson back by presenting him with his own skeet equipment: a customized, packaged deal consisting of a brand-new Remington 12-gauge, specialty reloaded ammo, protective glasses, earplugs, and a shell bag, all carried in fine cases engraved with Aaron's name. He worked on the gift for months, gathering and fine-tuning.

When Aaron's first tenth-grade report card came home, Elizabeth's worries became a reality. His grades had plummeted. She and Michael talked to him about it that day in his bedroom.

"What's happening, Aaron?" asked Michael. "This isn't like you."

"I don't know," Aaron countered. "I just don't like school."

"That's no excuse," said Elizabeth.

Aaron wasn't making eye contact. He sat on his bed, fiddling with his guitar. "I don't see why I should have to do something I don't even care about."

"I can't believe we have to explain this to you," said Michael. Elizabeth could tell he was getting angry, but he kept his tone even. "Music is one thing, but you need to be able to support yourself. Chances are, the guitar isn't going to be enough."

Aaron just shrugged. He no longer cared about school. He only wanted to play his guitar. They tried a few more times without success to get through to him. Whenever they approached him, his eyes glazed over, and he'd stare off into the distance. His teachers began calling home with their concerns: he often slept in class, made zeroes on missed assignments, and acted as if he were out to lunch whenever called upon. His parents took away his guitar and forbade him from playing in the band until he brought his grades back up to his usual As.

"I don't know how to reach him anymore," said Elizabeth to Michael late one night after Christmas, lamenting the sneers of contempt that had replaced her son's beautiful smile. "If he keeps looking at me with that shit-eating look of disgust, I'm gonna beat him with a rolling pin." They'd spent the holiday break bickering with Aaron over his constant pleas to see his bandmates. He refused her offers to invite over friends from school—kids his own age. He insisted on socializing only with his bandmates and pouted in protest, making everyone miserable

"He's too old and too big. But I know what you mean. It's unbearable to watch him destroy himself, which seems to be his intent." Having spent four months tutoring him in his homework, grounding him, and taking away his music and friends without making any progress, Michael also stood at a loss. "I just pray this is a passing phase."

School resumed, and Aaron's behavior remained unchanged. Elizabeth resorted to buzzing her son's hair, forcing him to wear a coat and tie, and accompanying him to school. "If all you care about is being Mr. Cool, then I'm going to class with you until you get your priorities straight," she said after he brought home his third report card full of failing marks and comments about his unsatisfactory behavior. For three weeks, she sat beside him all day. If he didn't pay attention, she prodded him during class and said, "Aaron, listen up!" or "Why aren't you taking notes?" This method worked while she was there. Once she left him to his own management, he reverted to earning Fs.

Wilbur didn't help his daughter, as he punctuated his every visit with negative remarks about Aaron. Most Sundays, he and Marilyn came to dinner to catch up on the news and spend time with their grandchildren, and after finding out the latest disappointment, he'd say, "It's because of his damn guitar, you know. It's poisoned him. He's not the same child he used to be." Then he'd shake his head in disappointment, as if all hope were gone. His remarks angered Elizabeth to her core. She hated the way her father had detached himself from Aaron completely; Wilbur related to Aaron now only if Aaron spoke first, and then Wilbur would reply tersely, "I don't know. Go ask your buddies." She knew her father had held a grudge ever since finding out Aaron had quit the skeet team and seeing the lovingly prepared gift stored away under the bed, unused and unappreciated.

On Sunday night, August 18, 1995, Aaron stood on the front porch with his family, including Wilbur. Aaron wished that Wilbur hadn't come over and that his mother had stayed inside. The look on her face—as if this were the worst day of her life—burned itself into his mind. "Please don't make me do this," he said to them. His mother didn't respond except to turn away from him. He could hear her tears.

His father had already packed the family Suburban with Aaron's belongings. "It's too late now, Son," he said. "The time to prevent this is long past. The car's all loaded." That was enough. Aaron knew it was unavoidable now: they were sending him to Fork Union Military Academy in Virginia.

Elizabeth turned back to him and enveloped him in a crushing hug. The way his mother was crying, it was as if she feared she'd never see him again. She choked on her words and held on to him until the last second. Aaron bawled too. He'd never believed his parents would follow through on their threat, and its reality seemed surreal; he waited for their cruel joke to end. His mother's tears told him that it was no joke. Seeing their conviction, he bucked up to the task and let a glimmer of his old self shine through as he comforted his mother. "It'll be all right, Mom. Don't worry."

Michael got in the car and started the engine. Aaron saw his grandfather standing in the background and walked to him. "Good-bye, Grandpa," he said, holding his arms outstretched to hug him, his face streaked with drying tears.

The gesture startled Wilbur. He backed away and gave Aaron his hand. "Oh yes. Good-bye, Aaron," he said with a handshake.

Elizabeth witnessed the chilly interaction and flew into a rage. "What's wrong with you?" she yelled.

"What? What do you want?" said Wilbur.

"I want you to love your grandson, not toss him aside because he's no longer a puppy! Who's the bigger man here?"

The blowup rekindled Aaron's tears. She embraced him harder and walked him to the car, apologizing for her father. "Don't mind him. He's just a sad, lonely man. I love you so much. You'd better make all this heartache worthwhile." She smothered him with kisses, and then he and Michael drove away.

Wilbur ambled through the house, unsure what to do. Elizabeth's words had cut deeply; she'd never spoken to him like that. He noticed Megan looking forlorn and confused. She was now ten years old. He hadn't had much use for little girls, not while he'd had Aaron to keep him company anyway. He loved her from afar but didn't really know her, and she responded in kind with distanced affection. "Hey, sweetie. How's about you come home with me? We'll let Mommy rest awhile," he said, hoping his daughter would see his gesture as an apology. Megan agreed, and they drove off soon after, leaving a note for Elizabeth.

The day left Elizabeth and Wilbur's relationship with new, unspoken boundaries. Wilbur feared upsetting his daughter and began watching his words carefully when around her. Since he couldn't find anything nice to say, he never spoke of Aaron. Elizabeth's sharp intuition knew why he acted so, but it didn't matter. In fact, his avoidance of all things relating to her son increased her anger at him, and she simply tolerated Wilbur's presence. As a result, she and Marilyn became closer, while Wilbur sought friendship in the only friend he seemed to have left: Michael.

As usual, Wilbur went to West Virginia for Thanksgiving. Unlike in previous years, though, Elizabeth spent a day visiting Marilyn. Without Wilbur, mother and daughter felt relaxed and comfortable.

"At least Wilbur has Michael to talk to," said Elizabeth.

"He certainly needs someone," agreed Marilyn. "Have you heard from Aaron much?"

"He has two mandatory phone calls twice a week, but he's been calling more often. Oh, I hope we're doing the right thing for him."

"Time will tell," said Marilyn. "Or not. I'm still not sure anything we did was right for your brother."

"He manages."

"Well, I hope you're doing more than managing. It certainly looks like it."

"It's funny. You know how one thing can overshadow everything else? It's kind of like that. I'm so worried about Aaron that I can't tell if Megan's getting everything she needs."

"It'll all work out," said Marilyn. For once, things seemed hopeful.

Wilbur had long been looking forward to the Thanksgiving respite from walking on eggshells around his immediate family. *At least no one expects anything from me there.* By his second day, he'd already killed one buck. He took it to the basement to take care of it. When he emerged and found the rest of his family at dinner, he was in a good mood.

"What a hunt," he said, filling his plate. "There's nothing like the air in these woods—I tell you. I saw lots of tracks but only followed one. Turned out to be the right one, though. It's only a six-pointer, but I bet I can double that!"

Everyone enjoyed his hunting story—at least that first time. By his third buck, however, they'd grown tired of the subject. Wilbur noticed, and he toned things down. He also noticed how bent Sarah was as she moved through the house. He didn't like seeing her in this state, so he spent more of the day in the basement and the woods. He didn't want to say what he was thinking—that she wasn't infirm at all but just liked the attention her alleged ailments got her.

Sarah, now seventy-eight, and eighty-two-year-old Vance were growing tired. Bob, Danny, and Mary, now grown adults, still lived at home. Their lives consisted of working good jobs, going to church, and taking care of every possible need their foster parents had until the day they died.

Though he was older, Vance's health remained better than Sarah's. He still drove his truck anywhere he chose, washed dishes, and ran errands. Sarah had undergone two unsuccessful surgeries last year for a weakened bladder, which had left her drained. Walking more than eight or nine steps fatigued her to the point of stumbling. After she fell several times, everyone agreed to wait on her hand and foot. Vance bought her an electric recliner to help her to stand and sit, Mary got her a wheelchair, and the boys took turns wheeling her from room to room. She balked at the idea at first, refusing to give up her independence, but she quickly grew accustomed to their fawning and now willingly accepted their help. Once the one and only mistress of her kitchen, she presided over the cooking by overseeing Danny as he prepared the meals, directing him from her wheelchair.

In the ten days he stayed, Wilbur killed and butchered five bucks, including a prize twelve-pointer that he sent to be mounted. Sarah and Vance were not unhappy when he left. His presence jarred their rhythm, and his negative observations about their life made everyone uncomfortable.

Driving home, Wilbur felt uneasy about his visit but couldn't pinpoint why. They hadn't argued, at least not that he recalled. He reviewed his actions, trying to find anything they might have misconstrued, but other than wanting his mother to fend for herself, he thought he'd behaved exceptionally well. *I'm just being paranoid,* he concluded as he arrived home in Jones County.

Glad to be home and relieved of his thoughtful burden, he turned onto his property—and was met with shock. He double-checked the street sign to make sure he'd taken the right turn. He had. But this place didn't look like his home anymore: most of the woods surrounding his land had been deforested. His property had once stood among one hundred acres of trees on the edge of town, but now, cleared land lay in every direction. His ten acres jutted out like an ingrown hair.

Panic filled him as he parked in his driveway. He'd been driving all night, and the sun was barely up, but he ran inside and woke Marilyn, demanding answers. "What the hell happened?"

Startled awake, she knew what he wanted. She'd had her answer prepared since the destruction began the week before. "All the land's been sold to some developer. They're going to subdivide and build houses all around us."

His heart sank as he remembered getting a few calls last summer asking if he'd sell his property. He'd said, "Hell no," and then hung up and thought nothing more of it. Now he wished he'd asked some questions of his own. "Goddamn it. There go the deer."

"I'm sorry. I didn't know it was coming either. They started clearing the day you left, and I couldn't bring myself to tell you over the phone. We couldn't have stopped them anyway."

Confirming his jaundiced perception of life further, he chalked this up to yet another conspiracy and thanked God (or whoever was responsible) he could still hunt in West Virginia.

With Aaron gone and his daughter's continuing coolness, Wilbur felt lonely. He managed some excitement when Aaron called—clearly at his mother's insistence—to tell Wilbur that he was home for the summer. Wilbur drove over right away and was pleasantly surprised to see that Aaron's bright personality had returned, as evident by Aaron's smile. "Hi, Granddad," he said.

"Glad to have you back, even if it's just for the summer," said Wilbur. He tried to hug Aaron, but the boy had his guitar strapped around his body, so the embrace didn't work out. "And how are your grades?"

"They're up from last year," said Elizabeth. She was beaming.

"That's something, I guess, though it would have been hard to make them worse," said Wilbur. When Aaron flinched at the backhanded compliment, Wilbur tried to salvage the moment by saying, "I see you're still playing your music."

"Sure I am," said Aaron. He sat down on the couch and began tuning the guitar. Wilbur found himself not knowing what to say. He felt as if he and Aaron had nothing in common anymore. Having him home, Elizabeth seemed her old self again, but Wilbur still felt her anger. She somehow blamed him for persecuting her son, and it made him uneasy. He hadn't realized how much he depended on Elizabeth and her family for comfort and society. Since Michael worked all the time, Wilbur's attentions turned to the only person left: his wife.

Marilyn liked his change of attitude. Waiting on her hand and foot, cooking supper every night, he'd tell her to rest on the couch since she worked all day. The routine lasted six months, and if he'd never done anything else, Marilyn would have been satisfied. However, when he got dressed up one Sunday morning in April, putting on the one suit he owned as she dressed for church, she had to ask what had gotten into him. "Are you having an affair?"

The question blindsided him. "What?"

"Well, it looks like you're going to church with me. And if you are, then you're feeling awful guilty about something."

He laughed. "Maybe I'm feeling guilty for letting you go by yourself all these years. Do you mind if I go?"

"Certainly not. But everyone at church will think you've risen from the dead."

Nestled into his pew seat, Wilbur felt completely out of place. Everything around him seemed too big—the stained-glass windows, the arches above the nave, the way everybody dressed up. It all was too ostentatious. Then the minister started talking. Wilbur was ready to scoff, at least on the inside, but on some level, he was ready to hear the message. That was what had brought him there in the first place:

his readiness. He found himself nodding along, hearing echoes of his own ideas but with a religious slant. Surprisingly, he found comfort in church. The members weren't crazy, weak, or stupid people, as he'd expected. They were just nice folks looking for solace in a cruel world, as he was. They dressed up because they respected the church and the truth behind it. Leaving one's burdens at the cross did help. Believing a heavenly reward awaited him helped even more. Surely, if Wilbur accepted the gospel as truth, Jesus had a throne waiting to his immediate right with Wilbur's name on it for all the suffering Wilbur had borne during his life on Earth.

Needing more information, he asked Marilyn what she thought about going to Sunday school too, seeing as how the sermons didn't explain the Bible enough for him. She would have done anything to keep him involved, and she wholeheartedly agreed. After three months of Mass, they began attending the preworship classes every week.

As with all of his learning experiences, Wilbur didn't dabble. He wanted the distinction of summa cum laude in Sunday school and immersed himself in reading the Bible and participating in theological discussions. He was always the first person to raise his hand in answer or question when the priest opened the floor. By the end of June, he'd read the entire Roman Catholic version of the Bible.

Long a committed heathen, Wilbur felt his lack of belonging and began the Rite of Christian Initiation of Adults, or RCIA, program in July as a unbaptized inquirer into the faith, called a catechumen. The process consisted of four periods: inquiry, study, purification and enlightenment, and mystagogy ("leading into the mysteries"), marked by three major rites—the Rite of Acceptance, the Rite of Election, and the Sacraments of Initiation. Conversion to the faith normally required a yearlong journey of purging oneself of a lifetime's accumulation of evil and sin through meditation, prayer, study, and ritual. Of course, Wilbur embraced the process, taking the accelerated course, and completed it in nine months.

The first time he stood at the altar and publicly bared his soul for the Rite of Acceptance, he felt uncomfortable, exposed, vulnerable, and naked, worrying about whether anyone thought him weak in character. *Lord, give me the strength to be humble,* he prayed. The priest marked him with the sign of the cross on his ears, eyes, lips, heart, shoulders, hands, and feet, symbolizing the joys and costs of Christian discipleship, and Wilbur felt the intimacy of the ritual. It was like the intimacy present when Jesus bathed the feet of sinners. *Who am I to feel superior to him?* he thought, gaining a newfound knowledge of how his past perceptions of strength had been signs of human weakness. Ideas, theories, explanations, and questions crowded his mind as he struggled to identify the strange emotions taking hold, wondering if the Holy Spirit had filled him or if he was just thinking too hard. His head ached from overstimulation. He became anxious, fearing he might panic.

Suddenly, without any effort on his part, his mind cleared. Feelings of serenity and peacefulness begged him, *Accept without question.* The need to debate disappeared, and he spoke out loud, repeating, "I do," even though no one had questioned him.

The ceremony proved so profound that he looked forward to the next two rites with anticipation, happy to stand before the crowd.

The disappointing Rite of Election came shortly after, during which he received the Call to Continuing Conversion. This rite only involved his assignment to a sponsor (an established member of the church) to help him reflect on the scriptures. He fasted, prayed, and exorcized evils for six months in preparation for his upcoming baptism during the third rite, the consummating Sacraments of Initiation, the final stage in becoming a full-fledged Catholic.

"Hi, Elizabeth. What are you guys doing for Easter?" Marilyn asked over the phone.

"Nothing unusual. Aaron's coming home from school. Do you want us to come to vigil with you again?"

"Yes. With me and your dad."

"Dad's going?"

"He's not only going; he's going to be baptized right before vigil, along with twelve other people in his RCIA class."

"What's been going on over there? I sensed a difference lately but never expected this."

Marilyn related the past year's events with joy, explaining how relieved she felt knowing her husband wouldn't burn in hell and how close the experience had brought them. "So that's why we've missed our Sunday dinners."

On Maundy Thursday in 1996, after sixty-one years of agnostic doubts, Wilbur knelt in humble acceptance of Jesus Christ as his Lord and Savior in front of a crowded congregation and his family. The experience was so moving that Elizabeth cried for him, knowing her father's heart and the strength it had taken for him to relinquish his control and acknowledge his pride. Admitting his faults, weaknesses, and human frailties was the hardest thing he'd ever done. Seeing him kneel with his hands held in prayer and a white sheet draped over his shoulder, signifying his conversion, weeping as he cast off years of denial, was a sight to behold. Even Michael shed a quiet tear in admiration and awe. Marilyn sat in the congregation with her daughter and family. Neither mother nor daughter dared to look at the other, fearing they might discover how much they really did love each other.

Sunday dinners with the family resumed, and Wilbur surprised them all by giving a table blessing, followed by making the sign of the cross. Elizabeth thought it funny they'd never done so when only her mother had believed. Megan joined them, repeating, "In the name of the Father, the Son, and the Holy Ghost." The girl clearly liked the sense of ritual. Having joined their local Presbyterian church years ago, Elizabeth found the Catholic traditions odd, and a quick glance at Michael told her that he was as out of sorts as she was. But even after all that, they weren't prepared for her father's rant, which now focused on religion instead of government and the economy.

"Michael," he said, sliding the butter along to Marilyn, "I've been wanting to tell you that you really should bring yourself and your family back to the Catholic Church. I mean, it really is the only church Jesus intended to start."

Michael arched an eyebrow in Elizabeth's direction. She was stymied. "Is that so?" he said."

"It is," Wilbur said. "I know you think denominations aren't important, but the fact is that they just are."

"That's an interesting perspective," Elizabeth said. But she thought, *Where were you when I was growing up?* She tried not to be critical, but it seemed he'd conveniently forgotten the example he'd set and the confusion he'd instilled in her and her brother. Elizabeth wondered where his humility was now. However, whatever the price, the serenity he'd gained was worth the blood she drew in biting her tongue. The real problem was that he didn't stop. Suddenly, every Sunday evening was a second trip to church for the whole family, with Wilbur in the pulpit.

Marilyn understood Elizabeth's careful words around Wilbur. When he and Michael disappeared together after supper, she'd commiserate about Wilbur's exhausting intensity. "You know, I've been Catholic all my life, and now he's telling *me* how to be faithful. He even argued with the priest in Sunday school this morning," she said.

"I don't know how you can stand it, Mom. He's either all or nothing. There's no middle ground."

"He joined the choir last month. Now I've got to listen to him sing every minute of the day while he practices at home—and he's not very good. I used to turn on the radio and listen to music while I cleaned house. I don't dare now. He'll just sing along."

Aaron returned to Fork Union in the fall of 1996 for eleventh grade. His parents offered to let him come home, but he asked to return. "I think I'd like to go back. It's not so bad, and I'm doing really well in school. Let's try one more year."

This reaction astonished his parents. Aaron explained that he liked the exacting schedule, knowing where he'd be and when. Having too much free time on his hands had confused him. "Besides, they have music there too, and I've got a really great band put together."

Hearing the real reason, they still agreed, since his grades were all low As.

In early November, Wilbur began preparing for his annual hunting trip while Marilyn made plans to visit retired friends from Willow Grove who now lived in New Orleans, when Sarah called him on his birthday.

"I just called to say happy birthday," Sarah said. They exchanged pleasantries and family updates—her health continued to decline. As Wilbur wound down the conversation, she added, "By the way, Vance isn't allowing anyone to hunt on the property." Vance had previously allowed local acquaintances to hunt, in addition to Wilbur. "He found two of his cattle shot dead last year, one of them a prize bull, and people keep driving their trucks where he's told them not to, trenching up the pasture." She rambled on nervously.

"What do you mean 'anyone'? I'm not just anyone."

"Well, that includes you. I'm sorry, Punk. Won't you come up and visit anyway?" She hollered at someone else in the house and didn't wait for Wilbur to reply. "Well, I got to go. Mary needs me in the kitchen. Bye, dear. Come see me."

"But—"

She'd hung up. Wilbur held the receiver in disbelief and then anger. *Anyone? I'm lumped in the same category as just anyone.* In disbelief, he passed the five hours until Marilyn got home from work by exploring any possible reason to justify his mother's words; there weren't any. *How could she?* he asked over and over. With no one home to provide answers, he fell into despair, letting painful memories and unspoken truths—personal insecurities of being unworthy, substandard, and unloved—resurface.

Marilyn came home to find Wilbur sitting in his recliner, his face expressionless, his soul dejected. "What are you doing?" she asked. He never sat with the television off and the house silent. He looked at her as if she might help him understand his world and told her the news.

"What? You're kidding. Does she realize what she's said?"

Wilbur shrugged, unable to find words. Enraged, Marilyn began listing the assaults he'd endured from Sarah all his life. The more she talked, the more depressed he became, knowing everything she said was true. The past excuses he'd made for his mother were unveiled as emotional denial: she didn't love him—not really. He doubted if she ever had. He was unworthy of one word spoken on his behalf. Surely Vance would have allowed him if she'd presented his side—if she'd explained that he came for his soul and not for the deer. *I'm not her family. Her foster children are.* His childhood memories had meant nothing ever since she'd replaced him—her only surviving son—with strangers.

Chapter 17

In the spring of 1997, Wilbur fought hard to keep the last few crumbs of happiness in his life.

Last year alone, some agency had deforested all the land around Wilbur's house, and Wilbur's mother had denied him access to his beloved and hallowed woods, leaving him with nowhere—and nothing—to hunt, stealing his lifelong passion from him. Aaron remained estranged. Elizabeth did too, but to a lesser degree. Adding insult to injury, the Dow had the nerve to skyrocket past 10,000, while he had dozens of worthless gold coins stashed in the attic, bought at more than twice their current value.

At ten o'clock in the morning on Wednesday, August 12, he forced himself out of bed. He had to be on the base by noon to attend Marilyn's retirement luncheon. *I'd rather take a beating*, he lamented, thinking about the demands of socializing with people he wouldn't give a rat's ass for, but he thought he needed the excuse to get up anyway. He ambled to the toilet to relieve himself of the uncomfortable basketball inside his bladder. He took his customary stance and waited. He waited some more. *Why can't I pee?* In desperation, and again without success, he tried the other toilet in the house, as if the problem lay in the facilities. He called Elizabeth at noon, asking her medical advice.

"You've got to go to the emergency room, Dad. You need to be catheterized."

He balked at the suggestion. "Maybe if I drink some coffee, it will force it out."

"It's already full. It's a mechanical problem—and a relatively common one for men your age." She explained how enlarged prostates affected middle-aged men and the simple facts about catheterization.

"I don't want to wait for hours in some hospital just to spend hundreds of dollars on a damn doctor. All he'll want to do is cut on me."

"What if Michael meets you there?"

Knowing he'd have Michael as security against quacks, Wilbur agreed.

Marilyn came home from work upset with Wilbur for missing her retirement party, but she forgave him when he told her about the day's events. "So what did the doctor say?" she asked.

"I have an appointment on Friday. They'll take this contraption out then." He showed her his catheter bag.

Wilbur kept his appointment and saw the doctor Michael had recommended, refusing his wife's offer to come along. If he'd known how to remove the tube from his penis himself, he wouldn't have felt it necessary to go. After the doctor pulled out the catheter, the urologist's examination revealed an enlarged prostate. The doctor recommended surgery. "Here's a prescription for catheter supplies in case you can't urinate on your own. My nurse will demonstrate how to insert one before you leave. Like I said, if you're still having problems by Sunday, give me a call." Wilbur listened, his suspicions confirmed, as the doctor explained what the surgery entailed. Wilbur thanked him for his time and raced home to await the return of his urinary function.

Despite drinking two pots of coffee and a gallon of water, he had to reinsert the catheter before going to bed. His flushing-out theory accomplished nothing but hours of discomfort as he walked around distended to the point of looking pregnant, trying to urinate every thirty minutes, until he couldn't stand it any longer. When he finally relented and inserted the catheter, Wilbur's bladder drained more than two and a half liters of urine, to his extraordinary relief.

Wilbur did not own a computer, so he spent the weekend at Elizabeth's house, searching the Internet for everything he could find remotely relating to the prostate, putting faith in articles written by untrained, unlicensed strangers who promised nonsurgical remedies. He favored sites that lambasted doctors, and he felt comforted by the number he found. Finding so many people who thought like him confirmed his theory: doctors (and lawyers too) were parasites on society, taking advantage of the ignorant masses for financial gain. Wilbur didn't need surgery; he needed vitamins, supplements, a strict diet without estrogen-laden fats, a little grape-seed extract, high-dose garlic pills, and other remedies, and he'd be cured in no time.

But after two weeks, he started to walk funny. Wearing the large catheter all the time had made Wilbur sore. Every leg movement wiggled the plastic tube against his already-bruised and bloodied urethra.

Michael tried to talk to Wilbur to assuage his fears of the unknown: the surgery would be minor; he'd be as good as new in no time; and the surgeons had no intention of "cutting his manhood out," as Wilbur put it. Elizabeth explained about the damage and risks he took: likely infection and sustained loss of bladder function if he didn't allow it to fill properly and trigger the need-to-go response. He cast aside everybody's advice, thinking, *I'll show them. Just wait and see.*

His obstinacy wore on Marilyn too. Now that she was retired, both of their lives seemed to revolve around his toileting. Catheters and bags hung over the shower rod as he rotated their use, cleaning and air-drying ones in between. She talked him into leaving home once to go see a movie. His leg bag detached during the show, spilling urine down his leg and pants. After that, he refused to go anywhere except Elizabeth's.

Marilyn waited for him to tire of the routine, thinking he still considered surgery an option—until they sat watching a Discovery Channel show about medical procedures, and he announced, "I will never let them cut on me. I don't care if I have to wear this damn thing for the rest of my life." He spoke venomously, as if he had to defend his life against everyone's advice.

She hadn't known he harbored such resentment. "So you don't care about my quality of life—of ever making love to me again. And you think your family wants to harm you by encouraging surgery. You think those quacks on the Internet have more concern for your welfare than me, Elizabeth, and Michael?" He didn't answer. "I don't appreciate the way you think about us. I'm sick and tired of your conspiracy bullshit," she said, and she went to bed alone.

Three months later, he called Elizabeth early one morning. "Voilà! I can pee!" he shouted.

"Really? Wonderful. I know you're happy about that. I guess you were right all along. Was it a full-fledged pee?" She let him gloat but knew from her medical experience that his catheter use had just dilated the bladder enough to let him go a bit. His victory would be short-lived.

"It was enough to encourage me."

He never called with any more good news. The next time he came over, she noticed his careful walk and the bulge of his leg bag through his pant leg.

In May 1998, Wilbur apathetically decided he'd had enough. He'd lived like an invalid for nine months with the godforsaken rubber tube stuck in his penis like a tether, chained to a bag and to his house. Wiping away dried blood from its constantly irritated tip every morning had taken its toll. The damn bag had come off sometime during the night, soaking the mattress with urine—again. He'd paid a price for not making love to his wife in months: a distance had crept into their marriage, and he couldn't blame her. He felt it too. She'd taken a job in a local dress shop, saying she wanted some extra money, but he knew she wanted to get away from him. He wanted to get away from himself.

He tried going to church for a while after his troubles started. The church had hired a new choir director, but he thought she stunk; the skeleton choir—the few who chose to return—sounded like caterwauling felines preparing to fight. Sitting in the pews for ninety minutes hurt, so he quit going and hadn't been for the past six months. He hadn't hunted in eighteen months and hadn't talked to his mother since her phone call forbidding him from hunting. Aaron was home all summer and stopped by to see him often. Wilbur enjoyed his visits and noticed what a nice young man the military school had made him, but something still felt amiss—strained. Aaron always hugged him good-bye, and when he tried to reciprocate, he couldn't. He wanted to, but he physically couldn't bring himself to do it. *What's wrong with me?* Questioning his inability, he'd end up resenting Aaron for making him feel inadequate and calling attention to his own inability to express love.

He was tired. Living a life in fear of intimacy, surgery, and failure seemed pathetic. Spending every day hoping to take a piss was pathetic. *I'll just stay right here in bed, where it's warm, safe, and comfortable. And boring.* No one cared anyway. Who was he but a lonely, disconnected man? His life never affected anyone or anything. He was an anonymous face in a sea of desperate people, alive for no good reason.

The phone rang, interrupting his pity party. "Hi, Dad. How are you?" said Elizabeth.

"Oh, same."

"Look, I know you're not feeling well, but Aaron's graduation is this Saturday, and you have to come."

"I can't go to Virginia."

"Yes, you can. And you will. Michael and I have rented a camper to drive us all up. It's got a bathroom and everything. We're not taking no for an answer. You owe it to the family, sick or not." Though her words sounded harsh, she said them with love in her heart.

He tried arguing and even thought of bolting himself in his room when the time came, but he eventually agreed to go. *I'll do this one last thing before I ...* He shook the notion from his mind.

Wilbur made it to Virginia without any trouble—for himself or his family. He sat in the back of the camper like a lump of coal and let everyone else take charge, doing as he was told and keeping to his thoughts when allowed. They arrived at Fork Union Academy an hour before the ceremony was scheduled to begin. Aaron met them briefly in his dorm before joining his classmates in the auditorium.

"Hi, Mom, Dad, Grandma, Grandpa." He hugged each person.

"You look so handsome!" cried Elizabeth, emotional at the sight of her baby all grown up.

He looked more than handsome. His hair was cut short and parted neatly on the side, and he wore his cadet dress uniform—he looked dashing. His beaming grin, confidence, and welcoming attitude complemented his looks most. "Tonight is gonna blow you all away," he said.

"What is it, Son?" asked Michael.

"You'll see in about an hour. I've got to go now. There are front-row seats waiting for all of you. Come on—I'll show you to your seats."

"Can I use your bathroom first?" asked Wilbur. Everyone groaned, knowing it might take a while.

"You go ahead, Son. We'll find our way," said Michael.

"How did Aaron manage to get us such good seats?" asked Marilyn upon reaching the auditorium thirty minutes later. They sat front and center, four rows back, behind the school's dignitaries.

"I don't know," replied Elizabeth. The aisle marker read, "Reserved for the family of Cadet Aaron Armstrong." She sat beside Michael, holding his hand and keeping a ready supply of tissues in the other. Megan sat to her right, and then came Marilyn and Wilbur, who wanted to sit on the end in case he needed to make a hasty exit to the restroom. Excitement filled the air; Marilyn jabbered on nervously, unable to contain herself.

"I wish you'd shut up," said Wilbur.

Taken aback, Marilyn replied, "I wish you'd stayed home. No one wants to be around a killjoy."

"Hmph." *I didn't want to come anyway.* He turned away to continue his pouting. *All this fuss for a boy who misbehaved to the point of getting sent away. He's to be congratulated for his parents having to spend thousands—tens of thousands—of dollars to straighten him out?* Comparing Aaron's situation to his own school performance, Wilbur thought him undeserving. *Had he stayed home, behaved, and made As in a public school, not some hoity-toity, pampering prep school, I'd be impressed.*

Aaron led as the students filed in, filling the front right section. He offered a wink and smiled at his family. He and the boy before him stood out; they were the only two wearing ornate gold sashes around their shoulders. Twenty or so others had similar sashes, but theirs were not as fancy. "What's the collar for?" asked Marilyn.

"It signifies belonging to the honor society," said Michael, whispering over his wife's shoulder in reply. Elizabeth was too busy wiping away tears to answer.

"Why's he first?" Marilyn said.

"I guess because his last name starts with an *A.*"

"Oh, I forgot. Why is his collar—"

"Let us pray," said a clergyman, taking the stage and interrupting Marilyn's train of thought. After the invocation, the headmaster made his opening remarks, giving a history of the school and complimenting the graduates on their accomplishments.

"I know you all didn't come to hear me, so let us begin by recognizing our salutatorian." The headmaster introduced the young man sitting beside Aaron and had him stand to receive his applause. The young man sat back down, and the headmaster continued. "Our valedictorian came to us three years ago, having lost his direction. A former achieving student, he had succumbed to peer pressure, rebelled against his parents, and made a conscious decision to fail. Though this is a common thread that runs through many of our students, his accomplishment is remarkable—not only because his 3.94 grade point average is higher than anyone else's but also because few young men come to understand the error of their ways, as he did. Even the ones who do often find the task of climbing back up their mountain of failure too daunting to overcome completely. They may come close, but none have made it to the top like this fine student. By the end of his first year at Fork Union, he embraced our standards and ideals. When his parents gave him the opportunity to leave, he chose to stay. And I thank him. The students, teachers, and faculty have been blessed by his presence, as he infected everyone around him with his enthusiasm, free spirit, kindness, intelligence, and music."

Wilbur was transfixed, staring intently at the speaker. He glanced around, sure that the headmaster was describing Aaron and hoping to see confirmation on the others' faces. Marilyn sat with an empty smile on her face, as if she weren't paying any attention. Elizabeth and Michael, however, beamed. They'd figured it out too.

It can't be Aaron. He would have told us. Wilbur's heart raced at the idea. He listed reasons it couldn't be true, convincing himself that the real valedictorian coincidently had the same characteristics as his grandson. The headmaster's next words jolted him.

"Ladies, gentlemen, friends, parents, and grandparents, I proudly introduce our valedictorian, Aaron Michael Armstrong."

The audience erupted with applause. Elizabeth sobbed in Michael's arms. A lump the size of a watermelon choked Wilbur's throat. He didn't notice the tear rolling down his face.

The room fell silent as Aaron thanked the headmaster and began his address.

"Everything he just said is true: I was lost. In preparing my speech, I reflected on my journey. How did I go from ranking first in elementary school to a flunking troubled teen to high school valedictorian? Why did I put myself, and my parents, through years of emotional turmoil just to end up where I first started? Did I learn anything while the alien invader took control of me?" The audience laughed. "I concluded that I did. I think I would not be standing in front of you today if it weren't for my past. I learned from my mistakes, and I had a solid foundation of love, family values, and appreciation of life's gifts—a foundation laid in my childhood—to fall back on." He thanked his parents for putting up with him and loving him enough to make the hard choices they'd made, and he told them how much he loved them. Then he got to the heart of his speech.

"My earliest lessons, other than cleaning my room and taking out the trash, were taught to me by my grandfather. Before I could walk, I knew he was there for me, only learning much later how he held me and cared for me when I was a babe. He taught me how to fish, hunt, and trap, and I spent every single summer day at his feet, happy in our outdoor adventures together. I didn't understand then the life skills he subtly included in having fun: what it meant to be an adult and the importance of taking responsibility for our actions and fulfilling our obligation as human beings by caring for the world around us. When he'd always tell me, 'Say what you mean, and mean what you say,' I didn't understand what he meant at all—until I arrived at Fork Union and had no one to blame but myself. His lessons directed my actions. His words rang in my ears as I made my way through school. His own history of being the class valedictorian was an aspiration I dared to dream of. My success today is microscopic in comparison. Knowing the obstacles he overcame to become the first person in his lineage even to go to high school, let alone graduate first in his class and earn a National Merit scholarship, inspires me with awe. And it shames me, for my obstacles were placed in my way by my own hand.

"I've always taken his guidance for granted. Now, with your permission, I'd like to thank him." He looked at Wilbur with loving pride, telling him with his eyes to get prepared, and then said, "Wilbur Weaver, will you please stand?"

Wilbur rose to his feet as if pulled up by cosmic force. Never had anyone revered him so. He'd never heard anybody else so honored. Feeling proud beyond measure and weeping like a child, red-faced, he let the world look at the man Aaron spoke of. "Thank you, Grandpa. I love you," said Aaron.

In response, Wilbur stood tall and saluted his grandson. The crowd roared. Those who weren't clapping and screaming were too busy wiping away tears. The family did both. Before he sat back down, Wilbur blew Aaron a kiss and mouthed, "I love you too."

Aaron ended his address and returned to his seat. The ceremony continued with the presentation of diplomas.

"Can you believe what just happened?" Elizabeth said to Michael.

"I'm in shock. What a wonderful kid we've got. This is the second-happiest day of my life; the first was when I married you."

"When we get home, let's buy him a car," she suggested. He laughed, agreeing.

Marilyn fidgeted in her seat, not knowing what to do with herself.

Wilbur was affected most. He sat transfixed, smiling, lost in his thoughts as tears ran freely down his face. *I did reach him. He remembers everything. I wonder how many other lives I've touched. God had a use for me all along; I exist for a reason. I am loved. I am worthy. Life is great.*

The next Monday, he called Dr. Klein and scheduled his surgery.

THE END

Lightning Source UK Ltd.
Milton Keynes UK
UKOW01n0048291016
286395UK00002BA/19/P